AF415306

Cover and Book Design by Dreams2Media

Edited by There for You Editing

Published by Vamptasy Publishing

Dedication

This is to never giving up. Whatever your dream, keep striving, hoping, and believing. Success may be just around the corner.
For my husband who shares me with the characters in my head.
Just Keep Your Head above. Swim ~Jacks Mannequin

Playlist

Hail to the King: Avenged Sevenfold
Him & I: G-Easy (With Halsey)
Hells Bells: AC/DC
Back in Black: AC/DC
Carry on Wayward Son: Kansas
Heathens: Twenty-One Pilots
Laugh, I Nearly Died: The Rolling Stones
Ramble On: Led Zeppelin
One Way or Another: Blondie
Born on the Bayou: Creedence Clearwater Revival
Midnight Rider: The Allman Brothers
Dig: Incubus
If You Want Blood: AC/DC
Love Hurts: Incubus
The Mixed Tape: Jacks Mannequin
Try: Pink
The Resolution: Jack's Mannequin

Glossary

Youngling—new vampire
Court—group of vampires
Lord—vampire in charge of large territories
Bondmate—vampire version of a soul mate
Speciesim—racism against species
Lady—female leader (co-ruler) in charge of large territories

Translations

Frumoasa—Beautiful

Deep into that darkness peering, long I stood there, wondering, fearing, doubting, dreaming dreams no mortal ever dared to dream before.

Edgar Allen Poe

The oldest and strongest emotion of mankind is fear, and the oldest and strongest kind of fear is fear of the unknown.

H.P. Lovecraft

Hail to the Queen

USA TODAY BESTSELLING AUTHOR

SHYLA COLT

Chapter One

I nudge the crumbling dirt around the exterior of the grave with the toe of my black combat boot and peer down into the gaping hole recently filled in. The freshly turned soil is still loose and damp. It emits an earthy aroma that reminds me of gardening. A four-foot angel lay on it's back, a mockery of the being it resembles. Its marble wings lay in pieces. Cracks run through the base of the tombstone, obscuring the messages chosen by loved ones for Imelda Agustin. The blatant disregard and disrespect for a final resting spot is cringeworthy. Chaos in a spot meant for eternal peace sickens me.

The black coffin at the bottom of the six-foot descent looks like a bomb has gone off inside of it. Splintered wood juts out at jagged angles. Scarlet drops, rapidly turning a rusty red as they oxygenate, stand out against the white satin lining. *There's no blood in a body post-mortem unless we're talking the undead.*

"I think you might've downplayed it when you said you had a problem," I say dryly.

I glance over at Donald Woodman. Clad in a pair of gray overalls, the lesser earth Faerie looks completely human thanks to magic. His warm ivory skin tone, dirty blond hair, and slight frame wouldn't turn heads at a glance until you looked closer. An angular face, upturned nose, and thick lashes framing gemstone-like sea-green eyes make him beautiful. Only, not inhumanly so. Over time, the Fae have learned how to blend in.

Like many of his kind, he chooses to pass his time in the human realm, performing a job that keeps him close to the element he has an infinity for. As a witch, I see him as he's meant to be. From the tips of his curved and pointed-tipped ears to the unblemished porcelain skin, cupid's bow lips, and ash-blond wavy locks, he's perfection.

"Any clue what happened here?" I scan the area he's roped off for signs of who or what could've done this. Other than a few shoe impressions, there's nothing obvious, which tells me this is purely a supernatural problem.

"No. My crew and I finished burying the body last night around seven o'clock. We packed everything up and went home for the evening as usual. When I came in today and did a walk of the grounds, I found this." He gestures toward the body less grave with his hands.

"Has anything like this ever happened before?"

"Nothing remotely close. We've gotten the occasional grave robber in, but they're looking for jewelry, not bodies." He shoves his hands into the pockets of his dark blue jumpsuit and shrugs his shoulders.

That makes sense. Grave robbing is an outdated and obsolete practice. "I'm going to take some samples for testing. You'll have to keep this part of the cemetery sealed off. Tell them you're having an issue with drainage. Reroute. Postpone. Do whatever you need to, including using your *gift* of persuasion. We can't have rumors about the dead reanimating and walking around." *Even if it is true.*

"You know we're not supposed to tamper with humans," Donny says quietly. Relations between humans and Fae have always been tentative at best. The deals brokered to afford peaceful cohabitation are stringent.

"Louella Esçhete is giving you the sanction. There will be no backlash. You're doing the community a favor." Some perks come along with the complications of belonging to a powerful magical family.

He ducks his head. "Okay, Lou."

"I'm going to take care of you, Donny. Don't worry." Crouching down, I study the impressions left in the soft soil. The dirt holds multiple sets of footprints. Unless there were two people buried in one coffin, we've got a serious situation brewing. *Why, what, and how many, are the questions foremost in my mind. Vampires?*

It's rare to have a vamp attack go unmonitored. Younglings aren't known for restraint. Having baby vamps bursting through the soil like daisies and attacking people would blow their cover. It's a code among them—they handle conversions with care. After what happened last summer, they'd tightened up on the rule breaking, and rogues that slipped through the cracks. Unlike Bella from *Twilight*, they don't come equipped with the ability to control themselves. It's a taught trait. Still, dead things tend to stay that way unless tampered with.

"I need to have the coffin exhumed." I want to see if something broke in, or out. I rise and wipe my clammy palms on my thighs. The first step is eliminating the obvious. I scanned the paperwork on the body before I came out. There was nothing out of the ordinary about the victim. If this was more than a body nabbing, I need to know about it. "I'll send people to take care of it." Lifting the Cannon camera around my neck, I begin to take shots of everything.

We've upped our game over the past six months as we iron out the kinks in our business. To appease everyone involved, we've come up with a blend of modern and magical techniques to solve our cases. Plenty of skeptics remain out there ready for Sacha, Felicite, and I to fail. Others have begun to come around to what we do. We're the youngest generation. Our changes are bound to make waves. Witches are so used to being closed off and exclusive, we don't know how to reach out to other supernatural beings for help. If Witch for Hire can act as a bridge between everyone, I'll consider it a success.

Replacing the lens cap after pictures, I approach the black case I set aside earlier, pop the silver buckle, and pull out the plaster mix and a bottle of water. The older cemetery is secluded. In the middle of an underdeveloped area surrounded by woods, it's the perfect place for the crime. The tombstones are aged, but well-cared for. The grass is neatly trimmed, and the dirt rows are defined.

A decent number of graves have flowers or other trinkets left in remembrance. Casting the molds, I call the office while they dry.

"Witch for Hire, Sacha speaking."

"Sach. The *disturbance* in the cemetery was a gross understatement. I'm going to need all hands on deck."

She whistles. "What happened?"

"If I knew the answer, I'd be a lot less worried. We have a fresh grave disturbed, a body missing, and nothing left behind other than faded footprints, a few drops of blood, and a shit ton of property damage."

"What the hell would do that?"

"That's the million dollar question. I'm having the coffin brought over to Cristobal's for Miles to run forensics on it. I sincerely doubt it was a baby vamp."

"We'd have heard about an attack by now. Vamplings are ravenous when they first wake," Sacha mumbles.

"Exactly my thought. I'm waiting for my molds to dry. I wanted to capture them to bring back with me before the prints degrade any further."

"Do you want us to close the office and meet you at Cristobal's?"

"Yes, as soon as you finish going over the info Donny sent over on the body. This case takes top priority. Humans might be prone to denial, but theft of dead bodies is going to be noticed sooner rather than later. Donny's damage control can only prevent discovery for so long if there's a rash of similar crimes."

"Fel and I are currently looking at all things Imedla Agustin. We'll head over as soon as we're caught up." I thank the powers that be, that my cousin, Felicite, said yes to joining Witch for Hire when we were getting up and running. The case load and research often required would swamp two people.

"On the plus side, we have good eats and expensive coffee at Cristobal's."

"When are you going to stop saying his and admit its now 'ours'?" Sacha asks.

"Not today." I disconnect before she can respond. Finally, I get the last word. I smirk. Simple pleasures keep me from going stark raving mad in the face of the evil we see. No one calls us in for baptisms, weddings, or house blessings. We come in after things have gone *Lord of the Flies*. Folks tend to try to tackle things themselves until they're forced to wave the white flag of defeat when things become unbearable. Perhaps it's human nature.

I press my hand to the tender area of my side. Last week a shakedown with a Werepanther went pear-shaped. Victory always comes at a price. Some are higher than others. Cristobal called my refusal of his blood stubborn, but I'm still wary of the bond we share, and the fact that death with his blood in my system would mean life as one of the undead.

I'm not ready to commit myself to that reality. Witches and vampires are total opposites. We revere life and the balance of nature. Their very existence is an affront to all we stand for. Undead, they exist by stealing life. It's made the truce between our people tenuous at best, and now I'm bonded to the Lord of the city, and the Cortez Court. Critobal is a force to be reckoned with. A master vampire charged with a territory, Cristobal keeps the peace, governs the lesser vampires, and holds my heart.

Me, the future Matriarch of the Esçhete witches. It's a union some see as an abomination. As I prepare to take my place as Lady of his court and my own family, we continue to deal with the changes the mating bond is causing.

I gather my things and try not to think about the tangled web of complicated situations and oddities my life has become.

I admire the breadth of Cristobal's shoulders in the soft gray T-shirt as I walk into the kitchen. Following the tug low in my belly, I found him with ease, thanks to our bond. Few get to see this powerful man, dressed so casually, or in such a relaxed state. Still ruffled from sleep, tufts of chocolate-brown hair fall across his broad forehead. Golden highlights glint like silverfish in the ocean waves, winking here and there beneath the overhead lighting above the kitchen island.

I love him best like this. He flashes me a lazy smile, and my stomach drops to my shoes.

"You're back early. Is it safe to assume you didn't stop by to have lunch with me?" Cristobal lifts a thick brow.

"I wish I could prove you wrong, but I'm here to accept a delivery coming in and have Miles fire up the lab. Besides, isn't this more like breakfast for you?" I step up beside him and run my fingers through his soft hair, massaging his scalp. He moans, leaning into my caress. There's a reason vampires have been called creatures of the night. While the sun doesn't harm them, the penchant for late hours remains from the time when they were forced to hide.

"Semantics. What are you waiting for?" His clear baritone is pleasant to my ear. He turns toward me, nuzzling my neck.

"A coffin that was broken into or escaped from. The jury's still out on which way it happened."

He pauses and pulls away. "Accidental vampire?" His shoulders tense.

"Highly unlikely. I found multiple tracks out by the gravesite."

He studies me with dark pools of brown surrounded by ridiculously long lashes. "You have a theory?"

"No. I need to look into the woman who was snatched first. It might've been about more than food."

His lips turn down at the corner. "You saw signs of this?"

"Uh-uh. It's more like wishful thinking. Anything that eats human flesh is bad news."

"Hmmm." He cups the side of my face. His warmth seeps into me. People think vampires are cool to the touch. The fact is, they're not. Their core temperature is lower than ours is, yes, but nothing unpleasant. "Eat with me."

"I don't have time—"

"I can feel your hunger and exhaustion. You're burning your candle at both ends of the wick. None of us can afford to have you down, dove." The pet nickname clinches the deal. The tone of his voice changes when he uses it. It softens, sheds some of its magical qualities as if he's baring the very essence of his being to me. I imagine it's as close to his original human voice as he can get.

"I know." One coronation takes a good year of planning. I'm attempting to arrange two close together, and one requires learning the intimate workings of a culture that's been so shrouded in shadows and myths, I'm learning everything from scratch. The fatigue threatens to overtake me. My shoulders slump. I could fight, but a good leader knows when to conserve their energy and admit their shortcomings.

I want to be superwoman, always there to lead a rescue, loyal, and just. Though, right now, I'm a witch stretched too thin, stuck between my people and the vampire court who've claimed me as their queen.

"Then come, sit, let me feed you."

I admired the fluffy pile of French toast artfully coated with powdered sugar and piled high with fresh strawberries in front of him.

He pats his lap, and I allow myself to be swept up in his insatiable need to provide, protect, and pamper. I lean back against him, embracing the tender moment among the insanity. He kisses my temple and closes me in with his arms on either side of me as he cuts the bread with graceful movements. I soak up his steady calm. Cristobal Cortez is fast becoming my refuge. The thought is alarming.

He spears a small pile of squares, taking care to add strawberries and a bit of whip cream. I pull away, slightly, and open my mouth. Sweetness dances along my tongue. I moan.

"Good?"

"Mmm hmm." I lick my lips, and he fixes his intense gaze on me. I could catch on fire from that look alone. The bond between us comes to life. Flooded with energy and comfort, my body tingles. I gasp. Warmth forms in my belly. *Let me help you bear some of this weight. You are no longer alone, dove.*

After so many years of running from what exists between us, relaxing into this connection takes effort. Setting aside my pride, I allow myself to feel. The corners of his lips curve upward. He offers me another bite. "Thank you."

I swallow. "For what? Letting you add inches to my waistline?"

He chuckles. "For allowing me to take care of you. Control has never been something you relinquished easily."

"Would you have tried so hard if it was?"

He smirks. "I could have done nothing less. You're worthy of the effort it took for me to convince you, Reina."

He feeds me until I'm ready to burst.

I turn my head away. "I can't eat another bite."

He sets the silverware down dead center on the plate, in an x. His polite, precise movements have become endearing. Control is a prized possession among vampires, and my man has it in spades. I catch slivers of his contentment and admiration through our bond. The scent of leather, woods, and masculinity winds around me. He wraps his arms around my waist, pulling me to him.

I all but melt into him as he nibbles his way down my neck. "My sweet, dove." His lips ghost over my pulse point. My breathing grows choppy. Retracing his journey back up my neck with his tongue, he returns to my lips. When we're together like this, nothing else exists. His tongue slips between my lips, and I press my chest against his. A growl in the back of his throat sends vibrations straight through my body.

We adjust our heads, deepening the lip lock. I lose myself in the irresistible combination of French toast and him. His clever mouth sets my body ablaze with desire. Heart pounding in my chest, I suck air into my aching lungs. He helps me maneuver my body to straddle his lap.

I meet his glowing amber eyes before our lips reattach. Our tongues circle lazily. I grind into his lap, and his breath catches. I smirk. It's a game of dare between us. Pushing buttons, we play to see who can outlast the other.

His fangs skim against my lip. *May I?* I ignore the voice telling me to say no. *Yes.* A sharp pain follows, and we both groan. We take turns sucking the wounds, mingling our blood. Hunger wakes inside of me. Power surges. My level in my magical well skyrockets.

A throat clears. Pots and pans rattle, and the dish clatters onto the counter. I groan as we pull apart, resting our foreheads together.

"Don't stop on our account," Marcellus drawls.

"How long until our next vacation?" I whisper, thinking of the enchanted two weeks we'd taken off from everything over six months ago.

"Too long." Cristobal clears his throat. "I assume you have a good reason for interrupting us."

"There's a coffin out front. Does that qualify as a semi-emergency?" Marcellus asks.

"Oh, that's mine."

"You're taking this vampire kink thing to a whole new level, huh?" Luz says.

"What? No. It's for a new case I'm taking on." I wiggle free, and hop down from Cristobal's lap, kissing his cheek before I head toward the front door. Duty calls.

Chapter Two

The laboratory is a blast from the past complete with bunsen burners, candles, and slate-topped workstations. It looks more like a mad scientist's playground than our forensic headquarters. Dressed smartly in a pair of black slacks, and a white labcoat, Miles is every inch the professional. He's tamed his chestnut curls with a shortcut and a side part. I'm proud of his conversion from absentminded librarian to the brilliant scientist. Since we've started to give him cases to work on, he's downright gleeful. Minds like his require constant engagement.

"What exactly am I looking for?" Miles asks. He glances down at the modern microscope that blends seamlessly with the mix of old and new he's merged in his space. I never appreciated his past as much as I have recently. A scholar, he was at the forefront of medical procedures in his time, which makes him the perfect lab tech.

While his methods may be outdated, his results aren't. Given his voracity for knowledge, he'll be caught up with the modern techniques and procure better equipment in no time. There are no limits to what an inexhaustible amount of money can do. Vampirism brings out the best and worst qualities a person possesses, exaggerating them until they're a new individual with hints of the old.

"Honestly, I'm not sure, and I don't want to sway you in any particular direction." I hold my hands up. "So I'll let you do what you do best."

"After observing the coffin, I can already tell you they took the body. The angles of the breaks in the wood and the lack of skin and hair don't fit with her breaking out. Someone or something definitely broke in to get her. I'll be matching the skin cells I've recovered against the ones on the lining, and then we'll see what we come up with. They smell different, and they look different, but I need to do a more in-depth analysis before I make any conclusions."

I can almost hear the gears in his head grinding together as they spin.

"Once you've isolated the samples, I may be able to work some magic. Right now, everything's too jumbled together. I wouldn't be able to get a clean reading." As convenient as magic is, everything has its limitations, and my powers aren't exempt from that rule of nature.

It's drilled into every young witch's head that each choice we make has a consequence, and what we send out comes back at least twice or thrice fold. It's a built-in check and balance system. I have to admit, it works for the most part.

"I'll put a rush on it."

"Thank you, Miles." I pat his shoulder and step back to let him focus. I'm proud of the way my court has come together like a puzzle with intricately carved pieces. We're learning how we fit to connect as one moving part. Vampires and witches never vibed. Witches worship nature, and by their very definition vampires are unnatural.

"I'll be in the library with the girls." Slipping out of the lab, I make my way toward the front end of the home. The house used to feel too big, and now its just walls, like any other. I admire the high ceilings originally meant to trap hot air. The ornate ceiling medallions done in shades of red and gold remind me of Cristobal's heritage. There's a hint of his origins spread throughout the building if you know what you're looking for.

It's the touches of personality that helped ensnare me in the first place. He wears humanity better than most vampires I've met. The time and the changes mentally and physically take some of them too far away from the people they once were. Others prefer to forget. The change can be a desperate decision made in an attempt to escape an unbearable life. Many a reinvention was made on the back of an undead life. Kings, queens, mercenaries, and more have ascended from the ashes with a clever backstory and powers that bent the human brain and willpower.

Door capstones and moldings add to the grand environment, boasting craftsmanship and history. They painstakingly refurbished the home with original materials and skilled labor. Colorful art brightens up the deep ocean blue walls along with the ornate pineapple-shaped wall scones. From the thick textured glass warped to mimic the outer shell of the fruit to the spiky iron worked tops, the pieces are miniature masterpieces. I run my fingers over the beveled glass as I pass, pausing to enter the library. The house is a riot of colors. The walls here are a cool gray that contrasts with the dark wood of the bookshelves.

Sacha's blondish brown curls obscure her face as she bends over the table. The cook left a colorful array of finger sandwiches, scones, pastries, and soup served on a three-tier serving platter. The traditional high tea is mouthwatering.

Three sets of tea cups and saucers accompany a matching teapot, sugar bowl, and creamer cup. We don't do anything in halves in the Cortez Court. The china tea set with a ring of turquoise and tiny pink and green flowers is probably the same age as the house itself.

Felicite looks up from her laptop and offers me a small smile. Her dark hair falls around her round face in a shiny black bob. "The tea's still warm. You'll want caffeine for this."

"It's that bad?" I take a seat on the opposite side of the girls.

"Or that good, depending on how you look at it." Sacha blows loose strands away from her face and rakes her hands through her hair as she straightens and rolls her shoulders.

"The woman is as clean as a whistle," Fel says with a sigh. "I'm upset because she lived her life so righteously. How jacked up is that?' She wrinkles her nose and scowls. "It feels awful."

"As far as anyone knows, Imelda was a model citizen. The forty-five-year-old Filipino woman taught fourth grade at Cypress middle school, attended church regularly, volunteered, and had the nerve to be healthy, too." Sacha grimaces.

"She seems to be exactly who she appears on paper," Fel adds.

"The only odd thing is the way she died," Sacha says.

"How's that?" I pour myself a cup of Rose Hip tea, add three sugar cubes, and move my cup and saucer to the side to make room for the manilla file Sacha slides over toward me.

"An aneurysm."

"Uncommon, but not unheard of," I mumble. I scan the obituary, coroner's notes, and important files. It's amazing how we all leave paper trails that draw a picture of who we are and how we live our lives. "There's got to be shady behavior. At the least a neighbor she's feuding with, a sibling she didn't get along with, or a rival teacher. No one's life is perfect."

"Well, she's an only child, so you can rule that one out right off the bat," Sach replies.

I roll my eyes. "You're a real helper."

"We'd have to talk to people to get the inside scoop, but with people posting, 'She'd give you the shirt off her back, and never had an unkind word to speak about anyone,' I doubt you're going to find the kind of dirt you're looking for," Fel says.

"Then why the hell would anyone take her body?" I ask out loud.

"Welcome to our nightmare," Sach sings, emulating Ozzie Osbourne. I admire her cheerfulness. I get the feeling we're going to need it.

I pull up behind Fel's car in Mémé's driveway. Soon this place will be flooded with family. A few months ago, this would've been impossible. Death has brought us all together. It's sad that it takes the end of life to wake everyone up to the fact that our days are numbered, and we never know when we'll meet our end.

Putting the car into park, I grab my bag off the passenger seat and slip out. The air is full of potential. Untapped magic taints the air, lending a spicy sweet scent. Breathing in through my mouth, I can almost taste the flavor combination.

Tonight, for the first time in ages, we'll dine and perform magic as a family. Not for a tradition, but to restore balance, and realign our magical cores. We share a special bond. Like any link, abuse or misuse can dampen its potency. Gone ignored, it can begin to decay and rot. Our family numbers are dwindling, along with many of the older families. Fresh blood and close ties are essential for survival. We have to pierce the festering wound that's become a rift between us all and rebuild. It's been a painstakingly slow process.

I brace myself for the opposition as I climb the stairs leading to the porch. The front door opens before I can knock and Fel grins.

"Show off," I say.

"I happened to be walking by the front door and heard you pull in. No magic involved." She gives me a cheeky grin.

"Ugh. I just hope no one ends up dead when it's all said and done."

She laughs. "Since looks can't kill, I think we'll be all right."

I roll my eyes. "It's going to get easier eventually, right?"

Fel pats my arm. "If anyone *can* reunite us, it'd be you. Look at us all gathering for fellowship, and magical practices. We haven't done this since we were kids. Family dinners were strained at best, and magic was done on a necessary basis. We lost a part of ourselves when that rift occurred that turned us into a shell of a family. You're trying to mend what's been broken for years. It'll take time. Honestly, I think you're doing a smashing job of bringing us back to the start."

"Thanks, cuz. I needed that vote of confidence." The smell of sage greets me as I move into the house. There's a tentative calm settled over the atmosphere. The kind just before a storm breaks out where the pressure can build or dissipate. My goal is to navigate us to the next step without detonating a bomb.

"You two stop moving those jawbones, and get in here and help us," Mom yells.

I laugh. "Yes, ma'am."

The cool air brushes over my skin and I thank God for air conditioning to combat muggy, Louisiana days. My blue ombre T-shirt sticks to my flesh and the khaki shorts that hit mid-thigh feel too long. I close the door behind me and trail my baby cousin into the kitchen. It's been a month of Sundays since I saw the Esçhete women gathered in the kitchen like this. Wearing aprons with silver diadems that represent the elements nestled into their hair Mémé, Mom, and Aunt Heloise are a contradiction of coziness and power. The vine and leaf, moon and stars, and wavelike patterns represent their element to call.

"Today we're cooking not just to nourish our bodies, but our very souls. We're adding magic, hope, and love to every dish we prepare. That means boosting our natural powers to make sure the emotions sink in as we prep with intention."

"Wash your hands, and join us," Mom says.

I remove the necklace woven with copper and Pietersite from my purse and slip it over my head. The dark gray and rusty reddish-orange stone represents earth. Today I am the grounding magic wielder. I will weave the strands of magic together harmoniously while Mémé steps back. In her own words: 'The time for hand-holding has passed. You have a lot to prove to me and everyone else watching your every move.'

"Why don't you tell everyone what we're preparing and why?" Mémé says. I feel like I'm at Show and Tell with much higher stakes.

"I chose this meal carefully. We need to come together as a family, to heal old wounds and move forward, so I focused on grounding, love, healing, and protection. Mémé and I prepared the roast last night, so it could slow cook. We focused on strength, protection, and grounding. I'm worried about Av and Vit with their mother gone. Every sheep is precious in this flock. The roasted potatoes and honey-glazed carrots will echo the grounding, as well as providing more healing and protection. The homemade bread is the binding element, representing kinship, and the Mead is love. I want you to focus on these attributes, and the healing, cleansing, and rebuilding of the Esçhete name. Let all the pain and dissonance of the past stay behind us where it belongs. "

"That's easier said than done," my mother says quietly. I feel for her. She and Aunt Odette always clashed the most.

"Have we become so petty and small-minded we'd let bickering and disagreements impede our magical legacy? Our numbers are dwindling, and yet we remain at odds. This family is close to falling out of favor with the ancestors and facing extinction. The universe has not been kind nor giving to us in recent times. If we hadn't distanced ourselves from the old ways, we might've noticed. The cracks started small. Our separation was a slow process. The rebuild will be much the same way." I gave them all time to get used to being in the same space regularly. I cannot afford to be delicate any longer.

"We had our grieving period. Now we move forward. We'll honor her memory by making a better future possible. You are the heads of your family. I expect you to be the backbones of this family the women have always been. Tonight we start the task of mending our foundation." I glance at Mémé who gives a nod of her head. I meet the eyes of the women I've grown up respecting. They've placed their trust in me. I can't let them down.

"Old habits die hard, cher. We can learn new tricks, but it won't happen in a day," Tante Heloise says.

"All I ask for is an open mind and genuine effort. The rest will take care of itself in time," I assure her.

I can see the cynicism in their gazes. They think this small step is pointless. There's a method to my madness. We can't work bigger spells without trust. Forgiveness has to start somewhere. "Aimee and Vit have always followed their mother's lead. Right now, they're lost. If we don't guide them, someone else will. I won't let the darkness take them the way it did their mother." I ignore their looks as I move to the sink to wash my hand and settle in beside Fel. "What do you say we take the roasted potatoes?" I ask.

"I'm game." Fel's voice is cheery. I draw strength from her unflagging support. As my first cousin, literally months apart from me in age, she's been my built-in partner-in-crime.

"I want us to all make an effort with Aimee and Vit. I invited them, and I'm hoping they'll show up soon. We need to come together, or everything I have planned is going to be for naught. Our power is only as strong as our bond. We've got all eyes on us, and we need to seal those cracks in our foundation and paint them over." I harden my tone, letting them know without words this is not negotiable. Being a leader means ruffling feathers. I feel like I've been in constant conflict since Mémé announced that I'd be taking over. We're a broken lot, but it's not irreparable.

"This has been a long time coming. I should've acted long before now. A mother can be blind to the realities of her children's fault. I downplayed the animosity that sprung up, allowing a wedge to form. Because of my ignorance, Louella has a lot of work ahead of her." Mémé's voice shakes.

"Mama, it's not your fault," my mother says.

"Yes, it is. As the matriarch of this family, everything that happens or doesn't is my business. It's the burden we agree to carry when we take on the title. I have hope for the future. It won't be easy. I won't lie to you." Mémé shakes her head. "It'll be a rocky ride. Esçhetes have never been weak-willed. We can fix what's broken. The lean, hard times build character. They teach us about who we truly are what abilities we have, or in some cases, lack."

"You've seen something," I state.

"Non." Mémé shakes her head. "It's more of a feeling ..." she places a hand on her belly, "here." Her lips twist. "A sick feeling tells me the darkness isn't done with us. It's gotten a taste of Esçhete blood, and it's hungry for more. With power, comes danger. We've had a great period of peace after the last uprising. It's made us soft. None of you has had to fight or live through casualties. By the time I was twenty-five, it was a way of life. Bargaining with the Weres and vampires wasn't something we took lightly. It was necessary. The losses we took were significant."

I hang on every word. Mémé doesn't talk a lot about the Reaping. The period when hunters pooled their resources and launched a co-ordinated assault on our area and the magical beings inhabiting it is a sore topic for all involved. The Reaping pushed the vampires and witches into a tentative truce. The chain of events set of the start of a co-mingled paranormal community and the shrinking of prominent families. I lean forward, holding my breath as I wait for her to continue.

"But that is a story for another time."

The breath rushes from my lungs. Mémé smiles sadly. *Soon,* she mouths. I nod my head as we return our attention to our dishes.

"Is it me, or is Mémé spilling secrets like tea these days?" Fel whispers.

I chuckle. "It's not just you. I mean, I knew Mémé was a bad ass, but now I'm wondering just what she's gotten into over the years. I spent a lot of time researching paranormal things while I was gone. I'm ashamed to confess I neglected our history. I know the things Mémé's mentioned over the years, but that's nothing but a drop in the bucket." We cut up potatoes, onions, and garlic, place them in a large white bowl with mustard yellow designs that's older than the both of us, sprinkle on spices, and mix them up. We make bundles with tinfoil and carry them out to the grill.

Free from eyes and ears, I feel the stress roll off my shoulders. We take a seat at the long, wooden picnic bench.

"I never realized how stubborn the women in our family are," I mumble.

Fel snorts. "Really? 'Cause you're one of the most mule-headed."

"What?" I laugh. "Come on, I'm not that bad."

"That's just what a stubborn person would say," Fel taunts.

I narrow my eyes. "Uh huh. I suppose you're not stubborn?"

"I'm far more agreeable. Mostly because I take after my father in that aspect." She shrugs.

I give her a playful glare. Her laid-back approach is part of what makes her element to call water. Steady when situations get hectic, she always keeps a cool head. She has a slow burn temper much like water. A calm body of water is a beautiful, tranquil thing to behold. Rile it up, and it turns deadly.

"I was surprised when she started talking about the Reaping," Fel says in a hushed tone.

"Me too. She usually avoids the topic like the plague."

"It's like Vietnam. Most of the people involved won't speak a word about it. Do you think it means something? Her opening up?"

"Yeah. She knows she's getting a bit long in the tooth to hold onto secrets unless she plans to take them to the grave. I think we're all in for some shocks," I say, thinking of her tryst with a certain vampire in the Cortez Court. I never would've pegged her as a rule breaker. There's more to their story than we know. So far, I've kept my mouth shut out of respect for Mémé. I'm not sure how much longer that's going to hold.

"It's hard to think of her as a person. That sounds awful, doesn't it?" Fel laughs. "I don't mean it that way. It's just, she's always been such a wise older woman with graying hair, and a regal bearing, regardless of the responsibilities she's shouldered. Youth syndrome makes us forget our elders have lived a life long before we were even thought of."

"We should actually get the cooking started before they realize how long we've been gone and come and check up on us." We pile the sachets onto the long shelf, and I turn on the gas. I imagine energy flowing through my body to my palm. A flame flickers to life on my palm, and I light the gas.

"It comes so easily to you now," Fel marvels.

"After the sessions Mémé's been putting me through, it'd better." I shudder as I think of our crash course in training. "She's tried her hardest to shove years and years worth of training and information into a thirteen-month period. If I'm not looking in grimoires or old journals, I'm with the court learning etiquette, sword play, and how to think like them. Their customs are nothing like our own, Fel. It's like falling into the upside down and the past in one go round." A strange blend of dominance, power plays, and an almost European-style of royal hierarchy, the courts are a tangled web, impossible to navigate without knowing all the nuances.

"Want to take a walk?" I ask, eager to steal a few more minutes of quiet with her.

"Yeah."

The bright purple lavender calls to me. I make my way through the knee-high rows, skimming my fingers over the tops. Pausing, I inhale the sweet fragrance. "I missed this place when I was away."

"What are they like?"

I cock my head to the side. "The court?"

"Yes." She bites her lip and toys with a sunflower stalk a half a row away.

"I don't mind talking about them." I frown as I chase the thoughts in my head. "Putting it in words is difficult. Their instincts can be extremely primal, and animalistic like Weres. What makes them so different is their ability to think rings around our best strategist. Their minds would rival Machiavelli. Constantly calculating minds, they think like people play chess, anticipating the next best move. Their main goal is always survival. Though loyalty and honor are a very serious matter.

"Despite the passage of time, they have maintained something medieval. A fact we should all be grateful for by the way. If they ever abandoned that code, I dread the ravaging that would follow." Kept in check and controlled by a carefully kept code, a stringent set of rules, and powerful players ready to enforce them, the vampire population runs like a well-oiled clock. If they ever made a true go at world domination, hell would be unleashed on earth.

"That is a frightening thought." Fel shifts her weight uneasily.

"Believe me, I know more than I ever wanted to." I grimace. "The brutality they deal in is a lot to take in. Once you've seen, there's no such thing as unseeing." I shudder.

"Suddenly I don't envy you and your vampire boo the same." She pouts.

I snigger "Vampire boo?"

"It's what I call Cristobal in my head," she admits sheepishly.

"Please say it out loud one day," I beg. "His face would be priceless. He'd be properly scandalized. We're dragging him into the twentieth-century kicking and screaming." Imagining his unamused expression, I chuckle.

"You walk the line between two worlds. Be careful you don't trip and stumble headfirst into one of them." Fel's words are hollow.

I turn to look at her. "Fel?"

"You are the bridge between two worlds. To prepare for what will be. You must discover what once was. Things in the darkness have been waiting for an opportunity to return. Alone we will parish. Together we can vanquish." She blinks.

"Felicite?" I whisper, grabbing her arm.

"What?" she asks, dazed. Her eyes are unfocused, and her voice is weak.

"Do you remember what you just said?" I study her carefully as I grip her forearms gently, supporting her weight.

"That I call Cristobal your vampire boo in my head?" she says huskily.

"No. You just …" I pause. "I think you just spoke a prophecy."

"What? No. I've never done that." Felicite shakes her head.

"Yes, I'm pretty sure you just did. The sight runs in the family."

"I don't want this, Lou." The fear in her wide eyes guts me.

"I'm sorry, Fel. It seems like the time of what we want is behind us. Now we're all doing what we must."

She grabs my hand. "Don't tell anyone. Not until we're positive that's what it was?"

"You know I can't withhold something this important indefinitely, right?"

She closes her eyes and nods. "I know."

"It won't be tonight. We've got enough on our plates, but make your peace with it?"

She gives a bitter laugh. "One prediction does not a Seer make."

"No," I agree. "However, it does show your inclination for it."

"I'm going to say what we're both thinking. It feels like we've all gotten a power upgrade along with you after this bonding."

"Or maybe it's the family coming together. Strength in numbers?" I suggest.

"It'd be in accordance with the old teachings," Fel agrees. Silence settles between us. The sound of a car pulling up front reaches my ears.

"They came."

"Who?" Fel asks.

"Aimee and Vit."

"You can hear that?" she asks.

I push aside the embarrassment. This is who I am now. Shame isn't going to change my reality. I nod. "I can hear a lot better than I used to."

"And it doesn't frighten you?"

"I'm adapting. I spend half my time with people whose senses are far more superior to my own. It keeps me from being completely blind." I wasted enough time running. It only prolonged the inevitable. "Come on, let's greet them."

I look around the table at the relaxed faces of my kin and clear my throat.

"I invited everyone here because I wanted to have fellowship, and work magic. Familial magic. The kind we've long neglected."

"Everyone has to be welcome to do that," Vit snaps.

"At this table, everyone is. We're all equals here." I keep my voice even and remind myself that hurt people, hurt other people. It's a cycle.

"You expect us to believe that, after everything that happened with our mother?" Aimee scoffs.

"Yes. If you want it. I can't force anyone to do anything. If you don't want to be here, I won't hold you. What I'm offering is a chance for a new start. You aren't your mother. No one is holding you accountable for her actions. Both of you were trapped by her way of thinking, and self-imposed shunning. I don't want you to remain trapped in the shadows. I want to free you. Which is why today we'll be creating a family altar and casting a circle."

Aimee and Vit look at one another. "Is this a joke?" Aimee asks.

"No." I hold out my hand. "I would never do anything like that."

"You know how little magical aptitude we possess. So why call us in to be part of the team now?" Vit asks vehemently. I flinch. His anger is a living flame, ready to burn anything in its path. We deserved his distrust. It's disgraceful how we allowed them to remain on the outskirts.

"That's no reason for you not to be included in everything this family does. Things are going to be different now. I promised you that. I plan on keeping my word."

The siblings exchanged a look. "You never answered me. Why now?" Vit regains control of the conversation.

"You're overdue for this. Whether we want to admit it or not, we all need each other now more than ever."

He presses his thin lips together tightly. "You mean we need you, right? Poor little, orphaned siblings have lost their mother. Let's throw them a bone—"

"No." I slam my hand down on the table. "We're not going to fall back into this cycle. No shade or judgment. There are no hidden meanings in my words. This is me extending an olive branch and asking you to help me set a new normal. You never lacked bravery. Don't fail me now."

He cocks his head to the side and peers at me through narrowed eyes. "You're serious, aren't you?"

"I am."

"We'll give this a shot, Lou. For you. Don't make us regret it," he cautions.

"I appreciate that, Vit. There's been wrong on all sides. I was out of the loop being gone. I'm caught up now and ready to make changes. I'm new. There's going to be an adjustment period for all of us. Communication is paramount."

Vit smirks. "Tell me, fearless leader, how shall we proceed?" I let his smug look slide because his tone is tempered with the one thing we all need—hope.

Chapter Three

You are leaving the office early today, and not coming back until tomorrow after ten o'clock," Sacha announces from in front of my desk.

I struggle to focus my strained eyes on the sandy-blonde haired nonconformist. "What?" I stare at the pile of paperwork on my desk. "You see that, right?"

"We took a vote. It's two to one, you lose," Fel adds in a singsong voice.

I spin in my office chair to face Fel. "What is this? My office mates plotting against me?"

Sacha spins my chair back around to face her. "Yes, because you're stubborn, obviously exhausted, and in serious need of some fresh air. And maybe," she gasps, "a little fun."

I cross my arms over my chest, resisting her charm. Half a day off puts me even further behind. "I don't blame you for being sick of me. I've been frazzled recently. There's a lot on my plate at the moment, and it's got me feeling snowed."

"All the more reason to take better care of yourself," Fel says.

"Let's go. We'll hit up New Orleans. How about Café Du Monde, my treat, and your choice of restaurant for dinner," Sacha urges.

The thought of the puff pastries coated in a layer of powdered sugar makes my mouth water. I can smell the river water, and taste Acme Oyster Company and pralines. Stress eating is an indulgence I can get down with if we're heading into the city.

"Not even you can resist the lure of chicory coffee and beignets." Sacha points at me.

My stomach growls loud enough for everyone in the office to hear. *Betrayed by my own body.*

"Fine," I concede. The girls cheer, and I laugh. "What would I do without you two?"

"Starve, and possibly harm someone while hangry," Fel replies sweetly without missing a beat.

"Have I been that big of a witch without a W?" I ask. They exchange a look that makes me cringe. "I'm sorry, you guys."

"Hey, it happens to all of us. Just let me handle all this." Fel scoots her chair over, grabs the paperwork in front of me, and wheels back "You two enjoy a day out of the office."

I throw my hands up. "I surrender."

"Quickly, Sacha, take her before she changes her mind." Fel shoos us away with her hand.

"I don't know if I'm flattered because you care so much, or I'm insulted by how badly you want me out of the office," I mumble as I gather my things and rise to follow Sacha outside.

"The first one," Fel cries with a waggle of her fingers.

I climb into the passenger of the aquamarine beast with Sacha and lean back in the seat. With the window down, and the wind blowing through my multi-colored sunset red, orange, and blonde hair, I feel free. I've gotten stagnate. I let the weight of the tasks coming down the pipeline toward me pin me in place. I massage my scalp as I inhale the sweet Bayou air.

"Feeling better already, aren't you?" Sacha asks.

"I didn't realize how long I'd been cooped up in the office, or some other stuffy room learning this or that. I've missed the sun more than I can express." The rays beam down on my face, and I soak them up like a flower.

"Glad I can be of service."

"How are you, Sach? I know I've been a horrible friend recently. These coronations have me wrapped up tighter than a mummy."

"You haven't missed much." She pauses. "Though, there's been a recent development on the family front."

"Good things?" I ask carefully.

"You know, I'm not sure yet. My mom came to the house the other day, totally unannounced, which is very bizarre for her. You know how she is about punctuality and politeness. I think maybe she was afraid I'd tell her not to come if she called and asked me."

I turn my body toward her. "I bet you're right. What did your mom say?"

"That she missed me, and she'd spoken with my father. Do you believe that? For once in her life, she stood up for me." I can hear the amazement in her voice. That was a huge step for her mother.

My heart swells with happiness for my friend. *About damn time, too.* The Morels are a patriarchal family. Her father calls the shots, and her mother never goes against his final rulings.

"He didn't admit to any wrong doing on his part, but he agreed that perhaps he'd been hasty and heavy-handed with his response to my refusal of the engagement. Because, of course, disowning me is just a *little* over the top." She scowls. "He went so far as to say an unhappy match would hinder the magic of both husband and wife."

"Coming from your father, that's practically a heartfelt apology," I say drolly. The proud, arrogant man was a throwback to a time when men ruled the world and their family without question.

"I know, right? He even asked me to join them for the family holiday. Well, technically Mom did, but you know he had to okay it."

She's trying to downplay her excitement, but it's seeping through every word she speaks. I understand her reason for walking away from her family when they throw down the ultimatum. Arranged marriages are archaic and cruel, and Sacha isn't built to settle down and be solely a homemaker. Which is exactly what her ex-future husband had been looking for. The whole thing was a mistake. This girl finds adventure wherever she goes. I can't see her ever fully giving that up. Despite the bad call on her father's part. Her family had always been close-knit. The separation, while necessary, was hard on her.

"I think you've earned your father's respect."

Her hands clutch the wheel tighter. "After all this time, do you even think it's possible? I feel like my entire life has been a contest where I vied desperately for his attention and approval. Him giving either is such a foreign concept at this point, I can't imagine it."

"What you did, walking away from your home and inheritance, took guts, Sach. More than most people have. Even if he never says it to your face, trust me he knows, and admires it."

She flashes a crooked smile. "Thanks, Lou."

"Anytime."

"Do you think it's a trap?"

"The holiday? No. I mean, it's not as if he can ambush you into a surprise wedding. I think they missed you as much as you missed them, and everyone raised hell until your father figured out a way to relent without losing face."

She chuckles. "Now there's an image. All of them giving Dad shit over me. I wish I'd been there to see it."

"What did you tell your mom about the holiday?"

"That'd I'd think about it, but I needed to check in with my boss."

I smirk. "I think you should do it, Sach. Family is important. We fight and disagree, but it   doesn't change the connection between us."

"You're right. I'm just nervous. After being on my own for a year, I'm not the same woman, and I don't know how they're going to react to this version of me."

"Well, for the record, I love every version of you, but this incarnation is my favorite to date because for the first time you're truly happy."

"I won't go back to being that person constantly concerned about their approval and bound to their rules."

"Nor should you."

She gives a shaky laugh. "I needed to hear that. For the first time last year, I felt like I could breathe. I always dreamt of tasting freedom. I figured short of leaving everything I knew behind I would never discover it. They almost brainwash us from the start to follow the rules with the family duty, proper manners, and traditions. There's beauty and darkness in that."

"I'll always be straight with you. Even when it's not what you want to hear."

"Can you spare me for two weeks, though?" Worry creeps into her tone.

"Don't worry about it. We'll make it work. This is important."

"Thank you, Lou."

"Anytime."

"Now that you're caught up with me, how are you really? I know you're tired, but that's all physical."

"Oh, we're diving deep, huh?"

"It's a nice road trip. We may as well. If you get to check up on my headspace it's only fair I do the same."

I sigh. "I don't know how to answer that question honestly. My emotions are all across the board. Stress doesn't look pretty on me, and switching gears is a tough job when you're dealing with two vastly dissimilar groups of people. I don't want to embarrass anyone or disappoint, and it's been one test after another one since the announcement went out that I'd be stepping up."

"I can imagine. What you're doing is unprecedented. People are going to be jealous and petty as hell."

"Believe me, I figured that out fast. I thought I'd be used to it dealing with the upper-class witches, but they have nothing on vampires."

"No?"

"People like to talk about having royal blood. Some of these men and women arc royal, and they don't let anyone forget. There are so many tiny details to remember. Knowing Cristobal and the others are putting their necks on the chopping board for me doesn't help either."

"Why? You bring a lot of good things to the table."

"I'm also a high-risk factor. If I offend enough people, fail to fit in, or turn off enough people, he could lose his standing. I'm not about to let that happen. So, I have to be damn near perfect for them to believe I'm not a subpar creature. Being a witch helps, but some of these vampires would make Death Eaters look like teddy bears."

"Jesus, Lou. At least you can never doubt his love. He risked everything to be with you. It's what we all dream about. A soul deep kind of love that you'd sacrifice everything for." She sighs.

"Is that love?"

"What?"

"Where do you draw a line between obsession and love?"

"Are you doubting his feelings?" she questions, shocked.

"No. I think he loves me as much as he's able to, or in his way. What concerns me is the fact that it's not organic. Our connection is otherworldly. Did he have a choice in the matter? I'm his bondmate. Destiny picked me. The universe said I was the one for him and twined our what … souls, consciousness? No one knows. Is that romantic or a matter of chemistry and genes?" *And what happens if someday I don't live up to the hype?* I toy with the edge of the seatbelt.

"You've thought about this often, haven't you?"

I nod. "There are times when it's like a record with a scratch, that won't stop skipping in my head." Sacha is the least judgmental person I know. I don't have to worry about unloading my warped thoughts on her. "You've seen Cristobal. He's powerful, masculine, handsome, and suave. What if I never fit into his world the way he needs me to? There's no place for him in ours, so where does that leave us?" My mind begins to spin out of control. Once I let the cork pop off the bottle, it's hell to shove back in.

"Has he said anything to make you feel this way?" Her voice grows icy.

"No. Cristobal doesn't have to. All our biggest arguments stem from our different ways of thinking. He can't understand where I'm coming from, and I feel the same way about him."

"No couple is perfect, Lou."

"No, but there are times when I understand that we are two different species. And if I push myself to become more like him or the bond changes me, then who am I? What am I?" I'm speaking more to myself, but it feels good to purge.

"Have you talked to him about this, Lou?"

"With all my spare time? No."

"You can't keep this bottled up."

"No, I made my bed, and now I have to lie in it."

"I don't prescribe to that malarkey. You deserve to be happy."

"I am. It's just …" My lower lip trembles. "When I squint, I'm not sure how much I like the picture I'm painted in."

Reaching across the console, she grabs my hand. "I know you can't get perspective because you're in the midst, so let me remind you. You are Louella Heloise Esçhete. My bad ass, loyal, talented, beautiful, and let's not leave out powerful, best friend. If you weren't in this one-hundred percent, you wouldn't have agreed to acknowledge the bond. You left for years, Lou. So, you can say there were other options. You explored them. They didn't fulfill you. You chose him. That's important to remember."

Her words make me smile. "I did, didn't I?"

"Damn straight. I remember it clearly because it made the elders catch the vapors, your Mémé cackle, and single girls everywhere cry."

"You are so full of it." I laugh.

"Hey, I'm sure that is a legitimate story."

The sour mood lifted, we turn on the 90s station and sing our hearts out the rest of the way.

We lapse into silence as she weaves her way through the city traffic and manages to snag a decent parking space.

Out on the sidewalk, my eyes drink in the city. The old buildings possess a rugged charm, and the clusters of people are rich and diverse. From smartly dressed businessmen and women, to eccentrically clothed artists selling paper and performers, the streets are teeming with life. Bright splashes of purple, gold, and green catch my eyes as the city displays its colors proudly. Even the tourists have a charm of their own with their wide-eyed wonder and cameras at the ready. We travel alongside them, catching their contagious enthusiasm, as we view the city with fresh eyes again. I smell Café Du Monde long before I see it. We join the lengthy line of people waiting for their fix and grab a table out front. The classic green umbrella makes me smile and blocks the wicked sun from my face.

"Seeing as how we have the rest of the day to ourselves, are you up for helping me with a little project?"

"Sure. What do you have in mind?" Sacha asks as they deliver our pile of beignets.

"I'm ready for a new hair color. I need to shake things up." *And be in control of something for once.*

"What color are you thinking?"

"Pink. I figure it's about time I mark something off my bucket list and freak out all the uptight elders planning my coronations."

She barks a laugh. "Well, there's one way to be passive aggressive."

"To change and taking back control." I raise my mug, and she clinks glasses with me.

They city is always lively, but it comes into its own at night. We wander the streets, hunting up treasures as the day slips its skin and night arrives in all its majestic glory. We stop to dance to a jazz band playing in the street. I'm lighter than I've been in months. We laugh as we link arms and continue our way back toward the car.

"Do you think you had enough oysters back there? We can always pick up a third order to go."

"You helped me with those."

"Just a little bit." She holds up her thumb and index finger. We are halfway through Jackson square when I feel it. The knowing tug of power.

"Do you?"

"Yeah?" I answer, scanning the area.

"It's her." Sacha nods her head toward the slender woman with olive skin, dark hair, and a simple black dress. Seated in a red fold-out chair, she blends in with the others pedaling their wares. There's no fanfare, only a beautifully drawn chalkboard with a gypsy woman inside a crystal ball, and her prices.

She smiles and waves us over. Her golden bangles click together. *Romani.*

"Come on. This'll be fun." She drags me the three feet to the woman.

Doesn't she know fate and me are on the outs due to her heavy-handed treatment of my life?

"Hello, my friends. My name is Sabrina. The spirits are anxious to speak with you tonight."

"How much?" I ask.

"For Louella Esçhete and Sacha Morel, free of charge."

"Job perks," Sacha crows.

She flashes a rakish grin full of mischief and knowledge. Clairvoyants have always been a bit spooky to me. They possess a disarming quality. Because not only do they look at you like they see inside your soul, there's a huge possibility they just might.

Sacha lowers herself into the chair first, and I sit beside her. "What kind of reading would you like?"

"I'll let you pick," Sacha says with a shrug.

"You like to go with the flow. Continue that habit. It will take you to places you've never dreamed of being before." She pulls a worn but well-cared for set of cards from a black velvet pouch. The rectangular objects radiate a power all their own.

"These have been in my family for centuries, and they always read true. I use them for my most special clients." She winks. Slightly faded and dappled around the edges, the beige cards have thinned over time. I hold my breath as she moves the stack forward over her black velvet table cover.

Sacha sucks in her breath when she touches the card.

"They're saying hello," Sabrina says. "I want you to cut the deck two times. Good. Now, shuffle the cards, keeping your mind blank, and stop when it feels right."

Sacha nods and gingerly begins to shuffle them respectfully.

After a minute she stops. Sabrina takes the cards from her, spreads them into a fan, and holds them out. "Pick the three cards that call to you. We are going to do a simple Past, Present, and Future."

Sacha carefully picks a card off the end, one in the middle, and one to the far right.

Sabrina places them down.

"This will tell us about your past." She flips the card over to reveal a card with Gabriel blowing his trumpet, and two people standing under him. "The judgment card. In your past, you had a lot of self-doubts. You tried to make yourself fit into a mold you knew wasn't meant for you. You were out of tune with who you were." Sabrina turns the card in the center. A hooded Skelton greets us with a grim smile. "Death. The beginning of a cycle is starting. You've renewed your spirit and healed long-standing wounds. You know who you are now, and how to play to your strengths and avoid your weaknesses. The universe has been watching you blossom." The final card is the lovers. Two couples embrace passionately. Sabrina grins. "The

Lovers. I see a very powerful union in your future. It will frighten you at first, but trust in the universe and your strength."

Sacha nods. She turns to me, beaming. "Looks like I'll be getting a romance of my own soon." Her eyes are dark diamonds in her face as they sparkle merrily under the lamp light.

"You next."

I eye the cards nervously.

"No cards I think. Perhaps something a bit more traditional for you."

She rummages in her purple satchel and comes out with a rectangular length of animal hide. She smooths the supple skin over her tablecloth and reaches back in to produce a red velvet bag. The contents clack together as she moves them about. They call to me.

"Yes, this is a much better fit isn't it, my dove?"

I stare at her, stunned. She winks. "It's been a long time since I have thrown the bones. Let's see if they'll cooperate. They have a lot to say to you tonight." She lifts the bag and begins to shake. I feel like the fabrics of fate are rubbing together. She drops bones, shells, trinkets, and curios on to the mat. I swallow to moisten my dry mouth. A golden joker face stands out. She lifts it up. "There's a trickster on the loose. He hides behind many faces and brings a great danger." She shudders. "You have to be careful here." She moves on to a small sterling silver figure. "The swan represents royalty. I think for you, that is self-explanatory, but if you look right beside it, you'll find this bone which represents the masculine. You'll rule alongside a loyal partner. Don't doubt what he would do for you." It's like she listened in to our previous conversation. The weight should be lifting, but instead, I feel tossed about on a raft by the universe. "Beside that, you can see a crown, but it's upside down. You're conflicted. If you want to be successful, you need to find balance within yourself. Like the canine tooth, which is both dark and light. Each of us has the capacity to do good and evil. Duality is the natural way of things. Its center in this reading, so it's very important you remember that. The bones have had their say," she says quietly.

"Thank you, Sabrina" I reach over and squeeze her hand. There are many who feign having the gift, but she is not one of them. We leave the table after tipping her, and I muddle over the things she said.

"Do you feel better?" Sacha asks.

"I'm not sure what I feel. I think fate pretty much told me to sit my ass down, though?"

Sacha laughs. "She did, didn't she? I always heard she was kind of a bitch."

"I can't wait until our roles are reversed," I mumble.

"Me either, Lou. It's been a lonely couple of years."

I shove the sunglasses on top of my head as I walk into the mansion. It's a welcome sight after a few days away and family togetherness. After centuries, the court has mastered the art of giving one another enough space to breathe. I inhale the scent of the bergamot and sage incense Ada constantly burns. I walk inside, greeted by the silence.

"Anyone home?" I ask.

"I'm in the parlor. Join me for tea. I received the labs," Miles says as I walk into the living room.

"And?" I take a seat beside Miles on the dark gray settee. The silver tea set shines like a treasure. Porcelain cups and saucers with tiny tea spoons are set out, in case someone happened by.

He blinks. "Well, this is a new look?"

"Do you like it?" I run a hand through my flat-ironed, chin-length fuchsia hair.

"I adore it." He beams. "Tea?"

"Yes, please."

"Sugar?"

"Two lumps, please."

"Cream?"

"Just a dash."

Patiently, I wait as he prepares the brew. There are certain things I've grown used to. When it gets real, the tea flows like water in this house. Refusal is seen as an insult, so, I always accept. Settled back with our porcelain cups, we resume our conversation.

"It raised more questions than it answered. The sample is from a human."

"What? How is that even possible? I mean, you saw the photos from the gravesite. Is it possible there was a witch, and I missed it?"

He shakes his head. "I highly doubt it. Witches have a certain smell."

I wrinkle my nose. "Yuck."

Miles chuckles. "Not a bad one. Simply distinct. Your magic smells sweeter and more robust, like a wine made from grapes harvested at their peak."

"I don't know if I'm fascinated or skeeved out, Miles."

He shrugs. "It's okay to be a little of both in this case."

"I don't doubt your information, but I'm having a hard time imagining an average Joe causing this much destruction and barely leaving behind a trail." I cross my ankles and run over a list of reasons an everyday person would need a corpse.

"I could only assume they employed some magical assistance since I found no residue that would suggest explosives or machinery."

"I didn't sense any magic." I mentally re-assess my investigation.

"Perhaps they masked it?" Miles suggests as he refills his cup.

"Nothing's impossible, but it would take one hell of a powerful witch or maybe a Faerie, who are way too hoity-toity for that kind of dirty work."

"A lesser Fae fairly called and enslaved wouldn't have a choice."

"Yes, but how many humans know how to summon a Faerie these days? And I repeat, what the hell would they want with a corpse?" I swirl the tea in my cup to keep my hands busy.

"Perhaps she was a changeling?" He arches a dark brow.

"Let's go with your theory." I salute him with the mug. "What good could she be to them, deceased?"

"They honor their species. Perhaps they wanted to bury her among her own people in their land?"

I wrinkle my nose. "They're careful. If Faeries crossed over, we would never ever know."

"Yes. Faeries are far too cunning. Unless their goal was to make mischief?" He poses his question like a query.

I shake my head. "That'd be morbid. Even for them."

"Are you sure there was nothing was unusual about the victim?"

"Trust me, Miles. We all scoured her records, house, school, and online history. The woman should be instated to sainthood."

"Hmmm." He picks up a packet of Jammie Dodgers, opens the wrapper, and shakes two out for me, keeping two for himself. He knows my pension for British sweets. I take a bite of the buttery biscuit with jelly filling and hum my approval.

"Perhaps," he pauses to chew and swallow, "they were making something?"

I cover my hand with my mouth. "What?" I ask around the cookie.

"The humans. Maybe they needed the parts for a spell or a magical weapon."

I wash down the cookie with tea. "Short of bringing a monster made of pieced together parts to life, I'd say nay. A hand of glory requires a murder's hand. Things of that nature tend to come from beings who exude serious darkness, so it doesn't fit."

"Or the opposite. Sometimes what's needed is purity."

"Then we'd be getting into virgin sacrifices and blood magic. She was dead already. It wouldn't do any good to take from her."

"And we're at an impasse." Miles sighs. "Perchance it was a random bout of human insanity. People don't always have a reason for their strange and horrific actions."

"I'd feel better about leaving it at that if I knew the *how*." There's a riddle I have no idea how even to begin to solve. How does one remove a body from a grave, cause catastrophic damage concentrated in one place, and only leave behind faint footprints and a few drops of blood? What group of people could gain power from that? Is it a cult with some whacked out initiation process?

"Did you run the DNA through the database?"

He sniffs. "Of course I did." His words are acidic. "*Whoever* it is has never committed a crime … that they were caught for at any rate."

I grunt. *Another dead end.* "Sorry, Miles. I want to get this figured out. I know you're a pro at what you're doing."

He grants me a smile. *I am forgiven.* "I can tell you the person who bled is a male, more than likely Caucasian. Admittedly, I garnered more information from the prints you took. You're looking for at least three males. In between the height of five-foot-nine-inches to six feet. They range from anywhere from one-hundred and seventy pounds, to two-hundred. I can tell you the make and model of their shoes, but to summarize two were in a pair of cheap steel-toe boots, and the other in gym shoes."

"They don't sound like they were very organized."

"It wouldn't appear so. Lucky for us, or we wouldn't have prints or blood."

"All we have to go by is three men, possibly tall and lean. At least one Caucasian, and all of an undetermined age?" The list of suspects that fit that description could fill a stadium.

"Indeed," he says glumly.

"That's broad as hell, Miles." My shoulders slump. I feel the resolution of the case slip further away. I want to solve every case, but the truth is, a good chunk of them we can't. I can show people how to protect themselves from further harm, but tracing the source isn't an easy task.

"It is now. Later, after we've gleaned more information, there may be more we've missed. Forensics is a puzzle. You can only get the big picture one piece at a time. This is a patient man's game." He sips his tea, pinky up, and I swear he has never been more British. Right now, he's the equivalent of a vampire Sherlock Holmes. All he needs to complete the look is a pipe, a tweed jacket, and a matching cap. My lips twitch.

"Did I say something amusing?" His puzzled expression is adorable.

"No. Promise me you'll never change, Miles."

"Who else could I possibly be?"

"That's the spirit, old chap," I say, adopting a British accent as I wink. He pinches his lips together, but the humor in his blue gaze softens his sternness. I finish my tea because to him it'd be blasphemous to do otherwise. "Thank you for looking into this for me."

"I remain at your disposal. What do you plan to do next?" He brings the cup to his lips.

"Wait. My gut tells me this isn't the last odd occurrence we're going to see. Mark my words, this is too weird to be a one-off." I pat his knee. "Thanks for the cuppa." I set down my cup and saucer, and ignore the twinge of guilt at not taking the dishware to the sink. I've had enough of being berated by my *family* for doing what they pay good money for servants to take care of. I move toward the stairs intent on a hot bath when intuition tugs me in the opposite direction.

Retracing my footsteps, I head outside to the Moon Garden. The fragrant white blossoms of all shapes and sizes and the running water in the pond soothe me. The silence is energizing. I kick off my flats, and wiggle my toes, admiring the grass and earth beneath me. Grounded, I inhale the fresh air and exhale slowly.

This bricked-in area is a slice of paradise. A calming space to combat the chaos that exists outside the four walls. From its rounded entrance to the water lilies floating in the pond with its mini waterfall effect, and the fresh herbs surrounding the water line, it's everything I could want in an outside magical space. The knowledge that it was built by Cristobal using the memories of me he'd gathered increases my feelings of sentimentalism. Tilting my head back, I admire the moon. Full and luminous, it calls to me.

There's power to be gained on a night like this. My core temperature rises and my skin itches. I feel feverish. A low, inaudible hum of power travels up through the soles of my feet. I walk deeper into the garden, opening myself up to what the universe has to tell me. Warded, and spelled, this place is my sanctuary.

I sink onto the grass beside the pond, cross my legs, and inhale. I turn the issues weighing me down into smooth black stones. Mentally, I chuck them into the water and watch the ripples. Not all go so easily. I shed the worries like a snake slips an ill-fitting skin. Clearing my mind is kin to escaping a fog. After a time, I gain true clarity for the first period in days.

With the shroud of uncertainty, stress, and fear lifted, I'm free to connect properly with my surroundings. The moonlight caresses my skin, filling me with strength and calm. I lean back on my elbows, soaking up the rays like a beach bunny settling in to worship the sun. The moon is my goddess of choice, and her cooling tranquility is a blessing. A sudden wind ruffles my newly dyed pink tresses. The brisk breeze is an anomaly in the muggy weather. I sit up.

Nothing that means harm may enter this space. That doesn't mean a curious spirit can't. A prickly sensation climbs its way up my spine and down my arms. A lily-white feather floats down in a graceful back and forth motion before landing on my lap. I peer over my shoulder, sensing another presence at play. Hair falls on my face. I tuck the fuchsia strands behind my ears and remain still.

A gentle touch on my cheek brings my head back to the right.

The air sparkles. An image flickers in and out of focus. I get the impression of a woman in a cream-colored maxi dress with two tiers of flapper-styled fringe at the bottom and along the bodice. I gain my feet as the being solidifies. Delicate beading and embroidery along the bodice and waistline create a butterfly and floral pattern.

A headband of white daisies around her forehead places her firmly in the 1930s. With her almond-shaped dark eyes, caramel colored-skin, and dark curls framing her slender, oval-shaped face, she's familiar. I search my memory for her identity as she offers a sweet smile. Gentle waves of affection, peace, and kinship wash over me.

"Alida Esçhete." This is Mémé's younger sister. I remember her from old photos in the house. The spectral nods and waves her hand toward her, signaling me over. I approach cautiously. She reaches out her hand. Energy flows through me. The lush gardens fade. My stomach dips as images spin around me like a carousel. I blink rapidly, trying to stop the polarizing effect throwing me off kilter.

I place a hand on my churning stomach as the scene around me settles. A black and white world surrounds me. Like a ghost, I watch the people move, unable to see me. This is the city of Cypress as it was in the twenties. We move at a moderate pace that allows me to see the changes time has wrought. Old-fashioned cars traverse the roads. Storefronts have large windows that house elaborate displays. Men and women are dressed as if they're headed to a church service. We end up in a wooded area where a man and a woman stand. Despite the years, I know Mémé instantly.

"Are we not friends?" The voice and the face click. *Percival?*

"If that were all that lay between us, this wouldn't be so difficult." Mémé's voice wavers.

"Cypress is a small town. There'll be no avoiding each other. We must take care in public." Percival sighs. "Tell me what you know."

His voice and his eyes are soft as he leans into her. Alida stands a few feet back, watching them. Silent, yet observant.

"Yes, you're right. I'm here now for my family. Nothing more. We agreed distance was best." Mémé clears her throat and holds her head high.

"Of course, family always comes first." Percival sneers.

"Can you say your lord and his court come second?"

Percival growls. The foreign scowl makes me jerk. "No. But my people aren't so narrow-minded."

"We all don't have the benefit of decades under our belt."

Points to Mémé.

Alida clears he throat. "We're not here for this." Mémé and Percival turn toward her. "This is bigger than a failed romance not meant to be. People are disappearing on both sides."

Mémé seems to deflate. "Alida's right."

"How can I help?" Percival asks, suddenly looking ancient as the fight leaves him.

"Do you know anything about the witches who've disappeared?" Mémé questions.

"No."

"The unease in the witch community is growing. We've never been attacked in our hometowns before. I fear what they may do soon."

"They think this is vamp related then?" he asks.

"It'd be the best bet."

"If we were the ones causing this, why would our own be affected?" Percival reasons.

"Panic has never bred common sense."

He grabs her hand. "I will investigate further and see what I can find."

The scene fades, and we return to the garden.

"You want me to talk to them about the past, don't you?"

Alida nods. I turn the scene over in my mind. Mémé alluded to having a crush on Percival, but what I saw was much more than that. Perhaps I don't know my family as well as I thought. Alida was killed in the Reaping, the second wave of witch hunting; no one likes to bring it up. The scars physical, mental, and other run deep. With the ancestors are getting involved, the choice was taken from me. I need to prepare to have an uncomfortable conversation. Alida flickers out of view.

Soon.

Chapter Four

Seated at the long wooden table, I carefully strip the dried herbs from the stems and place them into their proper glass containers. Replenishing inventory is a tedious affair. We pride ourselves on having the freshest. Ensuring that statement is true costs hard labor and stiff fingers. Vain creatures that we are, it's a point of pride that keeps us harvesting throughout the year.

After an hour, I've found a rhythm. The stripping and sorting are almost cathartic. My mind is blissfully blank while I work. Today's hectic morning shift was exactly what I needed. That kind of pace makes worry impossible. That's the best part about helping others. You're literally too focused on others to worry about yourself. Today Mémé is in the shop. She only comes in twice a week, so it's always abnormally busy. At ninety, she deserves more time off.

"How are you doing back here?"

Speak of the devil. I glance up at Mémé and smile. "It's coming along. Did Mom come in to relieve you for a bit? I know Felicite is good, but the mini-mob was lined out the door."

"She did. It feels like everyone and their mother choose to come in today."

I hum in agreement. "It made the time fly, though."

"That it did." She takes a seat in the chair beside me, and I'm hit with thoughts of Alida.

"Mémé, I had an interesting visitor in my Moon Garden the other night," I say casually.

She chuckles. "What critter did you catch messing with your flowers? Do you need an old remedy to get rid of them?"

"Oh, it wasn't a living being." I study her from beneath my lashes.

Her eyes flicker toward me, and her pupils dilate. "You're seeing the dead now?"

I nod my head. "Only this one so far. I think it was more her projecting than me gaining a new skill."

"Anyone I know?"

I set down the herbs and turn my body toward her. "Alida."

"My sister?" she whispers. The color leaves her face.

My stomach twists like a tornado, and I question my judgment call. Mémé is not a young woman. Should I be burdening her with this? There's a reason I'm taking over her position in the family.

"What did she say?" Mémé whispers.

"She never actually spoke, but she did show me a memory of you and Percy talking about missing people." Blood settles in her cheeks and neck. "What was Percival to you exactly? Because he seemed like much more than some school girl crush."

"The one who got away, but never stayed gone. The ultimate temptation that's haunted me." The depth of her feelings leaves me speechless. "An ally in the darkest of times. My best friend." Her voice cracks. The longing and regret I once glimpsed in Percival's eyes goes both ways.

"I think she wants me to ask you about the Reaping."

Mémé fists her rose-colored, floor-length skirt. "Those were terrifying days."

"I know, Mémé. I would never ask this of you if Alida hadn't shown up."

"It changed everything, morphed people into strangers and friends into foes. Those troubled times turned brother against brother and mothers against children. We were so divided. It's a miracle they didn't slay us all. There were two major groups of thought. Those who saw it as every man for themselves, and sought only to protect their own, and others like me who understood together we'd be stronger." She trails off, eyes seeing something I can't.

"What happened to *those* people?"

"They were slaughtered.

"Their ignorance and rigidity made them vulnerable to attack. We lost so many. I tried to tell them this was more than a witch-hunt. It was too broad and well organized. Everyone was being hit. In order to survive, we needed to be bigger than our prejudices and band together with the others, the way the hunters had." The horror etched on her face burns itself into my brain. I've never seen her so distraught. Her entire body is trembling.

"They let people die. Pride was chosen over everything else. So much blood spilled." She places a hand on her neck.

"What changed?"

"Our numbers dwindled, and I came into power because Maman fell. I went against them all, brokered the treaties we now live by, and fought the resistance. I stood my ground. I had to. I severed connections that would have led to our demise at a great personal expense to myself. I've gone over it so many times in my head since that night. I can't stop wondering if I could've done it differently." A sob erupts from her throat.

Jumping from my chair, I move to embrace her. "Mémé?"

"I tore this family in two. Every time I think of how few of us remain I blame myself."

I rest my cheek against her head, wishing I could take her pain away. "What would have happened had you not stood your ground?"

"None of us would be here now. It took all of us working together to defeat the hunters." She sniffs.

"A wise woman once told me, being a leader means making the hard calls, and pissing people off."

She gives a half laugh. "Using my own words against me?"

"When you learn from the best, there's no reason to deviate."

"I've held on to these secrets for a long time. Perhaps it's time I air my dirtiest laundry." She straightens and wipes her face. "It starts off benign. A difference of opinions. Each family member picked a side. It was as if someone had drawn a line straight down the center of us all."

"Mémé. We have Fae." My cousin's panic-stricken face appears in the doorframe. The whites of her eyes stand out against her brown irises. Her dark hair falls across her forehead.

"We can't keep them waiting. Send them back."

What the hell is a fairy doing here? I stand.

Mémé raises her hand. "Stay, Lou."

Confused, I return to my seat. I try not to gasp when the porcelain-skinned goddess with flowing, wavy, black hair, pointed ears, and a perfectly symmetrical heart-shaped face slinks into the room. Her movements transcend gracefully and fall into the otherworldly category. Her skin is luminous, lit from inside as if she swallowed the moon.

Her black gown shimmers as it trails out behind her, rippling like a living ink stain with every step she takes. Two steps behind her twins follow in her wake. Their eyes are a shade of black no human could ever hope to possess. Full of reflected light and the knowledge of ages, they make my blood run cold. Despite their beauty, these men are deadly. Bone straight, black hair tumbles around their sharp, angular features. A strong jawline and thin lips lend to their androgynous appearance.

"Sebile."

"Witch." Her voice is like wind blowing through the trees, haunting and eerie.

"To what do I owe the pleasure of her royal highness?" Mémé asks amusedly.

Sebile throws her head back, delivering a deep, throaty chuckle that makes me want to scramble from my chair and run.

"Still spry enough to play the game. Here I thought I'd find a feeble old woman having her power pried from her clammy, cold hands."

"You mean you hoped you'd find me in a state that would allow you to have the upper hand?" Mémé asks.

"You wound me. I came to pay my respects, and greet the heir apparent." Her eyes flicker with purple flames. I tamp down my urge to flinch. I can't afford to show weakness right now. Unseelie—the dark Fae—are as slippery as eels. Born with black hearts, they respect power, cleverness, and the ability to play political games.

"Meet my granddaughter, Louella, future matriarch of the Esçhete family."

"Call me Lou." I smirk and wink, in that annoying way I've seen Marcellus do all too many times.

Sebile narrows her gaze. "Lou … how common."

"You know us mere mortals. We like to keep things simple."

"Quaint. I wanted to see for myself the woman who wound Cristobal Cortez around her human finger."

It's an insult. My hackles rise, but my training keeps me from showing it. "It's a mutual exchange of respect, affection, and power. I assure you no one manipulates my Lord."

"Lord? So, you admit to submission? That you are a lesser being?" Her eyes light.

"I admit to using proper titles. If I were lesser, I could never be a queen meant to rule at his side. We are equals with different strengths and skillsets. Together we can only be stronger."

"She's a clever one, isn't she? See how well swiftly she plays at politics. Perhaps the Esçhetes will survive this exchange in power after all," Sebile muses.

"Do you want to make your true intentions known? I can tell it's more than a curiosity when you bring Cein and Kul with you and arrive during the daytime," Mémé says, providing me with names for the heartbreakingly beautiful, deadly beings.

"Can't I visit an old friend?" Sebile asks.

"We've been many things, but friends was never one of them."

Sebile casts her gaze toward her guards. "Recently I've sensed a disturbance in the veils between worlds."

"People cross back and forth all the time." Mémé shrugs.

"Yes, but this ... felt different. Foreign and ancient."

Mémé tenses. "Are we in danger?"

"I've yet to determine intention or details. The hall of mirrors is vast, and I am but one. I thought perhaps you could come and tell me your impression?"

I'm shocked to find her gaze fixed on me. "It's been a long time since I walked among the Fae," Mémé says.

"Not you, wise one. She who's proved quite adept at walking between all of us. I want to see this balancing act. *We* all do. It's the first thing the courts have agreed on in ages." Sebile smiles happily.

I frown. "Surely you don't expect me to travel into the Fae lands by myself?"

"You're welcome to bring a trusted entourage of course. We wouldn't want you to feel uncomfortable." She flashes a smile that shows her rows of shiny, slightly pointy teeth.

"When do you want us there?" I fish for more information.

"I need to speak with the other courts. We wanted to know if you'd be willing to make the journey before we made any plans. You'll be alerted when negotiations have been settled." She rests her arms in the crook of her guards, and in the blink of an eye, they're gone. I've grown used to the speed in which vampires move, and this terrifies me.

"Choose your partners wisely, girl. Things are never as they seem in the Fae world. You'll need your wits about you, and senses you can trust without a shadow of a doubt."

"Are you telling me to take vampires?"

"I said no such thing." The upward curves of her lips tell me the exact opposite of her statement.

I'm like a schoolgirl with a secret burning a hole inside of me. For days I've digested what's been revealed. Now, I need to speak with someone I trust, or I might explode. Sacha is off on vacation mending the rift with her family, Cristobal is too close to Percy, and I'm fit to be tied. I've been faking my way through every day pretending everything is fine when it's not. Between planning, training, and work, it hasn't been that hard to do.

"Fel, I need a favor," I say as we shut down our computers and clean up for the weekend.

"What's up?"

"I need a girls' night in if you don't have anything planned."

"Oh, you're actually going to your house for once?" Fel teases.

"Stop it. I stay there plenty."

"Uh huh?"

"With Sacha off with her parents for the past week, it's been too quiet."

"Hey, you don't have to justify anything to me. If I had tall, dark, and fanged waiting for me, I'd be home with him, too."

I giggle as we hit the lights and step out into the muggy evening.

"Are you telling me one of the court's caught your eye?" I ask.

"Oh no, that's all you. I have my hands full with Esçhete business."

"You'd be amazed what you'll do for love," I say honestly. A year ago, I couldn't have imagined myself in this position. We're both compromising. We bend without breaking to meet in the middle.

"Wow. You're openly admitting it. Cristobal does good work."

"Denying it wouldn't make it any less true. Besides, new year, new leaf, and I hope a better me."

"The best you. I'll meet you at your place?" she asks as she walks to her car.

"I'll see you in a few."

I blast Panic at the Disco and sing along. The music transports me to a place nothing can touch. I tap the beat out on the steering wheel and get lost in nostalgia and the high only music that touches your soul can bring. Upbeat as I pull behind her car in my driveway, I grab my purse and step out with a spring in my step.

"You already look more relaxed."

"Knowing I'm going to get a chance to talk things out has definitely lifted a weight off my shoulders. Not to take away from spending time with my favorite cousin."

"Yeah, yeah, no need to butter me up." Fel rolls her eyes. "What's this about?"

I lead her up the porch to my front door. "I'm still trying to figure that part out."

"Does this have to do with whatever I walked into you and Mémé discussing the other day?"

"Yes. The information she gave me blew my mind. I've been sitting on it, and I can't keep it in anymore."

"Okay, now you're kind of freaking me out," Fel mumbles as we step inside.

I hang my keys on the hook by the door and lock it behind us. "We talked about the Reaping."

"Oh, Jesus. How did you manage to get her do that?" Fel asks.

"Before I launch into that tale, I need snacks and Hurricanes."

"The slumber party essentials," she agrees.

There's a special bond you develop when a friendship spans the time ours has. She provides an indescribable sense of comfort that eases me on my worst days. She's a lifeline to sanity and stability in a world of constantly shifting circumstances and roles.

"Do you want to borrow some pajamas?" I ask.

"Of course."

I toe off my shoes, and we move to my bedroom where we strip down and pull on oversized sweatpants and worn T-shirts. With the

A.C. cranked up, the heat of the day remains outside where it belongs. Dressed down, we relocate to the kitchen. The rust orange pumpkins that stand out on the black curtain and wall border make me smile. This is my happy space. I poured a lot of myself into this home.

"On a scale of buzzed to blitz what kind of Hurricanes are we making?" Fel asks as I gathered up the rum, passion fruit syrup, and lemon juice.

"Somewhere in the middle. I need to be able to tell my story, but I don't want to be feeling any pain."

I measure out the syrup and lemon juice and admire the healthy amount of rum going into the glass pitcher. It's going to be an interesting evening. We break out the traditional Hurricane glasses and fill them to the brim. The sweet concoction burns its way down my throat and settles in my belly.

I lift the glass. "Much better." Every queen needs a confidant. Who better than my own cousin, best friend, and a future council member to be mine? She's going through similar changes with her own training, and preparation for a change in station. She can understand my position in a way few in my life can. "How's *your* training going? I feel like one of us is always running off and fulfilling impossibly long to-do lists."

"That's because we are. It's no secret we've been shellacking on the concealer to prevent ourselves from looking like the living dead. Things are coming up fast. I can only hope I'll be ready. It's a lot to take in, and I know," Fel holds up a hand, "I'm preaching to the choir. How are things coming on your end?"

"A mixture of frustrating, overwhelming, and exhausting?" I shrug. "What are your adjectives of choice?"

"Slow, boring, and all-consuming. I'm spending more time with the elders than I ever wanted to." Fel rolls her eyes.

"What do you talk about?" I ask, genuinely curious.

"Rules. Ethics. Who's who? Family histories, and how it affects their politics and relations to others on the council. Yadda yadda yadda. It's a mixture of tradition, gossip, and people management."

I grimace. "I can relate. I don't envy you the one-on-one."

"Yes, because you at least have pretty scenery to observe," Fel whines.

"Trust me. It doesn't matter what they look like when they're running my human ass into the ground. There's no such thing as *taking it easy* on me."

Her brow furrows. "What do they have you doing?"

"Defensive training, sword training, because apparently, they cleave to the old ways even more than we imagined. With them, politics is a slippery slope as well. It depends on their age, rank in society, and in some cases their location. It's a confusing maze of what to do and what not to do." I shake my head.

"Holy crap, cuz. I think I'll stick with the witches. And damn, no wonder your body is looking bangin' these days."

I giggle. "Small perk. What complicated creatures we both are."

"What's it like spending so much time with them?"

I pause as I think about how to answer her. "Desensitizing? It's starting to become my normal. Things that unsettled me about them before are now simply a part of who they are. How do Muffuletta dip, Creole sausage balls, and spicy pretzels sound?" I push away from the counter. If we don't get some food in our bellies, we'll be leaving buzzed in the rearview mirror on the way to wasted.

"Perfect. Let's get the dip going first."

We continue to play catch up while we gather the ingredients, place the olives, and the pickled cauliflower, carrots, celery, and hot peppers we've picked form the drained Giardiniera into a food processor. We add the combination into a glass mixing bowl with cream cheese and chopped salami, then mix well.

"This smells heavenly." I moan as Fel sprays the cooking dish.

"Wait till we add the mozzarella cheese and bake it."

"I've been craving spicy junk food for days. I love the court, but their taste is over the top. I often wonder if their taste buds are duller post life."

"It's possible. You could probably write a book about them with all you're learning."

"Yeah, they wouldn't take kindly to that. They're so bloody secretive." I roll my eyes.

"I can't blame them, really. Our kind has been hunted and killed for being different for a long time. They remember it with a crystal-clear clarity we can't begin to come close to."

"It's true." We pop the dish into the oven at 350 degrees Fahrenheit and move onto the Creole sausage balls. Thirty minutes later, we're gathered around the table in the living room with *Pretty in Pink* playing in the background, our Hurricanes resting on coasters, and a mini feast spread out before us.

Stuffed, we lean back against the couch.

"Okay. Now I can attempt this," I say. spilling my guts.

"Wait. You're seeing ghosts now?"

"I saw *a* ghost. There's a huge difference. Like you told one prophecy. Which I kept to myself by the way."

"Uh huh. Keep going," she says skeptically.

I tell her what Alida showed me.

"Wow. So Mémé and Percival?"

"Yes. Whatever those two know must be shared. I almost got it out of Mémé. I don't see an issue getting her to tell me the rest, but there are always two sides to every story, and I know from experience, vampires view things completely differently."

"What are you going to do?" she asks.

"Well, that's where you come in."

"What?" She places a hand over her heart. "Me? What can I do? I mean, he's in your court."

"Exactly. I'm way too close to the situation and him."

"And I'm too far away," she says quickly.

"No, you're perfect. I've seen the connection between you. He's drawn to you."

"I'm not an escort."

I tsk. "I want you to befriend him, not seduce him, Felicitie."
She frowns. "I don't like it.

"I know, and I wouldn't ask this of you if it wasn't important."

Fel glances away, and I understand; the pull is mutual.

"The family needs this."

Fel sighs. "I get it. I know where my loyalties lay. I won't lie to him."

"I don't think you'll need to." My throat closes up around the order to abort the mission I know I can't give.

"How am I supposed to justify my sudden desire to spend time with him?"

"I'll take care of that. As a future council member, you need a mentor who specializes in vampire politics. If you ever get stuck ask him about our histories. I'll let him know I chose him to be your advisor. He'll enjoy it."

"Clever," she admits reluctantly.

"I'm trying. I don't want anyone hurt, Fel. I'm not looking to manipulate. I just want the truth."

"I understand. You've got the greater good to look out for. What did the Fae want?"

"Hell, I'm not sure. To test me? She invited me to visit her lands and look at something for her. Whether it's real or imagined, I'm unsure."

"You're not going, are you?" Fel asks, alarmed.

"I have no choice. To say no would've shown fear. I can choose a group of people to travel with."

"And Cristobal is on board with this?" She purses her lips.

"Well, he doesn't know yet."

"Ha. I knew it." She points at me.

"Even I require a few days of downtime every now and then. I'll tell him tomorrow."

"Good luck with that one."

I sigh. "This is the hardest thing I've ever attempted, and I'm constantly unsure if I'm making the right decisions. I haven't officially taken over anything, and I already feel like I'm over my head."

"I'd be more concerned if you didn't feel that way. There's a reason the phrase, Heavy lies the head that wears the crown was coined."

For the millionth time, I wonder if I'll be ready to accept the titles being bestowed.

Chapter Five

I gather my hair into a messy bun at the nape of my neck and prepare myself for a different kind of battle. I've learned the best way to deliver bad news to Cristobal is by softening the blow and throwing in a pleasant distraction. He sees it coming from a mile away, but his response is always muted from what it might be otherwise.

The emerald silk nightgown grazes the floor. The thigh high slit keeps it sexy, yet tasteful. The room is lit with candles, and the bubble bath in the oversized claw-footed bathtub is still steamy. My man is secure enough in his masculinity to appreciate the feminine things in life. I never knew about romance until he taught me and later converted me. There's beauty in pampering your mate.

I lean against the bedpost when I hear him approach. The door swings open and he gives me a rakish grin. His dark brown eyes turn amber, glowing in the dim lighting.

"Step inside and see what I have planned." He closes the doors behind him and meets me in the center of the room.

"I don't even care what bombshell you plan to drop later, I'm enjoying this," Cristobal says.

I giggle and crook a finger. "I want you to remember you said that later." I slip my hands beneath his soft navy blue jacket and hug him tight, inhaling the rugged and refined smell of woods, old leather, and sandalwood. He intoxicates me. Burying my nose in his neck, I allow myself time to simply be as he runs his large hand down my back.

"It's been too long since we've had time alone like this." He kisses my temple, and we sway to the non-existent music.

I pull back before he can weave his spell. "Tonight is about you."

He lifts my chin and presses his lips to mine, which part like a flower opening to the sun as I sigh. His tongue slips inside. I moan as he grazes the roof of my mouth. Heat spreads through my body. He tilts his head, molding us together as he deepens the kiss. Desire swirls up, threatening to wipe my mind of everything but him. I tremble as I fight the urge to get lost in the moment and yield control.

I nip his bottom lip and push his jacket off his shoulders.

"You're too tempting for your own good," I say shakily.

"Says the woman in lingerie."

I trail my finger down his collar. "I'm just giving you something pretty to look at."

"Oh, is *that* what you're doing?" he teases.

I wink and tug his shirt from his slacks. There's something sexy as hell about seeing this well-groomed man ruffled. I begin to unbutton his shirt one button at a time, never breaking eye contact. Looking away is a habit I've struggled to break myself of. Equals don't avoid direct gazes. I smooth my hands up his chiseled abs to his sculpted pecs. The muscles jump beneath my palms. I roll erect nipples between my thumbs and forefingers, occasionally tugging lightly. He groans.

"Are you testing my breaking point?" he queries. His accent is thicker.

"That would insinuate I wanted you to hold back." I toss the shirt to the floor and undo his belt. The trust he shows me as he allows me to undress him is indescribable. I hold out my hand and lead him to the bathroom.

"Will you join me?" He nods toward the bathtub.

"Not today." He steps into the tub, and I'm grateful I can honor him in this way. Growing up the youngest, he was left the dirty bathwater everyone else had used. Freshwater and being bathed by servants was for the extremely wealthy. At one point, bathing in his country was illegal altogether because they linked it to other *pagan* religions. His past has given him an unusual appreciation for the act of bathing.

I dip the black, Egyptian cotton washcloth in the sandalwood-scented water and lather it with similar handmade soap. I trace circles on his back, and he leans forward, allowing me more access. His eyelids drift shut, and his body relaxes.

I cleanse him with slow, careful motions, pouring my love and appreciation into every caress. Seeing a being this powerful place himself in a vulnerable state is exhilarating. I kiss his crown and lean back on my heels. "Lay back and let me wash your hair." I massage his scalp with my fingernails and smirk at the rumble that forms in his chest.

When the water is cooling, he steps from the tub onto the thick mat. I pat him dry and help into a thick, black robe. Once he's seated on the bed, I pour us both a glass of berry sangria. Snuggled beside him, I wait as he enjoys the sweet, crisp, cool drink.

"Just the way I like it. Thank you, dove. You've outdone yourself this time."

"How am I doing on relaxing you?" I trail my fingertips down his arm.

"Exceptionally well." I bite the inside of my cheek. "You're laying it on thick tonight. I'm starting to worry."

I toy with the stem of my glass, rolling it between my fingers. "We had a visitor at the shop today. Sebile."

He sits up straight. Instantly alert. "What did she want?"

I shrug. "To see me, be nosey, and test Mémé's mental health mostly. There's some strange activity happening in the hall of mirrors."

His jaw tenses. "And this would concern you why?"

"She wants me to monitor the portals and see if I can sense anything."

"And you told her what?"

"That I couldn't travel to Fae lands alone."

He nods his head. "Good girl. How did she respond?"

"Basically, that she wouldn't expect me to and that I could bring *whoever* I'd like." I widen my eyes and mimic her fake innocent act.

"And you're actually thinking of going?" Cristobal asks.

"I don't see how I could avoid it. For one, we can't let her think we fear her, and for two, provided she's telling the truth, we need to know about anything trying to pierce the veil and enter this dimension."

"I understand this. My concern is why she feels it must be you. It could be a trap."

"Perhaps, but I think it's a two for one deal. Solve the problem and see the new leader in action. The Esçhetes are the ones who brokered a deal with the Fae originally. You know this. I can't pick and choose which roles I place. It's all or nothing."

He growls. "What do you expect me to say, Louella?"

"That you're coming with me and we'll make sure everyone is safe."

"Was there ever any doubt?"

"No. We need to pick a good team of vampires and witches. I've never been to the Fae lands, and this is our first showing."

He takes my glass and places it on the nightstand beside his own. "Tomorrow is enough time to worry." He rolls me onto my back. "Tonight our focus is going to be elsewhere."

He covers my mouth with his and all my protests die as my brain fogs. He slides his hand up my thigh, and suddenly strategy is the last thing on my mind.

"What have you done to warrant longer lessons?" Marcellus asks as he peers over his teacup. He's always present. Be it hand-to-hand combat, politics, or manners, he's there adding his comments and opinions.

"Why does it have to be my fault?" I keep my voice even and my hand steady as I add two pink sugar cubes to my cup. The staff outdoes themselves with their attention to detail, and in some ways, I think all of the courts have their childlike quirks. The appearance of pink is all Ruby. The fiery Scot has no problem making up for all the things she never had as one of thirteen children born to loving but poor parents.

"Thank God you're rude enough to ask. I've been wondering the same thing myself," Luz says with a laugh.

"There was something tense in the way Cristobal informed us your timetable needed to be upped. Your manners are impeccable. It's your ability to hide your true feelings he's worried about. So, I have to wonder, what's coming up that you need to be prepared for?"

I keep my eyes glued to the cup as I stir my tea.

"It's not your fault really. You live your life tuned into your sur-roundings. Witches are grounded in nature and those around them. You're a strong, genuine woman who knows herself and trusts her instincts. Subterfuge has never been a part of who you needed to be. One-hundred percent Louella Esçhete as it were. You don't mute your shine for anyone. The good, the bad, the flaws and quirks. This way of life is a huge part of why you are so very dazzling to look at. We're drawn to your zest for life and sincerity. But we need you to learn how to emulate us. That means stepping into the land of the non-living. We weigh and measure everything we do by possible consequences. Our race is calculating, and hard-wired to ensure our survival. We play the long game because eternity is both the goal and a yawning black-ness if mishandled. So, you have to cast aside your concept or human mortality. Move past your preconceived expiration date, because as it stands, you're going to surpass it."

His words are a pile driver to my consciousness. I'm bonded to Cristobal. There's no telling what my aging process is going to look like. Struck dumb, I can only attempt to process the reality I'd yet to get around to thinking about.

"I don't think she's had time to think about all of this yet," Percival says.

"It's past time she started. In order to be the lady of the court and our queen, you have to become one of us. Get in touch with the new side of yourself. The court is also yours to command, call and depend on. Lean on us. Use our connection to your advantage. The power we have is in our loyalty and numbers."

"This connection is meant to be used between us all."

I flinch. The sound of his voice in my head is foreign.

"Keeping this form of conversation solely to speak to Cristobal does nothing to improve the way the court functions. You have to stop holding back."

I want to bite his head off. I don't because his logic is sound.

"You want to ease up there, brother?" Luz asks, jumping to my defense with a deep scowl.

Touched, I place my hand over hers. "No, le chat, he's right. We're running out of time, and I need to let go of everything holding me back … no, holding us back. I want to be an asset to the court, not a hindrance. People are watching our every move and waiting for failure. That can never happen."

"That's what I want to hear." Marcellus tips his head and I can't help but enjoy his approval. It's hard earned and rare. We didn't see eye to eye in the past, and since joining the ranks, he's been the one pushing me the hardest. I know he has the court's best interest at heart, and regardless of if I like him or not, I respect him for that.

"It's not she who's upped the timetables. It appears our unique situation is garnering more interest than we anticipated." Cristobal's voice is unmistakable. It's rare that he communicates with all of us this way. He does his best to respect privacy, but I imagine I'm the only one who feels uncomfortable with this type of communication. There are some things only time can shift into an everyday occurrence. *"It's okay to explain things to them, love,"* Cristobal whispers in my head.

"The Queen of the Unseelie Court came to visit at my family's shop." I relay the story to them.

"That's disturbing," Percival says after I'm finished.

"Understatement, brother," Renee remarks, walking into the kitchen to join us at the massive wooden table. The furniture is formal, but our gatherings rarely are.

"There are few beings who play the games as well or better than vampires, but Fae are even older and shrewder than we are. If she truly needs your help, we'll be fine. If this is all concocted as a means to test you, the court needs to be airtight and solid, along with the witches you choose to bring," Marcellus states with a frown.

"I know," I say.

Marcellus shakes his head. "You're far too young to remember what the Fae did to humans when they were able to move about unchecked. The things done in sport could make one of your serial killers look like a saint. In their realm, we'll be bound by their rules. Percival, get together with Miles, and pull every book we have about the night court and Sebile herself." Marcellus narrows his color-changing eyes. "You and I have work to do. Your face is a mirror. It can't remain that way. Your mental shields are strong. But they need to be stronger." He turns his head. "Luz. Go tell Ruby and Ada we're leaving." Marcellus stands.

"W-where are we going?" I inquire softly.

"Onto the streets where we all learned. Cristobal taught us, but the bond you share is powerful. It regulates without either of you having to think. This is why he's left your training to us. He won't always be there, and he needs to know you'll maintain your skills."

"We also need to bond," Ruby interjects, appearing beside me with Ada.

"Ruby and Ada have two of the most resistant minds I've seen. No one is getting into their noggins unless they want them to. They can teach you things even I can't."

"Coming from you, that's high praise," I say.

"Oh, we've had centuries to wear him down and make him see the truth of things," Ruby says.

Ada snickers. "He's practically civilized now, but it wasn't always so."

The words shock me.

Marcellus sniffs. "We all had our growing pains. It takes time and hard work to operate a unit when we're all quite different. What you have to learn in less than a year took us a hell of a lot longer to get right. I don't dislike you, Lou. I'm looking out for the family, which includes you. You have to be better. Because, in everyone else's mind, you're the weakest link."

"What do I need to do?" I ask, sufficiently shaken.

"Today we hunt, and you'll be prey. Don't let us confuse or overwhelm you."

"Three against one isn't odds I like," I admit.

"One of us will always be with you. The other two will attack at random, but never together," Marcellus assures me as we climb into the back of Ada's black Audi.

"The best defense is offense. We're going to work on recognizing when a skilled person is trying to influence you mentally."

"Like now. Look down," Ada instructs softly.

I glance down to see my fingers are tapping the window against my own will. I jerk my hand away from the glass and meet her gaze in the mirror. "How long have I been doing that?" I whisper.

"Less than a minute," Ada replies.

My hand trembles. "I didn't feel a thing."

"It's a trick, a gentle nudge that makes the person believe the idea has come from them. It's a slithering snake in your mind, carefully weaving its way through your consciousness. In order to sense them, you need to know your own mind. How it's ordered. The natural way your thoughts form. Once you understand this, it can no longer be used against you."

"What my sister is not telling you is she was a gypsy in her *human* life. This means her powers of persuasion were already high. Our vampirism heightens the best and worst traits, so she's basically a freak of nature."

"Jealous," Ada coos.

"Yes, you wench."

"Sisters," Marcellus mutters.

The absolute normalcy of the moment makes me laugh.

"I think we broke her. Bossman is going to be pissed," Ruby whispers.

"You're all just so …"

"Powerful?" Marcellus guesses.

"Stunning?" Ruby adds.

"Normal," I blurt.

The hisses that follow make me laugh harder. I wipe away the tears and focus inward. I breathe in and out slowly, as I allow myself to fall into a meditative trance. I imagine my brain is an apothecary. Each topic has a shelf. Each spice family is matched together. The wards on my shop alert me when someone tries to enter against my will or tamper with my products. I hold up my hands and cast the words, watching as my magic becomes visible. The brilliant green streaks form a neon perimeter before they disappear.

By the time we park and slip onto the crowded streets, I'm more aware of my surroundings in myself.

"I've actually got some shopping to do," Marcellus says.

Intrigued, I follow beside him, as the girls disappear into the crowd. Their ability to blend into their surroundings is frightening. They're built to hunt. My eyes drink in the shops we pass and the people. Sangria is a town I don't frequent often. Primarily for vampires, though humans mingle unsuspectingly as well. To them, it's an eccentric town for those who don't fit into the mainstream. Fondly referred to as the Austin of Louisiana, it's a best-kept secret. The energy here is different.

We slip down an alley and pause at a rusted door. Marcellus raps twice, and a tiny rectangle slides open. The piercing gray eyes are arctic cold.

Marcellus nods. The rectangle is closed, and the door opens, hinges creaking in protest. It takes an effort to make my feet work so I can follow him into the dimly lit space. The walls are black, and the blue lighting does little to brighten the space. Vampires of all shapes and sizes line the front bar. Like a predator with the scent of prey, they turn to study me.

Head high, I follow Marcellus, keeping the barriers around my mind locked down tight. We weave our way through the crowd, and down a hallway through a door that says staff only. The shop is unlike anything I've ever seen before. Plastic bags full of blood are lined up in glass cases, hanging on racks in refrigerators with glass doors, and actually bottled in cans and glasses.

My jaw drops.

"Welcome to the Blood Shop, My Lady. It's where we come to stock up on all of our favorites," Marcellus says. The title is meant a warning. All eyes are on me, and I need to act accordingly.

"It's amazing." I nod to the proprietor behind the counter dressed smartly in an expensive suit.

"You honor us with your visit, Lady. I'm Monroe, the owner and sommelier of this establishment. I make sure we have the freshest, tastiest, and free-range options."

I nod my head. *"Is he telling me this is all farmed from willing donors?"* I ask Marcellus.

"That's exactly what he's saying. Well done."

"We've come to pick up our order, Monroe," Marcellus says.

"I'll get it from the back. Is there anything I can get for you, Lady?"

"You're too kind, Monroe. I'll take whatever you think will suit me best."

I feel eyes focus on me.

"Hmm, do you prefer sweet or savory?"

"Sweet. I'm a fan of floral and fruity flavors, as well as savory and sweet, like rich chocolates."

Monroe nods. "I will add a special sample for you."

"Tell me I didn't just screw that up."

"You did well. Saying no would've been an insult. No one is sure how to treat you, so their default will be to treat you as they would a vampire in your position."

"Noted."

I feel the urge to tap my feet. I peer around cautiously, resisting the urge to obey the random desire, and tighten my mental barriers.

"Round one, point, Lou."

Monroe returns with a large paper bag with handles, and we leave to continue on our shopping journey. I see Sangria through new eyes. Those who belong to an insider. I wince as my head throbs in protest.

"You okay?"

"Yeah. Headache."

"We're done for the day, girls. Meet us at the car." Marcellus steers me back the way we came. It's silent until we reach the car and climb inside.

"You did well for a beginner," Ada says as she and Ruby settle in the back.

"It didn't feel that way when I found myself randomly tapping my foot, twirling my hair, or humming. How the hell are we going to get me where I need to be?" I rub my temples as I slouch down in the front seat.

"A lot more practice and headaches," Marcellus replies.

"Dude. Do you live to give bad news, or does it just come naturally to you?"

Marcellus chuckles. "It's a specialty of mine."

Chapter Six

I hitch the gray backpack higher and turn toward the skeptical group of young people gathered around me in various stages of sleep depravity. Aimee, Vit, and Felicite are here upon my request. Our flashlights carve hollows out of the darkness. The sky above us is a shade of blue somewhere between purple and indigo in the pre-dawn light. Trees rise up on either side of us.

"Are you going to explain why we had to meet you here at this ungodly hour in the wilderness?" Vit mutters as he rubs his eyes. I'll take the irritation in his voice over mistrust. I've been working hard to win him and his sister over and bring them back into the fold.

"There's somewhere we need to be when the sun rises."

"You know that's not really an answer, right?" Aimee huffs.

"Fair enough. Dawn is the time for new beginnings and new projects. The location I'm leading us to has been forgotten over the years. It was once a vibrant, active part of our family and their magical practices."

"Sounds like you're chasing ghosts, Lou," Vit says. *He has no clue how close he is to being accurate.* Unlike us, Vit has never been connected to magic. I want to change that. He deserves to claim his birthright. I sense an ability inside of him. Rusty, untapped, and stifled as it may be, it exists. There's a flickering flame on the verge of being doused. I plan to breathe new life into all of us.

"I know right now this seems a little out there, but I've brought us this far. Give me a chance to bring you through to the other side. I think you'll find it was worth the early morning wake up and hike."

I remove the thermos from the mesh side pocket of my bag. "I want everyone to drink this. It's an herbal tea blend meant to open our minds and heighten our abilities. It has chamomile, lavender, and rose."

Vit unscrews the top and takes a healthy gulp before he passes it to his sister. I admire the way he's always looked out for her. As an only child, I often wished for a sibling to share a connection with. Some things aren't in the cards. We pass the thermos around. The warm liquid seems to loosen everyone up.

"In order for today to go well, we need to keep open minds and hearts." I'd hiked this path a million times in my dreams and broke out an actual map to mark it on a format I could trust. The bayou and GPS have never been close friends. The signal is spotty at best once you get in too deep.

Alida, if you're out there, please help this trip go smoothly.

I set off at a moderate pace, guiding them on the overgrown path as the dark sky begins to light, and the area slowly creeps to life.

The chirp of birds, croak of frogs, and rustle of bushes make up our soundtrack. The deeper we go into the forested area, the more I feel a protective force surrounding us. The light scent of gardenias comforts me. I frequently check our map and compass.

"You sure you know where you're going?" Fel asks.

I shake the papers in my hand. "The map doesn't lie."

"Uh huh," she says, not sounding convinced.

"Don't worry. I cross-referenced it with the one our ancestors used."

"I'm feeling a little better," Fel says.

"You think I'd lead us out here if I thought we'd get lost?" I ask with a huff.

She laughs. "Me? Yes. Vit and Aimee?" She nods her head toward the duo a few feet behind us. "No."

"Gee, thanks." A light sheen of sweat coats my forehead and back.

"Do you feel that?" Fel whispers. Tendrils of power stretch out to us from our final destination.

"Yes, we're getting close."

"What is that?" Aimee whispers.

"The reason we're out here at O-dark-thirty. Vit, can you feel anything?" I peer at him over my shoulder.

"Yeah." He nods. "A pulse, like a heartbeat." He points ahead of us. "Out there somewhere."

Excitement sparks to life inside of me. With every step, the air grows thicker. We round a bend, and I spot the circle of trees. "This is the place where our ancestors often gathered to cast their magic. It has waited a long time for our return. Can you feel it?" I pick up my pace at the murmurs of agreement. "Today, we're going to cast a sunrise circle." I pause in the center of the clearing. The ground buzzes between my feet, wind whips at my hair, tugging it from its ponytail. Heat engulfs me, and what feels like a light mist touches my face. The elements move around me playfully. This location is starved for attention.

I turn to face the others. "We're here." They approach cautiously, peering around. "Can you feel the rightness of this moment? We're meant to be here." Strong feelings of harmony and unity wash over me.

Is this how it used to feel before pride and disagreements pulled the Esçhete clan apart? I walk over to Fel. A hazy blue aura surrounds her. I place a hand on either side of her head. "Water, my blood," I chant the words softly. Power flares to life inside of me, burning its way through my veins. I raise my voice until the magic is bumping against my skin, seeking an exit. I let go. She jerks. Her back arches and the power flows through her.

Emptied of the imaginary water, I feel air flittering around in my belly like butterflies. I walk to Aimee. Her light brown almond-shaped eyes are wide and full of hope and caution. I can see the eternal battle being waged in the windows of her souls. I wrap my fingers around the side of her neck and rest our foreheads together. "Be at peace." Her shoulders relax, and I move back. I can see the person inside of her caged and lashed tight by years of belittling and living on the outskirts of the family thanks to her mother's jealousness. Perhaps, that's why air is hers to call. She needs to feel the freedom it'll bring.

"Air, my breath." As I chant, her mouth opens. The magic is a living thing, climbing its way up my belly and exploding from my mouth into hers in a mystical white stream.

Breathing heavily, I stumble my way to Vit. I place one hand over my heart and the other over his. "Free my spirit." The power crackles to life inside of him, but like damp kindling, it refuses to catch. I frown, exploring it with my senses. I thrust the power inside of him, and the spark ignites. The blaze engulfs us both. Like a Phoenix rising from the ashes, the flickering orange-red flames with blue center explode and extinguish in the blink of an eye. I step away, stunned by the contented expression I've never seen grace his face before.

The others move in around me, and I focus on the power lingering inside of me. "Earth, my body," I whisper, claiming the element I'll be calling to me today. "We come here today to cast a circle and honor the ancestors who came before us and used this sacred space." I shrug off my backpack and kneel to remove my Athame, colored candles, incense, and salt. I face north, hold out my blade, and carve out an imagined circle of pure white light, leaving a small gap. "I cast this circle in perfect love and perfect trust of all who enter." I hold out the Athame. Fel meets my gaze and steps forward, trusting me enough to take her eyes off the blade. I repeat the process with Aimee and Vit. "The circle has been closed," I whisper as I close the gap. I lay down a physical circle with sea salt.

We take our places at the four corners. The magic wakes from its slumber. There are many ways to cast a circle, depending on what you seek to gain. This is a more casual calling.

"Spirits of the Air, I call on you." Aimee's voice is ethereal and whimsical. The blast of wind that circles us is undeniable.

"Spirits of Fire, I call on you." Vit's voice is powerful and full of confidence. A circle of controlled fire springs up as a barrier around the salt.

"Lou?" His voice shakes. "What's happening?"

"This was asleep inside of you. All I did was wake it. This is who you are, Vit. You're an Esçhete, equal to each of us. Don't you ever forget that." His lips twitch before they yield to a smile that threatens to split his face. His eyes burn with an inner light, unlike anything I've ever seen. He's a different person.

Laughter bubbles up inside of me, and I let it spill out. My family is healing.

Facing the west, Fel lifts her arms. "Spirits of the Water, I call on you." Her voice is bubbly and sweet like a brook running over stones. A fine water mist creeps in, surrounding the circle of fire without extinguishing it. The flames sway with the wind as the elements work in harmony, co-existing. The ancestors are pleased. Here in this place of power, I'm starting to see our real capabilities.

"Spirits of the Earth, I call on you." The ground trembles beneath our feet. I watch as a wall of dirt rises, three feet high and solid. It's stunning. I turn toward my cousins.

"Our circle is cast, blessed be."

I sense that I'm on the right path. It's the reassurance I've been searching for. As we peer into the sky, silence falls as nature puts on its daily show. The sky shifts from a blazing red, to a burnt orange that gives way to a light peach and pale pink as the sun coasts its way up onto the horizon. Peace fills me. As the sun shines down, a translucent dome shimmers above us.

Tiny, flickering flames come to life in Vit's palms. Bright blue and black butterflies dance around Aimee. Fel is an artist, creating bubbles of water on her fingertips. Crouching down, I bury my fingers in the ground. I find the struggling Irises at the base of the trees and send them my energy. I watch as the slumped flowers straighten, becoming a vibrant violet as the leaves turn lush and a rich green.

We spend the rest of the morning practicing our skills and meditating. As we leave the clearing, the newly developed bond between us is secure. *This is how family should feel.*

I wanted my two families to unite, but not like this. *God, never like this.* My stomach rolls at the sight of yards of fabrics draped across the table. Satin, lace, organza, and tulle all battle for dominance in a sickening display of shades not entirely white. Their eyes are all trained on me. Gil's intense oceanic blue, and my mother and Mémé's natural shades of amber and brown.

"What do you think, Lou?" Gil asks.

What do I think? That I'm suffocating under the weight of planning these insane, decrepit ceremonies meant more for show than an expression of emotion. Traditions, status, and etiquette have joined together to form a noose. The rope is tightening around my neck with every day that passes.

"What do I think?" I repeat the question slowly.

"Yes, these are your days. You need to be happy with them," my mom says.

I give a humorless chuckle. "Oh, no. They are anything but my days. Let's call them what they are: carefully crafted events to show everyone how beautiful, powerful, and *special* we are."

Her jaw drops and Gil hisses. His disproval rolls over me through our bond. *Bite me.*

I refuse to feel guilty for my honesty. I was never the type of girl who fantasized about having the perfect wedding. I don't like formal wear, stuffy parties, or worrying about seating arrangements. This planning is pure torture. "Look, you can dress me up appropriately, go over the important traditions, make sure I know who's who, so I can play the political game, and let me do what I do best. Work."

Gil sighs and glances up at the ceiling. "You are so bull-headed."

My mother gives a humorless laugh. "Trust me. You've only scratched the surface."

Murmurs rise as the *ceremony committee* whispers among themselves.

"Non." Mémé's voice slices through the buzz. She pushes herself up. "You will not shirk your responsibilities. This is more than a lavish party announcing your arrival to a meaningless position. The night will dictate how you wish to be perceived. It sets the stage, giving a glimpse of how you plan to rule. Nothing you've ever planned has been more personal or important. Is this a show of power? Absolutely. There have been too many cracks in the foundations and breaks from the old ways. You have a lot to prove. There'll be no stopping them from testing you, but you can scare them in to not coming for you until you and your man are ready. You're balancing a lot on two scales. You have to work harder than any who's ever held this position. Because if either side goes down, it's bad for the entire community."

"Mémé—"

"Non. It's time to grow up. The time for hesitation and selfishness is finished. Deep in my heart, I knew you were the one to lead us. I saw glimpses of your greatness from the time you were old enough to work magic. It's been an inspiring and terrifying journey to get here. You've stepped up, protected this family, and made some hard decisions. We all can see you're tired. But now is not the time to rest on your laurels. You've committed yourself to forging a new path. Own it. Forget about the way others ruled. Make this your debut. Celebrate the differences. You hear me, girl?"

Her response is multi-layered. She's reminding me of what's important. Ashamed, I duck my head. How quickly I've forgotten to put my people's needs first. A strong showing at the coronation could go a long way toward conquering fears and smoothing ruffled feathers. The supernatural world is watching. "Yes, I hear you, Mémé. I'll do better."

"Good. We can't afford for anything less than your best. These are precarious times. Can't you sense it? There's a cold wind drifting in. We won the battle over the black coven, yes, but wars aren't ended with a single victory."

I nod. I've felt the disturbance. I wanted to blame it on jitters. There are still dark coven members out there. Plotting, and possibly regrouping or recruiting new members. The attack shook the witch community. *And they don't even know the half of it.* Having my own aunt participate firsthand in an attempt to destroy us has me questioning everyone and everything I believed. Had she been influenced, or was she acting of her own free will?

Her past points to the later, but I cannot wrap my head around why. What makes a woman who has everything she needs and more abandon her very blood? I want to investigate further, but we've been laying low and playing the part of a family in mourning. I exchange a look with Mémé and silently pledge to dig deeper. She nods her head and sits back in her chair with a fluidity that mesmerizes me. She is royalty personified in every action, word, and movement. I've got big shoes to fill.

"If this is going to be *my* ceremony." I stand, stalking over to the samples, and push them off the table and on to the ground. "We're starting over from scrap. I don't want to be sworn into an office inside. I want to be outside in a sacred place out in the Bayou. We need to reconnect and get back to our roots. The earth will help ground everyone. The water nearby and the trees will help us dispel negative energy." For the first time, I'm enjoying this process. Mémé's words lit a fire under my behind. This *is* about more than a party.

It's my first time stepping out of Mémé's shadow. I need to make it memorable. Now isn't the time to hold back or let someone else take the reins. "I think we have moved too far from our magical roots. We need to rekindle that connection while maintaining an open mind. Things have changed. Modernization is forcing us to adapt. To survive, we must step out of the Dark Ages. I want to build a bridge between the old and the new, honoring our origins while showing where the future lies. We all need to remember the way our families came together. Our council was created for the greater good, and we've all got our roles to play. Losing sight of that would be detrimental. This isn't just my day. It should be our day, celebrating not only my new position but the bonds we've forged."

"This is the way a woman who leads speaks. Remember you speak for all of us, and those without voices now in every decision you make."

The heaviness settles over me like a wet blanket. *How could I forget?*

"Bring me the books that contain the history of all the houses. We're going to flip everything and create something brand new out of the old ways and the new ones." Armed with a plan of attack, I am ready to plot out my battle.

My jaw aches from the effort of holding the fake smile in place as I see the elders out of the house. The poking, prodding, and haggling of planning is ended for the day. I made leeway, but it was no less exhausting.

"Thank you all for coming and helping me with this momentous occasion." I give a slight bow as they leave the house one after the other. I close the door carefully, lean against it, and exhale. The quiet, stillness of the house washes over me. I close my eyes and soak up the calming energy. The refreshing essence of the court reinvigorates me after being stuffed in a room full of power and strong opinions

"Are you okay?"

I pry open eyelids that feel like they weight a ton and manage a small smile for Larkin. His brow is furrowed, and his dark eyes are full of concern. The brotherly vibe pouring off him is downright adorable. I've progressed leaps and bounds with my new family over the past year.

"I'm fine. Exhausted, and sick to death of all things coronation related, but hanging in there."

He smiles, and it takes layers off his dark countenance. Quiet, brooding, and immensely intelligent, with a sharp tongue, he's a modern-day Mr. Darcy.

"The best part is you'll only have to go through it once … well twice a piece, but you know what I mean."

"I do. Let's hope the city and everyone in it survive both ceremonies. It's a lot of powerful people in one place who don't always agree."

"Are you concerned about problems?"

"We're the supernatural Romeo and Juliette. Aren't we all expecting things to go wrong?"

Larkin shakes his head. "We're all expecting a good show. You rattled a lot of cages and knocked people down a peg who've long needed a reality check."

"You know me, pissing people off, and smashing age-old traditions to smithereens like a punk rocker from the 80's in their prime."

"It'll settle."

"Not soon enough."

"You've never had a taste for the spotlight. It's part of what makes you a shoe-in for being a good queen. You care more about the people than the title. I look forward to you stepping into the role of a lady. We've lacked a certain balance for too long. I think it'll be a change for the better."

"Are you done boring her and sucking up, Lark? What Lou needs is a stiff drink and some relaxation," Renee says as he comes down the hall. He flashes me a devilish grin, and I melt. The proverbial baby of the group, the mocha-skinned man with the irresistible smile and soft doe-brown eyes is a trouble magnet. "Isn't that right?" He throws an arm around my shoulders.

"You're incorrigible," I mumble, unable to hold back my smile.

Renee preens like a peacock. "Notice she never denied the truth in my words."

"I didn't confirm them either," I point out.

"She's got your number, Renee. You let your head swell anymore, and it'll be too heavy for your neck to support," Larkin says dryly. "A drink does seem in order."

"This court never needs an occasion to drink," I retort.

I let them both sweep me into the study where one of the numerous liquor cabinets is located. As we slip inside, I'm stunned to see Percy and Fel seated at a table—side by side with their heads close together. They're speaking softly to one another, wholly engrossed in a conversation. *When did she slip away with him? What are they talking about?*

Percival glances up. "I see we aren't the only people looking to get away after all that."

"They just left," I say with a smile. The happiness visible in his dark gaze twists my guts into a knot. "How did you manage to escape early?"

"We were just browsing through some historical records we said might help with planning." Fel shrugs.

Everything is connected to the past. The theme continues to reoccur in every facet of my life. It reminds me of the missions I've yet to progress on. Hearing the rest of Mémé's story and comparing notes with Fel about what she's learned from Percival have been thrown on the back burner. Time alone with Mémé has been impossible, and between work, training, and preparations, Fel and I haven't had a spare moment to compare notes or reconnect.

"Find anything good?" I ask pointedly.

"There hasn't been a Lady Coronation in centuries. It was interesting seeing how they laid out the one prior." She shrugs sheepishly. *That's a no then.*

"I figured it was as good an excuse as any to rescue her after we ran into each other in the hallway and she begged me for an out." Percival beams. The man is a white knight in shining armor ... who happens to have a taste for blood. No one's perfect, right?

"I see how it is. Abandoning ship when I wasn't looking, huh, Fel?" I shoot a mock glare.

"I had to. My brain was slowly starting to seep out of my ear."

"It's okay. The court has an incredible archive of the past. I don't blame you for getting lost, in the past or borrowing Percival's memory."

"Being able to remember everything has its ups and downs," Percival says.

"I can only imagine," Fel whispers. He smiles down at her. "One day you'll have to give me a Cypress history lesson from the first-person point of view."

The sincerity in her voice is so compelling, I wonder how much of her enthusiasm is feigned. I stow the worry away to examine later. My brain is currently at max capacity.

Chapter Seven

Memories from the past rush to the surface as we pull in front of the retirement home. I see grand-père, all angles and bones as he struggles to breathe. I close my eyes against the pain. Prostate cancer ravaged the once strong and powerful man who stood beside Mémé through the years.

I ball my fists. *This is about a case.* I know it's terrible when Carter calls us in. The redheaded wolf shifter and his pack mate, Marcus, work with the local PD.

As crime scene investigators, they help route the more suspicious cases appropriately. We have a few plants working in our version of a paranormal unit in town to keep the good folks of Cypress blissfully unaware.

"You doing okay?" Fel whispers.

"Yeah. I haven't been back in one of these since grand-père."

"I know. I was thinking about him on the way over here, too," Fel says.

"You want me to wait a few before I call Carter?" Sacha asks gently.

"No. Let's get in there so the coroner can come through and do their job. The boys are holding them off for us."

She makes the call, and moments later the familiar face steps out of the entrance.

"Here we go."

We exit the black sedan and meet him.

"What's going on inside there?" I ask.

He shakes his head. The freckles stand out on his paler than usual skin. A true redhead, he looks more like a Boy Scout than a shapeshifter who could take out a human with a few swipes of his claws.

"Pure evil. I've never seen anything like this." He reaches into the pocket of his white suit, removes some mesh booties, and hands them to us. "You're going to need to double up."

"Jesus, Carter," Sacha whispers

He nods his head. "We've been trying to keep everything under wraps. The last thing we want to do is panic everyone. Death is a prevalent part of life here, but the residents sense this is different. We've had cops in and out all day, taking photos and cataloging the scene. The call to wait this late to try to move the body was strategic. They can't see this." He holds the door open for us while we make our way inside. Clad in expensive slacks, low-heeled pumps, and blouses, with a badge on our hips, we're wearing what I refer to as detective wear. When the boys meet us, and we walk in with confidence, people don't tend to ask questions.

The smell of mothballs and industrial cleaning solutions mix to mask the other odors I'd rather not think about. The woman at the front desk nods at Carter as he leads us back. It's past midnight at Oak Hill's Retirement Home, and the members are sleeping, or nestled away in their rooms. The photographs and wreaths decorating the doors keep the sterile environment from feeling like a hospital. I smile at the group of teenagers posed on a photo probably sent by their parents to one of their grandparents.

Anger builds in my gut. These people shouldn't have to be afraid. They're here to peacefully live out their final days with dignity and grace. Only the lowest of low would go after the elderly.

We come to the door blocked with the yellow tape I've become all too familiar with. The strong tinge of copper and bowels punch me in the gut.

"Ugh."

"I know," Carter agrees.

"You already smell it?" Sacha asks.

"Yeah, I do."

"No," Fel says.

I feel their gazes glued to my back. I ignore them as Carter peers around and opens the door, holding the tape up as we can duck under. It takes me a minute to realize what I'm seeing. The walls are speckled with blood. Clumps of flesh and what I suspect are organs dot the floor. There are numbered signs everywhere. The gruesome scene has me afraid to look at the victim. I push past my instincts and peer at the man. My heart leaps into my throat. His face is twisted into a mask of pain and terror. His lips are frozen in a silent scream. Despite the white film of death that covers his blue gaze, I can see the pain etched in his irises.

I glance down and balk at the caved in chest cavity. My stomach roils. Saliva coats my mouth. Turning away, I press the back of my hand against my lips. His chest looks like pulp. Clawed to the bone, and dugout, it has the consistency of pulled pork.

"Jesus Christ. He was alive when this happened?" Sacha inquires.

"Yeah, he was," Marcus says softly.

"They took his heart," Carter states.

"Are you sure this isn't a Shifter problem?" I ask, thinking of the damage their claws can do.

Carter shakes his head. "No. We'd never leave this much meat. The only way we'd do anything this publicly would be starvation."

"So, none of you ever goes off the deep end?" Fel says.

"Even then. They would not work this hard just to eat the heart. In addition, as far as we can tell, the heart is intact. They must've needed it whole," Marcus explains.

"That's why we figured the ball goes into your court," Carter adds.

I peer around the room to keep my eyes off the man who's far too emotive in death. My gaze lands on pictures of him in a uniform. A shadow box boasts a purple heart. The man is a national hero. He deserved so much more than this.

"I won't say there are no rituals that use hearts, 'cause that would be a lie. I can't imagine why his would be worth risking exposure for though," Sacha says.

"Agreed. It doesn't make any sense," Fel seconds.

My brow furrows. "What do the police say?"

"They're more concerned about how this happened in a building full of people, and no one saw or heard a thing," Marcus drawls.

"Unless they did, and they're afraid to talk. I mean, if I saw what it was capable of, I wouldn't be lining up to narc," I say.

"Fair point," Carter whispers.

"I think we should let this settle down and come back and see if anyone will speak," Fel suggests.

My gaze is drawn to the wall beside the door. I carefully move over to it and wave my hand slowly over the area. "There's something here." I whisper a reveal spell and find a faint and rapidly fading serpentine-like squiggle with a hooked ending and slash like lines.

"Did you see it?" I whisper to the girls.

"For a split second," Sacha replies.

"I need paper and something to draw with."

Carter hands over a notebook and a pen and I sketch the sigil. This is the first break we've gotten. There's no doubt in my mind this is connected with the body snatchers. The odds of two bizarre incidences happening this close together are small.

"Does this mean anything to you?" I ask, holding up the crude drawing.

"I've never seen it before. It looks old, kind of like the Norse Runes our seer uses," Marcus says.

"Girls?" I wave the piece of paper.

"No, but at least we have a starting point," Fel says.

"It's more than we had before we walked in here," Sacha shrugs.

"What are you going to do?" Carter asks.

"Search for answers."

"Reina, you've been locked up here all day. What is it you're look-ing for?"

"Cristobal." I set aside the worn brown leather volume, remove my white gloves, and rise. I rush across the wooden floor of the library into his waiting arms. With the impending coronation, he has had his own duties to perform. It's been a long time since so many courts have gathered; egos need to be stroked, and treaties need to be revisited and confirmed.

"Miss me?" he asks against my temple.

"More than words can express. When did you get in?"

"A few hours ago. You were so focused on your research, I shield-ed to keep from interrupting you."

I peer up. "Maybe you'll know this sigil." I leave his arms reluc-tantly, twine our fingers, and guide him over to the table. The re-sketched symbol stands out against the thick, beige drawing parch-ment. Cristobal frowns.

He traces the sigil with the tip of his elegant forefinger. "This is old."

"You know it?"

"No, nor the language it derives from. Though, I feel confident in saying it comes from the Middle East."

"I thought the same thing. I've been trying to look in the oldest tomes we have focused on that area."

He picks up the book I'd been studying and thumbs through it gently. Unlike humans, vampires don't sweat or release oils from their skin, so there's no danger to protect the book from.

"I don't think you'll find the answers you seek in any books we have access to. Which means you will need someone who would remember this ancient dialect, provided it's human."

"You don't think it's human?"

"I do not know enough about Arabic to say definitively one way or another, but in those days, it was much easier for magical things to walk the earth. In those times, there were more others than humans. You believed in the magic and in turn … in us. This was all before my time. Yet, people still talk."

"What do they say?" I ask, intrigued.

"That left unchecked, we would have run the world, devoured humanity, and eventually each other. It was before the laws and the reconnection with rationality and what was left of our humanity. They were brutal times. Think of it as your caveman period. We had much evolving to do. There is a reason why we focus on control and hold ourselves to a much higher standard than humans. We stick to the old ways because there was refinement, restraint, and a code of honor and order. You play it fast and loose in the twentieth century. It's a freedom we can never know. At the very core lies an insatiable hunger we must always remain in total command of."

His words freeze the blood in my veins. I've never felt our differences as keenly as I do at this moment. "But we all adapt and grow, no?"

I nod my head, still mulling over his history lesson.

"Do you know someone I could ask about this symbol?" I ask.

"Not personally, but I can ask around."

"Thank you." I rest my head on his shoulder.

"How long have you been at this?" He closes the book and replaces it on the shelf.

"What time is it now?"

"Four o'clock."

I grimace. "Ugh. Seven hours. Jesus."

"How about you come up for air?"

My shoulders sag. We've gotten no closer to discovering what killed Mr. James Marsh, why, or if it'll strike again. "I wish I could. People are dying in this city, and I need to get to the bottom of it."

"Your nobility is one of your traits I have a love/hate relationship with. I admire your dedication to what you believe in, but I hate how often it takes you away from my side."

I run my hand over his jaw. "Soon we'll carve out time for us." I pull his face to me and share a bittersweet kiss full of greetings and good-bye.

"Where are you headed next?" he asks with a resigned sigh.

"I have a hunch I need to play."

He studies me carefully. "That's not an answer."

"I'm going to contact Halcyon and see if she'll meet me."

He tenses. I hold up a finger and swish it back and forth. "Ah. Don't say it. It's witch to witch, no vampire politics necessary or wanted."

He shakes his head. "Would it matter if I told you not to?"

"Right now?" I suck air between my teeth.

"Go. But be safe, and keep your GPS tracking on." His words are pinched and his jaw clenches and releases rhythmically. He's probably choking down all the things he wants to say. It takes a lot for him not to plow and smoother me with his good intentions. Slowly, we're finding our way together.

"Of course."

"Be safe," he implores me.

"Always." I grip the lapels of his suit was I go up on tiptoes to meet his lips. We pull apart breathing hard.

"Soon I'm going to whisk you away."

"I look forward to it.

Two hours later, I pull up in front of an adorable, pale blue, cottage-style home with a Victorian wooden porch. Stained glass windows and handcrafted railings add a classic elegance to the historic property located just outside of New Orleans. Shifting the car into park, I release a low-whistle. Fire engine red crisscrossing lines start from the edge of the curb and follow what must be her property lines. The pulsing crimson slashes emit menace and light up the darkness.

Any witch worth her salt would be able to see the do not enter sign forged with dark magic. Spells this visible come at a cost or with immense power. Even a human would find what appears to be a quaint home by all other accounts foreboding. My body is tense as I leave my car. A witch who tried to cross into this territory without permission would likely be killed. I am literally placing my life in her hands by trusting her word that she's allowing me admittance to her home.

Fear hits me as I step from the car. Clutching the handle of my black messenger back tight, I step forward with a confidence I don't feel. I keep my chin up, back straight, and cross. My skin tingles as the wards accept me. A bark of relieved laughter escapes as I continue toward the porch.

The front door swings open before I can knock. Hal greets me with a bright smile entirely at odds with the dark magic inside of her, slowly working toward gaining a foothold in the battle for control. The off-the-shoulder, ruffled top, pale pink dress goes well with her peaches-and-cream skin and golden blonde hair. Her cerulean gaze is lit with mirth.

"I'm so glad you came out to visit me, Lou."

"Thank you for having me over. Your home is gorgeous."

"Come on in, and I'll show you around before we talk business." The door closes behind me, and the wards buzz to life. Like an invisible fence, they separate us from the rest of the world.

The abundance of white walls and high-vaulted ceilings broken by splashes of pastel-hued furniture keeps me from feeling cloistered by the invisible partition.

"It's beautiful," I whisper, stunned by the open space despite the small amount of footage. The design is all crisp, clean, and soft. It encompasses a sense of peace.

"This is my sanctuary. Not many are allowed in. You're like family. So, when you came to me witch to witch, there was no other option but to invite you down." She clarifies the lines between us. As lead witch for the mighty Lord of New Orleans Court, Blazh, she has to be careful about our interactions. At the moment, he and Cristobal are on friendly terms, and allies, but things can change swiftly. As lord of a large portion of land in addition to Cypress, we're neighbors.

"Know I would do the same for you, Hal."

She smiles. "I believe you. You're the only visitor I've had here from back home."

My heart aches for her. "I'm sorry, Hal."

"Don't be. I knew what I was forfeiting when I made my choices. To date, the gains far outweigh the losses."

"I'm glad." Despite my avoidance of all things black magic, I'm pleased to see her happy. She deserved far better than her lot in life. Magic can do many things, but it can't fix a broken family riddled extreme sexism and dysfunctionality.

"Let me show you one of my favorite parts of the house. The kitchen." The white theme continues in the cooking area. White subway tile on the walls is a contrasting backsplash to her butcher-block countertops. The appliances are top of the line stainless steel, and the window above the deep-set sink overlooks a large, well-kept garden.

She beams. "I like to grow as much of my own produce and herbs as possible."

"I totally understand that. Spells are so much better when the ingredients are fresh."

The rest of the house continues to be equally light and airy with pops of soft colors, and high-end, engaging pieces of art and décor. Very little of her previous life exists here. Her pictures are sparing, and the embellishments all seem new. Suddenly, I appreciate my family, warts and all.

We end up on the comfy, powder-blue couch in the living room with a bottle of rum on the table and glasses half full of cola.

"Tell me what brings you over this way."

"I'm working on a case, and I ran into a sigil I don't recognize. It's old. So old even Cristobal couldn't pinpoint it. He's working on finding someone who might be able to, but I'm impatient. People could potentially get hurt if I let this go too long."

"And you don't want it on your conscious?" she says.

"No. I owe them better. What kind of leader would I be if I didn't get my hands dirty and protect them?"

"A normal one. You realize the queen is protected by the hive, not the other way around, right?"

"When have witches ever sat back and watched injustices unfold? I'm only going at it from a different angle.

"Hmm." She tilts her head. "Why do you think I'll know what he won't?"

"It's a shot in the dark, but I'm *doing* something. I've exhausted most of my sources, and the other I'm avoiding?"

She leans forward. "You can't say that and not tell me who and why."

"Mémé. I'm on planning overload. I mean, you'd think I was getting married."

"It's even bigger than that, and you don't get to choose who does and doesn't come, so I'm wagering it's worse."

"Maybe that's why it feels like I'm trapped in hell."

She laughs—a husky, honeyed smoke sound that makes me think of seduction.

"I was stuck in a planning session from eight until two with a room full of maternal witches and a few snobby vampires the other day. I'm still trying to recover from it."

Hal grabs the bottle of the rum and adds more to my class. "I think you need this more than I do."

I roll my eyes but take a sip of the potent drink.

"Better?" she asks.

I give a mock cough. "Getting there. How have you been?"

"Good. I'm getting to know the magical community here. It's different from what we grew up with. Practitioners are a lot more open-minded."

New Orleans has always been a melting pot. "How so?"

"Well, for one thing, witches like me, who choose an alternate path, aren't seen as pariahs. We co-mingle. There's a place for us, too. There are various shades from white to dark there, so it makes sense."

"That had to be a revelation," I say, picturing the scene in my head.

"The best kind. It gave me a clearer picture of what my future may look like." Having finished her drink, she places it on a coaster. "Do you want to show me the sigil?"

I dig into my handbag and pull out the paper. "I drew it on the fly, so this is my loose rendition at best."

She peers down at it and tenses.

My stomach drops.

"Where did you say saw this?"

"I didn't. The crime scene was at a retirement home."

She traces the symbol and shudders. I wonder what she can sense that I can't.

"I'm not surprised you saw it a crime scene. This is dark."

"How dark are we talking?" I ask.

"More than likely was never human."

Thinking back to the body, it's not hard to believe. "Maybe it was the signature needed to summon a demon?"

"You said it disappeared, though?"

"Yes."

"They might've been calling their master and connecting to power freely given. Can you tell me about the body?"

"Do you have a strong stomach?" I ask sincerely.

"I've developed one over the years." Her eyes harden.

I describe the victim.

"If it's demon, you have one of two things … a younger one, who came to do the dirty work himself, or one who's higher on the food chain, and didn't need to."

"I'm hoping for option one." I pause. "How can you tell?" The question is out before my brain can filter it.

The joy leaves her face. "When you become attuned to the darkness, you see things you wouldn't normally. It's like the sixth sense all witches have turned on its ear. You become aware of the creeping darkness. The disturbed and unnatural. It binds you to death in a way our kind is never meant to be."

I see a shadowy figure nearly hidden in the depths of her irises, longing to break free, and gain control. She blinks. It's gone, out of sight, but never forgotten. I dread the day I look into her eyes and see the person she used to be trapped and desperate to escape.

I've summoned entities before, but never demons. They're a different story altogether. The summoning needs to be airtight, and the summoner must be more powerful than the being he seeks to command to hold them. If this creature is as high up as she believes, it'd be dangerous to try.

"I wouldn't suggest trying to summon this thing unless you really know what you're doing. Demons are born tricksters. One misstep and they have their in." She paused. "I can try to make contact through a séance if you're willing to enter into a circle of protection with me."

"I've never done one before."

"It's basically the same rules as a circle. You can't break the protection, and you have to mingle your powers to call out to the creature you wish to summon."

I hesitate. Keeping my magic separate from black magic is more than a moral call. It's physically uncomfortable to mix incompatible magic types. Black magic feels terrible. Still, I owe my people their safety. There's no way of knowing how many will lose or have already lost their lives to this creeping silently in the darkness.

"I'm in."

"Let's go get the items we'll need. I want to perform the ceremony outside. I have a table that will work, and the weather's nice. We can actually use the earth to keep us grounded if necessary. There's no way I'm inviting anything into my personal space."

"Makes sense." I nod my head in agreement. I let her take the lead as we move to her closet and she begins to gather her ingredients. Ten black pillar candles, and a velvet bag later, we're seated around her mid-sized, black iron garden table.

"No matter what happens, do not let go of my hand. Once I'm in a trance, I'm a conduit. The spirits want to get out. They'll do anything to create an opening that'll allow them to escape into this realm, so be cautious and keep your mental shields up. We don't want anyone or anything hitching a ride out of here."

"No, we don't."

"Okay." She lights the candles with a thought and slips out an antique, silver-edged, circular mirror. The smoky glaze makes me gasp.

"A black mirror." Used for scrying and contacting the other side, the item is known to amplify power and increase psychic energy. She places the mirror in the center of the circle of candles between us and draws the sigil on the center with her finger. Straightening, Hal holds out her hands for mine.

"Here we go." We link hands, and her energy jumps up and latches on to mine. I wince. Her magic is like molasses, thick and cloying as it slides alongside my own, slithering like a snake on its belly. I grit my teeth, ignoring the sensation of tiny insect feet traveling along my skin. My magic balks. I force it to play nice and mix. Like oil and water, they float on top of each other, without real cohesion, but it's enough. The connection between us is made. Hal hums as she slowly rocks in a circle. I'm unable to take my eyes off her transition into a trance. Her expression goes slack, and her cerulean eyes glaze over. A frost covering turns them white.

She ceases all movement. "We seek the being summoned with this sigil." Her voice is sexless and louder than it should be as it echoes through the backyard. I can practically taste the power behind it as her call stretches out to the other side. My heartbeat kicks up a notch when the temperature drops. *We're no longer alone.* My palms grow clammy, and I tense.

"Come. Do not linger on the outskirts. We demand answers. You've come to a realm that is not yours and caused harm and chaos. Who gave you permission to do this?" The table begins to rattle. I feel a pressure beating against our circle. I grip her hand tighter and reinforce the circle as we're rocked back and forth like a ship in rocky waters. My teeth chatter and the air from my mouth makes white clouds. Chill bumps cover my arms, and my hands begin to feel numb.

"Speak," Hal demands. She jerks in her seat. Her eyes bleed black. It takes every ounce of courage I have not to let go of her hands as the entity rushes into her body, bringing the feeling of pure evil with it. Not Hal cracks her neck and focuses its attention on me. The menace is rolling off her in waves, literally, cause bile to climb its way up my throat. I swallow, forcing it back down, and know I am staring into the eyes of something that was never human.

"Who are you?"

Not Hal opens her mouth. The low hum coming from the gaping opening makes me tense. Her body shakes, and the hum turns into a buzz that vibrates her entire body. A trail of blood runs from her nose and eyes.

"Hal," I croak.

The bubble building explodes. A swarm of black flies burst from her mouth. I close my eyes as they rush past, brushing my face and burrowing into my hair. I tighten my hold on her hands, hanging on for dear life as everything in me tells me to scream. *Keep your mouth closed. Keep your mouth closed.* My thoughts are reduced to those four words as the being unleashes. I gather my power and toss a shield around Hal, cutting the connection between her and the being. She jerks like a marionette, pitching forward onto the table. The candles all extinguish at once. I scan her body for any signs of lingering possession. Her aura is the same pink tinged with black that it was prior, although the shade is a sickeningly dull puce. I release her hands and rush to her side.

"Hal." I tap her cheek lightly and wipe away the blood smeared on her cheeks and over her nose with my sleeve. "Show me those blues, so I can make sure you're the only one home." I slap harder.

She snorts, shaking me off. "W-what?"

"Don't talk, take a minute," I whisper. I stroke her silken locks, grateful she's still in one piece. I've never seen a manifestation like that. I rest my head on her shoulder. "Don't you ever fucking scare me like that again."

"Whatever it is, it's strong, and doesn't want to be identified," she says shakily.

"Yeah, I got that. Let's get you inside." I help her stand. Slowly we shuffle our way inside, where I lead her to the bathroom. I wet a warm washcloth and wipe away the lingering blood. She seems fine. Exhausted and lethargic, but mentally sound and whole. I dart to her closet, collecting quartz and salt. I line her room—to provide extra protection—and run a bath, liberally adding the quartz and salt.

"Get in."

"With my clothes on?"

"Yes. The residue is … bad." I help her from the toilet into the bathtub. I scrub her with salt, and move on to the crystals, rubbing them against her scalp.

"Dunk."

She goes under and sits up. "Betterish." I return to cleansing, weaving my magic in carefully. I siphon the excess bad juju, filtering it out. Her dimmed aura brightens to a Pepto shade. I lean back on my heels, relieved.

"Once more, and I think you'll be okay to finish up while I get your bedroom ready for you."

She goes under again, and the heaviness on my chest lifts. She surfaces.

"I'm going to smudge because I'm hella paranoid."

"When you get back, I'll have myself together." She reaches out and grabs my wrist. "Lou, I'm worried about you."

"Right now, I'm my worried about you. I'll be careful with this case, okay? I've seen what it can do."

She nods at me warily. "This is what I don't miss about being a white witch. You put yourself on the line constantly and get so little back." She shakes her head.

"The reward is in the helping, Hal."

"We'll have to agree to disagree," she says softly.

"*What the hell is going on?*" Cristobal's voice comes through the bond. The clarity stuns me. We're getting better at communicating farther and farther away.

"*Séance went wrong.*"

"*You did what?*"

"*We had it under control.*"

"*Obviously not.*"

"*We're fine.*"

"*I'm sending someone.*"

"*This is witch business, Cristobal. Bringing a vampire will only complicate it.*"

"*The spike in your fear tells me it got that way regardless. I'm sending someone to you.*"

"*No. I'm fine.*"

"It's non- negotiable. She'll have to understand. This is bonded business. That trumps everything."

It's amazing how the man can make me want to kiss him and strangle him at the same time.

"What happened at the séance?" he asks gently.

"Whatever it was answered, and it wasn't happy with being called up." I quickly relay the story.

"I want you home.

"I can't leave her like this, she's too weak, and it might double back. She was doing a favor for me. I owe her."

"We'll be talking when you get home."

Of course, we will be. I roll my eyes, grateful he can't see my expression.

"I know. I love you."

"I love you. I need you to understand how important you are now. You have to be careful about the risks you take. You're too valuable to place yourself in dangerous situations without backup. I know you're independent, but this comes with your new roles."

"I'll do better."

"I know you will, dove. Be careful?"

"You've already deployed people here, haven't you?"

His laughter is all the answer I need. I'll never admit it, but having some of my family close is comforting. The court has become more than a group of people I was accidentally linked to. They're pieces of my heart and soul. I'd kill, die, and fight for each one, no matter how much some of them annoy me. These intense and possessive emotions are a foreign concept. I know they're people, not property, but the instincts are animalistic. It makes me wonder what quirks and traits they may have inherited from being linked to a witch. As I finish smudging, I sense Lark and Renee drawing near. I send out my thanks before I move inside. The sage and my prayers go up in every nook and cranny of the house before I return upstairs to find Hal sitting on the bed.

"You look better."

"I'm getting there. I won't forget what you did for me."

"Hey, it's the least I could do. It's my fault it happened in the first place. I never anticipated that."

"Me either. I've never encountered anything like that demon. I'm afraid to even consider why someone would need to call up something that powerful."

"You and me both." I sink onto the edge of her bed.

"Are you heading back tonight?"

I shake my head. "Not if I can crash here."

"Of course. I enjoyed having you … honestly. It's nice to see some parts of my past still have a place in my life."

"I know that feeling well. When I came back, it was a culture shock, and everything kept changing every time I got halfway used to things. It's been one hell of a year."

"You're surviving it better than you think. People are talking about the powerhouse you and Cristobal will be once everything is official. The witches are chattering and looking toward the Esçhete family once more to see what moves they'll make. It's a good time to be you, my friend. Enjoy it."

"I never wanted this."

"And yet, you're meant to have it. No one else in our generation holds a candle to you. Felicite is talented and sweet, but a leader? Not so much. You did well placing her in the council spot. She's a nurturer full of wisdom, and the ability to soak up knowledge like a sponge. She'll also prevent them from crying favoritism and monopolizing."

"I thought so. I don't want people to think this was a strategic move. Bond mates aren't something that can be faked."

"There will always be haters and doubters. It's not for you to worry about the opinions of peasants."

I see an opportunity to learn, and I'm going to take it.

Chapter Eight

I should have anticipated retaliation. It knows we're seeking it now. Striking out and kicking its agenda into high gear is a logical step. I try to talk myself out of guilt as I fly down the highway, headed back toward Cypress. The 'notice me not' glamour is helping me chop the two-and-a-half-hour drive in half. The longer it takes me to get to the murder scene, the muddier the evidence becomes. It already took them three days to find the body. Literally. The corpse in the conservatory is headless. What stars and planets have to do with it is beyond me. I'm coming to think of them as ritualistic killings.

Every case has been bizarre in its own way, and other than the fact that they make no sense and have no evidence left behind, there's no one thing that binds them together. Though, I'm starting to think every incident is more outlandish than the next. We went from stealing dead bodies to removing hearts and now heads. What's next? And why in the hell would a demon need body parts? It has to be someone with a vendetta or a mission, but why and what? These cases deliver more questions than answers, and with the body count piling up, that's a severe problem.

Short of the Frankenstein theory, everyone is stumped. *Bad analogy.* A Golam is created from clay, not actual pieces, and a hand of glory only requires a hand of a murderer. What the hell would anyone need a head for? Not even a part of the brain, but an entire flesh covered skull. Can one feed a demon like they do a dog? As far as I know, they hunger for souls and chaos, not actual flesh. Is this some new breed of demon someone unearthed? *Why wouldn't it be? It's not like we have enough things to worry about.*

I'm the furthest thing from professional wear in oversized sweatpants and a white T-shirt. Cristobal's irritation and anger burn a bright red through our bend. He has slow burn anger, and it's been brewing overnight. When I got the call for the case this morning, it tipped him over the edge. He doesn't like letting issues lie. I swear I can feel the heat the closer I get to the city. I shift in my seat, uncomfortable, despite the air conditioning. This puts a whole new spin on the phrase *hot seat*.

Just when I think I'm getting used to the bond, a new quirk is uncovered. I understand why he is unsettled. Paranoia and plots come with any position of power. But I refuse to have bodyguards every place I go. Life is unscripted, and no amount of planning will keep me safe twenty-four hours a day. Not that I'd entertain the constant sentry.

Shifting into another lane, I kick the speedometer up a notch. The engine purrs, and I enjoy the perks of the upgrade. The black BMW is leaps ahead of the Toyota Corolla stick shift I'd been babying since I was nineteen. I glance down at the navigation center. Twenty-minutes.

An intense urge to switch into the far right lane slams into me. I obey. A loud pop makes me jump. I watch in horror as a fourteen-wheeler loses its rear tire. The mass of black rubber unravels and the car directly behind it veers to the right, directly into the car that would've been mine had I not moved. The white Honda plows head-on into the wall, only to be T-boned a second later. The hood flies up, and smoke begins to roll out. My heart beats erratically as I move into the emergency lane and grip the steering wheel tightly. Coincidence or pot shot at my life?

"Are you okay?" Cristobal's voice chimes in my head.

"Fine, just saw a nasty accident on the highway."

I keep my suspicions to myself. Accidents happen frequently, and I'm still spooked as hell by what I saw last night. *Who wouldn't be?* Calm, I rejoin the flow of traffic, hyperaware of my surroundings. I pull into the parking lot next to the familiar aquamarine Studebaker. Fel and Sacha step out of the car, and I feel like I can breathe.

Sacha raises my black duffle bag. "You owe us a story young lady," she crows.

"I do."

"No more running off to do dangerous things solo, please. There are three of us at W.F.H, you know?" Fel adds.

"I know. This was supposed to be an info run. I never expected anything else."

"Afterward we want all the details. Right now, this case deserves our full attention."

"Have you guys been inside?" I ask.

"No, we wanted to wait for you." Sacha nods her head at me.

"And to settle my stomach. There's gruesome, and then there are headless bodies. We've graduated to a new level of disturbing and horrifying." Fel mock gags.

"Who cuts a person's head off, and takes it home?" Sacha mutters.

"This is one of those times I really don't want to know," I answer honestly.

"Be a private eye, I thought. It'll be adventurous and glamorous, I thought," Fel says in an announcer-style voice.

"Shut up, no one told you that," I say.

She laughs. "No, they actually said, why the hell would you want to do that."

Her impression of her father makes me giggle.

"It does help people and pays the bills, though." I shrug.

"Tall, dark, and fanged would handle any bill you wanted him to," Fel replies slyly.

"Do we want to enter into a debate about the tall, dark, and fanged, cousin?" I flip the tables on her.

"I go on vacation and you what … start up a new relationship?"

"N-no," Fel sputters.

"No? Are you sure? 'Cause you were looking super cozy at the house."

"Friendship is not the same thing as a relationship, and don't you need to get dressed?" Her obvious change of topic makes Sacha and I laugh as she gestures wildly toward the bag.

"There's a gas station up the road where you can change. In the meantime, we'll give you the highlights of the case," Sacha says as she leads us back to her car.

The conservatory was closed over the weekend as Dr. Stanley Glants finished final preparations for his brand new, fully funded display. The murder occurred sometime Friday, and the body was discovered this Monday when they opened around eight in the morning. Doctor Glants was a healthy, forty-five-year-old astronomer with no family to speak of and no serious relationships. Married to his work, he lived for research, travel, and the stars he studied. Fairly "likable" but quiet, he came across as reserved, but polite. There didn't appear to be any obvious links between him and the other odd scenes we've been to recently.

I change quickly into a charcoal pants suit with low-heeled, black pumps, and an official-looking badge for appearances. Back on the scene. I try to brace myself for what's to come. There's nothing natural about murder, and every crime scene is unsettling in its own way. I don't know that I'll ever be used to seeing death this way. Nor would I want to.

The stench of rotten eggs and flesh greet me not long after we enter the building. The space is small and enclosed, and death is a potent breaking down of organic matter that gives off distinct odors.

"Ladies, if you'll follow us, we'll take you back," Carter says. His face is even paler than usual, so I know this is going to be bad.

"What display was Doctor Glants working on?" Sacha asks.

"They were opening up a Night Sky observation. Nothing incredibly fancy to big cities, but the high-powered telescope was a huge upgrade for our town. Along with the new sound system and screens, it was a much-anticipated addition to the community. They'd been working on the proposal for a while I hear. Dr. Glants was persistent, and it paid off."

"It doesn't sound like anything kill-worthy. The exhibit wasn't at anyone's expense, was it?" Fel questions.

"No," Marcus shakes his head. "As far as we know, Dr. Glants was looked at as a hero for getting the big wigs to pay attention to us down here."

I clear my throat as the smell intensifies. Blood mixed with the unmistakable odor of feces and cleanser creates a hot mess of stomach-turning scents. Carter and Marcus stop in front of the caution tape and hand us booties.

"You should double up on those," Marcus says.

"Jesus," Sacha whispers. We quickly cover are feet.

"Are you ready for this?" Carter asks.

"No," I reply honestly.

"Yeah, we weren't either." Carter holds up the tape as we duck under and round the corner.

I notice the corner is the first blind spot hidden from the cameras positioned around the room.

"And of course, this is in the blind spot. Let me guess, they didn't capture anything on camera," Sacha says.

"They didn't. There was also no sign of forced entry," Marcus states.

"That tends to mean the vic knew the killer," I say.

"Usually, yeah," Carter says skeptically.

"You don't agree?"

"You'll see," Marcus replies.

The words are ominous. Around the corner is an image from a nightmare. I'm looking at a meat suit. A body without a head is a lump of flesh. Arms, legs, and a torso with no identity. They've stripped this man of who he was. Our faces emote. It's the first line of conveying how we feel. The most powerful tool we have in our arsenal of communicative tackle. Blood splatter lines the walls and puddles of congealed blood line the floor in dark pools.

"This looks like a scene from a slasher movie," Fel whispers shakily.

"When you sever the head, the blood that pumps to the brain has to go somewhere," Marcus explains.

I cover my nose with my sleeve as I study the stump. Insanely clean, it appears the doctor's head was taken in one fell swoop. The wound is uniform.

"What the hell would make a clean cut like that other than a guillotine or an executioner's ax?" I wonder.

"I'm looking forward to seeing how the coroners spin this one when it comes to cause of death."

"You're the witches. Tell me why someone would need a head?" Marcus says.

Sacha shakes her head. "I wish we could tell you that."

"Is this some Macbeth level shit? They put into a cauldron and cook up a spell?" Carter asks.

I scowl. "That is not how magic works. Besides, there are far easier ways to procure a skull. Ones that won't draw police attention."

"They either needed it fresh or needed it from Dr. Glands specifically." Fel's voice is muffled by her sleeve.

"I want to see if I can find a power signature. Can you give us a few minutes?" I turn to look at Carter and Marcus.

"Yeah, we'll step out for a few minutes."

"We need to cast a circle," I say once the building is empty.

"Okay, why the precaution?" Fel asks.

"Whatever this thing is, it's powerful, and now it knows we're hunting it. We take every precaution we can moving forward when it comes to things connected to the sigil."

"You sound scared," Sacha says thoughtfully.

"I am, and you will be once you hear about last night. Cristobal doesn't get upset over trivial things." I hold my hands out. "The sooner we get this over, the quicker we can get out of here. The smell is strangling me."

We join hands, and I call down the powers of our ancestors, the elements, and the watchtowers for protection. I take the girls' offered energy and direct them toward the dome made of pure white energy we're erecting around ourselves. People often misunderstand magic. It's not a matter of which school of thought is correct, but the strength of the faith the practitioners themselves have. Their belief is the determining factor along with skill, practice, and some natural inclination. The air shimmers and I feel the shield settle into place.

Sacha waves her hand over the room, seeking signs of magic or summons.

"We're here too late to pick up anything." Fel's voice is full of disappointment.

"I still maintain there's no way these events are separate. It's too bizarre even for Louisiana." Sacha remains faithful to the serial magic worker theory.

"Maybe it's calling us out. This is incredibly public and brutal. Could it be warning us off?" I ask out loud.

"That's terrifying. You speak with confidence. You know what we're dealing with now, don't you?" Fel asks.

"Demon, a powerful one."

"I think it's time for that conversation. We've done all we can here for now," Sacha shakes head.

"Let's lower the circle and get back to the office." Fel goes into planner mode, and I take a backseat, relieved we didn't encounter the demon. *We're not ready.*

"Holy shit, Lou." Sacha whistles.

"Insects flew out of her mouth?" Fel repeats slowly.

I nod my head and huff. "I was there, and I'm still having a hard time believing it."

"How?" Sacha says exasperatedly. "It's not like Hal was possessed."

"No, but she was keyed into the thing, channeling and challenging it. Apparently, it's close enough to the same thing," I reply.

Sacha holds up a finger like she's about to make a strong point. "She's also got one foot in the darkness. Her resistance isn't the same." I fight the urge to roll my eyes. As if that's the answer to everything. Haven't we learned by now there are never any easy answers?

"Still. What the hell level of demon can do that?" Fel scoffs.

"I might be more concerned about who could control it. Hal is no lightweight, and it owned her," I counter.

"Maybe they're not. The demon is pulling strings and letting them think they're running it," Sacha suggests.

"That's the most likely scenario. A group of beginners stumbled on to a spell or a book and got in too deep. Now they're stuck," Fel agrees.

"All I know about demons is the bare basics. We need to change that immediately," I say.

"So, research," Fel mumbles.

"Seems like a legit place to start." Sacha nods.

"I think the court's library might be the most viable. We have a section dedicated to the subject."

"Shocker," Sacha drawls sarcastically.

"I saw that! I haven't gotten a chance to explore it yet," Fel says.

"Oh, have we been spending time there for reasons other than visiting our dear friend, Lou?" Sacha leans forward. "Please explain."

"Percival's been tutoring me, if you will, on how to deal with the different courts. It's nothing toward." The sparkle in her eyes and the slight upturn of her lips suggests the opposite of her words.

"Wait. How did this come about?"

Fel points to me. "She suggested it."

"Way to throw me under the bus. I did. I thought it'd be beneficial for everyone. They have to get used to more witches, and you needed a crash course in vampire politics. I'm still learning, so I can't teach you."

"See," Fel says.

"Oh ho. You like him, don't you?" Sacha questions.

"He's a likable man, so yes." Fel's dancing around the issue like a tap dancer at a competition.

"Don't try to pull that misdirection bull crap on us," Sacha scoffs.

"Guys, I enjoy spending time with him. He's funny, polite, and incredibly knowledgeable. It's not a hardship to be around him. It doesn't mean we're making a love connection. This isn't reality television."

"Uh huh," I say.

Fel shoves me playfully. "I'm only doing this because of you," she grumbles.

"Yeah, I said befriend him, not bewitch him *I Dream of Jeannie*."

She flips me off, and I laugh.

"What am I missing?" Sacha asks.

"We're trying to get an inside view of the Reaping period."

"Jesus, why would you want to bring that up? It's like asking a Vet about 'Nam?" Sachs frowns.

I give her a cliff note version of the past few weeks. "I've been having dreams and visits from ancestors pushing me toward learning about the past."

"Wow. What do you think they want you to do?" Sacha says.

"No way of knowing until I can get the full picture. It could be exactly what we're doing, bringing our two groups closer together. That period was a time of huge strides forward when it comes to relationship building between all of us."

"You know I'm here whatever you need," Sacha says.

"I do, and I can't begin to tell you how much I appreciate that." I move across the couch in the office to give her a side hug. A year ago, I wasn't sure if I'd ever feel this closeness with her again. My mass exodus from Cypress nearly bankrupted our friendship. It wasn't the leaving. It was the way I failed to share my plans before I uprooted my entire life. Looking back, I can understand her point of view, but hindsight is always twenty-twenty.

"We need a plan." Fel grabs a notebook and pen. "I know we want to research, but where do we even start?"

"All we have to go on is the sigil itself. When I showed it to Cristobal, he suggested a Middle East B.C. It's still broad, but it's better than nothing. He's looking for someone who might be able to help us, but it could take a while. There's no telling where they might be, or what they'll ask for in return for a favor. Everything is done with self-interest with them." I roll my eyes.

"You're telling me if vampires had a house it'd be Slytherin," Fel says, lightening the mood.

"Hey! That's my house, too," I protest.

Sacha grins. "It explains so much, doesn't it? Houses tend to stick together."

"And suddenly it's pick on Lou time?"

"No, we're just comparing notes, in front of you," Sacha says playfully.

"Oh, well that's so much better than being made fun of, thank you."

"You know we're your real friends because we care enough to say it to your face instead of behind your back," Fel deadpans.

"Evil witches." I snicker.

"Speaking of. What's up with you and Hal?" Fel asks.

"I don't want to give up on her because she chooses an alternate route."

"Eventually you're going to have to. You know what happens to witches who let the darkness in," Sacha declares. Things are still black and white with her when it comes to the intention of magic.

"Actually, I don't. I've seen the extreme side of it. Who knows what stages there are in-between."

"A snake can't help what it is, Louella," Fel whispers.

"I'm going into this with open eyes guys. Besides, I have to deal with her anyways. She's Blazh's head witch."

"Doesn't mean you need to connect with her on a personal level. You can't save everyone, Lou."

"I'm not trying to save her. Hal made her choices. She has to live with them. It doesn't mean I have to abandon her like everyone else. I think we all deserve a little forgiveness and understanding. Without it, I would've been screwed."

"Completely different circumstances," Fel replies.

"Yes, because I was lucky enough to have people who gave a shit about me. She never had that. You know how her family is."

Fel and Sacha exchange a look.

"Let's agree to disagree?" I plead silently with my eyes.

They nod, the moment passes, and we begin to go over what we know about magic that involves actual body parts.

Chapter Nine

"Why don't we call it a day?"

I lower my shield, grateful for the reprieve, and bow to the older witch who just gave me a run for my money in a dueling battle. I wipe the sweat from my brow and suck air into my burning lungs. Hazel Walden might be pushing fifty, but her power packs a serious punch. I wince as my ribs protest my movement. She landed her fair share of hits.

The muscles in my arms jerk as exhaustion sets in. Hours of casting have parts of my body feeling like they're made of jelly. Over the past few hours, I've battled a handful of powerful witches. Mémé is determined to condition me to endure and expect the unexpected.

Each witch had a different style and strength. I understand the *why* behind Mémé's methods. Unfortunately, understanding does nothing to alleviate the toll taken on my body.

"Thank you, Hazel." I bow slightly.

"The pleasure was all mine. I look forward to your coronation. You'll be a strong leader."

The approval from the older woman makes me smile.

"I'll see her out while you freshen up," Mémé says, giving me an escape.

I head inside the house to the guest room where I've set up shop since training. The lavender walls with violet-themed wallpaper trim are comforting. Once upon a time, this was my room growing up. Moving into the bathroom, I strip down, tossing my dirty things in the wicker basket in the corner as I turn on the shower. The sound of the water moving through the pipes makes me smile. Older homes have a charm all their own.

Slipping into the shower, I let the hot water beat down on my shoulders. Spent, I lean against the tile as the heat loosens tight muscles and takes away some of my soreness. I feel like I've been trapped inside the Mortal Kombat video game, and I'm one more hit away from a fatality. The steam puffs my hair up like popcorn being heated in the microwave, but I'm too tired to care. Appearance is the last thing on my mind at the moment.

I close my eyes and focus on renewing my energy. Refreshed, I step from the shower and don my comfortable pair of yoga pants and the off the shoulder 'Wifey' shirt Renee purchased as a joke. I leave the room and walk down the stairs, avoiding the creaky stair three up from the bottom. I follow the scent of old bay seasoning and a host of other spices into the kitchen where Mémé is seated at the table.

"Lunch?"

She smiles. "The least I could do is feed you after wearing you out."

"You're enjoying this a little too much, Mémé," I say as I move to the cupboard for a bowl.

"I am."

"Gee thanks." I take the lid off the gumbo and scoop myself a healthy serving.

"Not the pain. The gumption. Every time you rise to the occasion, you make us both look good. I'm proud of how you're taking everything in stride. It'd be too much for most people."

"It's not like I have a choice." After setting my bowl across from her, I pour a tall glass of milk to counteract the heat I know will be dancing its way across my taste buds.

"There's always a choice. You're doing well."

"That's nice to hear you say, 'cause it sure as hell doesn't feel that way. I never realized how bad winning could make a person feel," I whine.

She snickers. "Takes a lot of pain and sacrifice to look pretty and polished while you wield magic effortlessly. Talent will only take a person so far. The rest requires skill. That's earned with hard work and sweat. Do you think I got where I am by D.N.A. alone? Non." She wrinkles her nose and curls her lip. "You have to be willing to work for it."

"Even now?" I tuck into the jambalaya and hum as the flavor mingles to perfection. The heat hits me at the end of every bite, and I sip on my milk to keep it from overpowering me.

"Always. If you get lazy, your spell work will become sloppy and lack power. Being matriarch requires constant vigilance. You must hold yourself to the highest standard in order to demand the same for others. Lead by example."

I nod my head and gesture toward my food with my spoon. "This is so good."

"Thank you, cher. I do my best cooking when I'm thinking."

"Are we going to continue our story?" I ask between bites.

She sighs heavily. "It's past time we do. When the family revolted mid-crisis, I bound them."

I finish my final bite and place my spoon in my bowl. "Bound them from doing what exactly? Acting against your goal?"

She gives a hollow laugh. "If only it was that simple. No, I bound their magic."

"You *what*?" It's a punishment left for the most disturbed and violent. To be stripped of your magic is to have your soul crushed. It renders the magic wielder unable to tap into their God-given gifts. My stomach roils. Instantly, I regret my lunch. "How could you do that to your own kin?"

"I warned them." Her lower lip trembles. "I told them I'd cut them out of our line. They laughed at me." Her eyes glisten. "We'd just lost our parents, and I'd been appointed the matriarch. I was confused and looking to prove my worth. I didn't understand how important things like patience, mercy, and the art of persuasion could be. I wanted to make them respect and obey me. I was willing to use any means necessary, including force and fear. We'd lost so many. I couldn't stand the thought of another loss that could be prevented. I was desperate. Their refusal to assist also felt petty, and personal. It was my breaking point." She covers her mouth, and her slender shoulders shake. "I used my own blood and magic to bind and banish each and every one of them who stood against me and the mission of unity. I thought the price would be worth it, but in the end, it was too high."

"Why not take it back?"

"Once done, some things can't be rescinded." Tears roll down her face unchecked, and the sorrow visible in her eyes clogs my throat. "I severed our family line with a few careless words and blood magic. Once it was done, they all left. They had no choice really. To stay would mean enduring misfortune."

"What happened to them?"

"I don't know. None of them looked back or reached out. I let my children believe they were all missing in action. Misplaced in the Reaping and believed to be dead. That the sliver of hope kept me from erecting gravestones in the family plot."

"Jesus." The depths of her deception is chilling. *Do I really know this woman at all?*

"I've been a coward, too frightened to admit the truth."

"So why are you doing it now?"

"Because *you* can fix what I've done. Once I pass on the title, you have the power to remove the binding."

"If I do this what happens to them? Will the magic become retroactive? What about the children born with no inkling of their heritage? Unearthing that inside of them would be irresponsible and cruel. I have no clue how that might affect them, or if they have someone to teach them properly. At the very least, we should track down your siblings, make contact, apologize, and move forward from there."

"With what time? We both sense the danger and darkness in the air. We've already lost one of our own, and that coven was wounded, not killed. We'd be fools to think they won't try again to harm us."

"So we force those family members into this after years of ignoring their existence? No. We don't have the right to disown them and reclaim them when we need them. I saw what hate and resentment can do to a family, and those emotions were unjustified. These people would have every reason to hate us. I won't do that."

"You think you can always choose the high road?"

"No. I'm not naïve. But in this matter, I have options, and I'm choosing the lesser of evils." Reaching across the table, I grip her fisted hand. "You've trusted me with this family. Now you have to let me handle things my way. I promise you, I will make this right for you, and heal this family."

She presses her lips tightly together and gives a curt nod. "It's in your hands now. I can't carry it any longer."

After everything she's given me, I want to return the favor.

"I think Fel spoke a prophecy the other day."

"What?"

"I'm not sure. I've never seen one delivered, and it was only a few lines."

Mémé leans forward. "How did she behave?"

"Out of it. Her voice was strange, and after it happened, it was as if she woke up. She didn't remember a word she'd spoken."

"Tell me."

I repeat the lines.

"Hmm. It's nothing we didn't know. We haven't been able to tap into the site in decades."

"Is that a good thing?" I ask.

"I'm not sure. Change is coming whether we like it or not. The only thing we can do is hunker down and make the best of it. If this happens again, you need to come to me immediately. Some predictions are time sensitive, delivered in hopes of preventing a catastrophe, and others are more general."

"How can you tell which is which?"

"You can't always."

I leave the house conflicted. Confusion, disappointment, and fear blend together to muddy my brain. How could the wise, generous, loving woman I adore commit such a heinous act? To strip her kin of their magic and force them from the only home they'd ever known took a level of cruelty I wouldn't have thought her capable of. Not when it was directed at her own family.

My entire life she's preached tolerance, family values, love, and strength in numbers. Was it a lie? A carefully constructed persona she used to gain our loyalty and obedience? Or was the binding really her worst mistake? She seemed genuinely apologetic and regretful. At the same time, her confession was poorly timed and linked to a questionable request.

Did absolute power really corrupt absolutely? Was it a ploy to soften me up? Am I looking at an inevitable future? No one's perfect. Logically, I understand that. It's the viciousness of the situation and her solution to it that disturbs me.

My brain threatens to shut down, and I run to the one place where I can escape all things witchy and lick my wounds—the mansion. I could never imagine the day my family home would feel like a prison. I park the car in the driveway and follow the link to our room.

Stepping into the suite, I pause at the sight of the open suitcase. My mood plummets.

"Are you headed off for business?" I ask as I step inside and close the door behind me. The four-poster bed has been lonely without his presence.

"No, but we are leaving."

"We?" I smile.

"Mmm-hmm."

"May I ask where to?" Intrigued, I watch as he packs enough for a few days.

"You may, but I won't tell you."

I frown. "Cristobal, you know how I hate surprises."

"Only the bad ones." He shrugs.

I laugh. "No, those I hate more than the other others."

"You like mine, though." His arrogance never fails to astound me.

"I like any time I get to spend with you, and I humor you about your surprises."

"Now you're just playing hard to get."

I roll my eyes. "So full of yourself."

"No, I'm confident. I promise you, dove, you'll enjoy this. We're both in desperate need of time away. Everything can hold for two days while we take this break."

I sink onto the edge of our bed. "I can't—"

"You can, and you will. You're no good to anyone exhausted with a muddied mind and a broken spirit."

I bow my head. Drained, frustrated, and in desperate need of respite, I yield. There's nothing more I can do currently, and our people depend on our harmony. I have to think about more than myself. I can sense the tension growing among the court. Vampires on edge are a precarious situation. It's like having hungry wolves all in one den—they snap at one another at the slightest provocation. "I can't argue that."

"Good, because you'll lose. I'm not the only one who thought you needed a moment away to gather yourself. If you're a good girl, you'll get to pick out next excursion."

"Anything I want?" My mind fills with pedestrian things to drag him along to.

"I'm already regretting this. Yes, Louella, anything."

"Okay." A vivid image of Cristobal camping forms in my mind. After being plunged into a perpetual state of adjustment, it'd be nice to turn the tables on him for once.

"The court needs to settle. Call Luz here."

Like a spider's web made up of single strands, we're all connected. I can follow the path to each individual. And read them. I tug on the strand that leads to Luz. *"Meet us in our room, please."* I sense her in the hall seconds before she appears in the doorway.

"You rang, mother?" She scans the room. "Are the parental units going on a trip?"

Her words warm me. *Cute.* "As a matter of fact, le chat, we are."

"I'm putting you in charge of wrangling this restless bunch." Cristobal zips the luggage shut.

She barks a laugh. "No difficult requests, huh? It'd be easier to wrangle greased pigs."

"We're all feeling the pressure of living in a glass house right now. We can't afford to prove anyone right, or fall into any traps laid out," Cristobal says.

"We're not saying stay in the house, just mind yourselves while away, please." I lengthen the second syllable.

"I will not be pleased if this trip is interrupted for foolish reasons." Cristobal's voice is stern and fatherly. It makes me want to giggle.

Luz nods. "I understand. I'll keep everyone in line. Percival, Gil, and Lark can help. They're good at having a calming effect."

"Buena." Cristobal pats her face affectionately, and I'm awed by the relationship they've built. The parental bond inside of me flairs to life. Much like witches, the court has invisible cords connecting us all in different ways.

"When we get back, we'll all do something," I promise.

Luz walks over, and I embrace her, cherishing the closeness. It's been slow but steady progress to get us back to this point. When I ran from the soul bond Cristobal established without asking, it hurt her deeply. My rejection and years of denial felt personal, despite the way I reached out to her. She couldn't separate my intense anger and feelings of betrayal toward Cristobal with my desire to remain in her life.

When the love of your life activates an unbreakable connection without explanation or asking permission, it's like someone ripping your heart out. It broke every bit of trust I once held. Young, overwhelmed, and terrified, I did the one thing that would counteract the effects of the bond … I put as much distance between us as possible as fast as I could.

I don't regret my decision. I needed the time to grow up and become the woman I needed to be to deal with Cristobal and everything that came with him. I do wish I had handled the way I left better. I damaged many bridges. Some I'm still trying to mend. No one expects his or her first love to be eternal. Given the fact that I was twenty-one when I met Cristobal, I think I was fully entitled to my freak out.

Luz pulls away and graces me with a smile that could make an angel weep.

"Thank you for keeping an eye on things while we're gone," I say.

"It's my job." Second, in command, she wields a lot of power. "Besides, you need this."

I sigh. "That obvious, huh?"

She shakes her head. "Only to those of us who know you. It's been a non-stop roller coaster since you arrived home."

"My price to pay for jumping ship. I let fear rule me. It was a valuable lesson."

"You're here now, that's all that matters."

The words are a gift. I hold them close to my heart.

"I love you, mija, but if you don't stop delaying our departure, I'm going to be irritated," Cristobal teases.

Laughing, Luz holds up her hand. "Go, enjoy yourselves, I got things back here."

"We will." I wink.

Cristobal wraps an arm around me, guiding me out of the house with our suitcase in his hands. A man on a mission, his steps are quick and sure. He hurries me out of the house and into the car.

"Are you going to tell me what made you so upset today?" Cristobal asks once we're on the highway.

His words break a damn. I spill the story, unable to hold back the flow of words, or the tears. By the time I'm done, I'm emotionally and physically spent. I slump in my seat, resting my forehead against the cold glass of the window.

"Do you want to know what I think?"

"No." My voice cracks. "Right now, I want to think about anything else. Tell me about Spain."

His alto, descriptive words and the wheels on the road relax me. Beautiful imagery dances in my head. I can see the colorfully tiled walls and feel the bricked walkways beneath my feet as I let sleep take me.

I roll onto my back and allow the sunshine to coax me into consciousness. A deep peach ceiling greets my vision. I fought to recall our arrival late last night. Stretching my arms over my head, I embrace the peace that comes with being hours away from all my stressors. Snuggling back into Cristobal, I pull the crisp white sheets up to my chin.

"Morning, reina." His sleep worn voice makes me smile.

"Morning, mi corazón."

"Aaah, she's happy. The endearments have come out."

I playfully slap his chest. "I know I've been tense, but it hasn't been that bad, has it?"

"Tense is not a powerful enough adjective."

I prop myself up on my elbow and narrow my gaze.

"And why have I been so tense, dear?"

"The Esçhete Coronation."

"And?"

"Witch for Hire. New businesses take a lot."

I scowl. "And?"

"The Court Coronation," he says softly.

"Uh huh. And all that comes with it."

"My poor, dove." His playful tone is a reward in and of itself. He's loosening up a bit at a time.

"Look who's finding their sense of humor after centuries."

He rolls me onto my back, and his lips brush mine. "I'm learning lots of new things."

I bury my fingers in his hair and pull him down to me. Our bodies meld together, and our connection hums to life.

"I want to show you something," he whispers.

"I think I have an idea of what," I say cheekily.

"Here." He brushes his fingers over my temples. I swallow to moisten my throat. I nod my head, unable to speak. It's the first time we've intentionally connected our memories. "It's not pretty, but I think you need to see it right now."

"I trust you."

"Thank you, dove." He sits up against the headboard and pulls me into his lap. "Take a deep breath, relax, and clear your mind."

I focus on my breathing as I relax against him. My surroundings fade away as I tumble into the past.

PAST

Pain pulls me from the darkness. An intense searing pain unlike any I have ever known explodes through every part of my body. It slices through me, cutting so deep, I can't form sound. The coppery taste of blood fills my mouth as my gums are ripped and reformed.

"This is the hard part. The transformation. It's the final bridge you must cross from your old life to your new one." The heavily accented voice of my employer sounds overly loud in my ears. I come off the floor, arching my back as the agony sweeps its way through my limbs.

"What have you done to me?" I croak.

"I have given you the life you never knew you wanted. Your talent and intelligence would be wasted here, toiling away as a textile worker, barely able to create. No. You were meant for better things. I knew it the moment I first saw your work. Now you'll have eternity to do as you see fit with."

"You're speaking madness, sir. Please. I need—" My muscles clench and my stomach heaves. Rolling onto my side, I empty my stomach as the burning begins. My body catches fire from the inside out. My veins are a delivery system for poison. I fight against the blackness, as I try to climb out of bed. My limbs refuse to cooperate. They've become useless deadweight. I manage to pitch to the side.

Strong hands grab my arms and place me back in the middle of the bed, holding me down.

"It will all be over soon."   I drift in and out of consciousness.

The most delicious scent rouses me once more. Pushing myself into a sitting position, I open my mouth, tasting the air as I breathe it in. Saliva dribbles down my chin. I tilt my head and close my eyes, focusing on the one thing that makes sense—the hunger and the thirst, unlike anything I've ever known. I open my eyes and find a pretty maiden in a jade dress seated in a chair with my benefactor behind her.

"Ahhh, my son is awake."

"What is this?" My voice is distorted.

"Where you decide if you will live or die."

I focus in on her throat. The flutter of her pulse, calls to me. My body takes over. I gain my feet as a red haze lowers over my vision. I blink and find myself bent over her petite frame, ready to strike.

"No." I throw myself back.

"You will find the will to live is strong. I caution you. The longer you choose to fight, the worse the first feeding will be."

"I will never give in to this evil." I hunch over, squeezing my eyes shut. I open them quickly when it only intensifies the woman's scent.

"I will give you time to reconsider."

Vampire. The soulless beast who possesses life after death. How have I landed myself here? Damned beyond redemption, dependent upon the blood of others to live. Better to die now than live a life of sins I can't hope to cleanse myself of.

Every day Rasputin returns with another woman. They wait, clearly under the influence of his will, like living dolls in chairs. Lambs to the slaughter they smile down at me, never realizing the danger they're in. I lay on my side, fighting to breathe as my vision dims.

I am not ready to die. I give in to the beast, clawing to the surface, and let instinct take over. I fall upon the first girl.

PRESENT

I'm jolted out of the memory.

"You don't need to see the rest."

"Why show me that?" I whisper, shaken.

"Because I want you to understand. We've all gone morally bankrupt at one time or another and had to work our way back up from the muck and mire. Who we become after the corruption can be an entirely different identity. It's how we recover that matters most. I know you're hurt. You've never seen the ugliest sides of your abuelita."

"It was more than that."

He trails his knuckles down my side of my face. "I'm not belittling your situation. I know this is hard, and you have every right to be upset. But I encourage you to reserve your judgment and sort your feelings later when you aren't coming off a gut reaction. You're clouded by your emotions right now."

"You expect me to excuse her behavior?"

"No. I want you to remember we all have monstrous moments. It doesn't make us savage beasts. It makes us fallible humans."

His words are everything I didn't know I needed to hear. He kisses my forehead as the silence falls while I think on his words, and the vivid imagery I've lived. Sharing memories is more than a remote viewing. I was in his body. I struggle with reconciling the rabid creature with an insatiable lust for blood with the cultured man I know and love. I trail my fingers through his hair. I've never seen this vulnerable side of him.

"Thank you for sharing that with me. I get the point you're trying to make, but I'm not ready to deal with it yet."

"And you don't have to. I brought you here to get away."

I fall into the dark pools of his eyes and wonder what else he'll share. The man is an enigma I'm still decoding one secret at a time.

"Enough sorrow, and painful memories. Let's go explore the gardens. They're a part of the reason why I brought you here. I know how much you love to immerse yourself in nature."

"How did I get so lucky?" For forty-eight hours, I'm going to focus on this man, my bond mate, who I'm linked to for the rest of my days. The finality of the situation still shakes me to the core.

He cups my face and delivers a drugging kiss, clouding my mind, and carrying away the concerns and tension.

Chapter Ten

The speaker box chimes as the door swings open. I peer up from the desk and wonder briefly if the smartly dressed woman is in the wrong place. It's on the tip of my tongue to ask when she scans the room. Her gold and green elephant print dress and rose covered sunglasses are obviously designers. The two things alone could pay rent on the office for months, and that's before I add in the leather purse at her side. Her plump lips are not ones that occur in nature. The deep maroon lip color contrasts with her perfectly highlighted golden-blonde locks, which tumble around her shoulders like she's about to audition for a Herbal Essence commercial.

"Can we help you, ma'am?" Fel asks.

"I hope so. I have a …" She peers behind her like she anticipates being followed. Stepping inside, she closes and locks the door. "Problem with the new home my husband purchased. He may be in denial, as he travels for business and is rarely home, but I can no longer afford to ignore the incidents." She clears her throat, and peers down at her French manicured fingernails. Her voice is cool, but I can detect the undercurrent of fear. "Before I say anything more, I need to be assured you can be discreet."

"Of course, Mrs.?" Fel stands and moves toward her.

I lean back in my chair, content to observe, and let her take point. Of the three of us, Fel has the best *people skills.*

"Charlotte Addington."

I bet you think that last name means something to us, don't you?

"Please let me get you settled, Mrs. Addington." Fel guides her over to the suede charcoal couch in our receiving area. "Can I get you anything to drink? Coffee, tea, or water, perhaps?"

I glance over at Sacha and arch an eyebrow. *Is this chick for real, or are we being pranked?* She shrugs her shoulder and shakes her head. We get all kinds. Half of them have problems we can explain with science. Hauntings and paranormal issues are rarer than most people believe.

Mrs. Addington has yet to remove her sunglasses. If the scandalized and the shamed expression on her slender, oval-shaped face—with impossibly perfect, asymmetrical features—is anything to go by, she wishes she was anywhere but here.

"I'm fine. Thank you." Mrs. Addington's voice is sugary sweet. A proper southern belle knows how to maintain impeccable manners in any situation, regardless of how awkward it is.

"Here at W.F.H., we work as a team to produce the best results. I'm Felicite, and I'll be taking the lead in your case. These are my associates and co-owners, Sacha and Louella."

"It's nice to meet you," Sacha says. I echo her statement as we join them both in the receiving area. I want to see her eyes. You can tell a lot about a person by merely locking gazes and watching their response. Everyone has tells, and body language is only altered by the consummate liar.

"Please, call me Charlotte," she offers like an olive branch. "I must seem silly to you, showing up here in oversized sunglasses, but people in my neighborhood live for gossip. A person in my situation does not dabble in the occult. I can't risk damaging my husband's good name. Surely you understand that?"

We're being insulted and asked for help in the same breath. It's not the first time, and it won't be the last. I grit my teeth and hold my tongue.

"Of course, Charlotte. We know these things can be scary and hard to believe if you've never experienced a paranormal event. So, we understand your concerns about people possibly misinterpreting things. I assure you we are well-versed in the art of subtlety. We never reveal our clientele list."

Thank God, Fel's taken the lead on this case. She handles the blonde bombshell with warmth and professionalism.

"Can you tell us what brought you here today?" Sacha asks, gently steering them toward the main event.

Charlotte takes a deep breath. "It started off small. Things going missing, odd noises. While it's a new home for us, the building itself is hundreds of years old. I thought it was a matter of acclimating myself to a new property. When the strange occurrences continue, strange smells, sounds, and the feeling of being watched. I thought maybe we had a ghost or two. It's a plantation home. We all know the ugly history tied to such locations."

Ugly history. Years of mistreatment and inhuman living conditions, demoralization, and inhuman atrocities can be wrapped up in a proper sentence. I sneer.

"What changed your mind?" Sacha asks.

"The tone changed. I started to be afraid of being alone in the house. The knocking grew louder, more agitated, if you will, rattling doorknobs and shaking beds. Then I started to see them."

I lean forward, resting my elbows on my knees. "Them?" I ask.

"The shadow people," she whispers.

Chills run down my spine. "Can you describe them?" I ask, skeptically.

"They're not black. Not in the way we normally understand the color. They're darkness. A shape no light can penetrate. They're all long limbs, reaching to the ceiling and bending in ways no human could ever manage. They stand at the end of my bed, moving closer with every blink. I catch them out of the corners of my eyes in other rooms. They whisper to me."

Shit. The woman is one of two things: mentally ill or under siege. Part of our job is determining which is the case.

"Charlotte. We have to ask you a series of questions before we agree to take the case. They may be a bit personal, but we need you to answer them honestly. Please keep in mind, we're here to help, not judge."

"No, I'm not on medication, nor do I have a history of mental illness. I'm not a heavy drinker, and I wasn't under the influence of anything when I had my experiences," she says haughtily with a smirk. "I did my research. I've tried smudging, ignoring, and questioned my sanity a number of times only to come to the same conclusion. This is really happening."

"How long has this been happening?" Sacha asks.

"Eight months."

"That's a long time to deal with what you're describing," I state.

"I exhausted all other venues before I came here."

"Do you have a problem with witches, Mrs. Addington?" I lean back, narrowing my gaze.

"Not personally, but the open association with them would be bad for my husband's business. I'm a newlywed. It's too soon to be rocking boats. A girl's got to look out for number one." She flashes a faux smile.

"And how do you propose we help you with your issue without *'rocking the boat'*?" I air quote.

"Well, I'm not a saint. I can have friends over for girls' night." Her pleased grin has me struggling against eye rolling.

"Clever. We'll be happy to accommodate your needs." Fel schmoozed like a socialite, and I grit my teeth and remind myself not everyone is grateful for the help they receive. No. Mrs. Addington apparently feels she's entitled to it. Thankless jobs are often the ones most necessary.

I continue to take notes as we arrange a time and date to explore her home and see her out the front door.

"You didn't like Charlotte at all," Fel remarks a few moments after she leaves.

"I didn't say a word." I stir the honey into my rosehip tea and she snorts.

"Like you had to?"

"I was polite." I shrug.

"Yeah, and nothing else," Sacha echoes.

"Shut it, Sach. You didn't like her either."

"Yeah, but I'm a better bullshitter." Sacha winks.

"I didn't have it in me to pretend with another person. I have enough ass to kiss in everyday life. She rubbed me the wrong way."

"I think she knew it, too," Fel says.

"Bitch."

Fel laughs. "Meow. Put away the claws."

"Do you want us to drop the case?" Sacha asks.

"No. Last time I checked, being a bitch isn't a crime. Come on, we have another appointment to make," I say, eager for the road trip to the next site. I need time to shake this.

"How the hell could anyone do this?" Sacha asks.

I stare at the old battlement at Fort Pike historical site and shake my head. A massive chunk is missing from the brick and mortar. I crane my neck to peer up the decaying structure initially built in the early eighteen hundreds. The old cannon still rests atop the high wall constructed to see the enemy coming and give a perfect place to fire off from. The old girl's been breaking down for a while under the strain of hurricanes and aging, and land under the water level. It bore cracks and weak points.

It's the perfect slices taken out like a slice of cake that screams magical aid.

"Had to be magic. Nothing else could be that precise and go

undetected," I say. There's no sign of heavy machinery, and short of lasers, I can't think of a damn thing that could make a clean cut.

"Even if someone figured out a way to remove this section, how would they carry it away, and where would they store it?" Sacha asks.

"Why would they do any of it?" Fel adds.

"To move something this big magically, you'd be expending a large amount of energy. It doesn't seem worth the effort for a witch."

"You think it's the demon again?" Fel says, catching on to my train of thought.

"Yeah." I nod my head, straining to put the pieces of the puzzle together. Corpse, heart, head, and battlement? They're all random. If I stretch it's possible the parapet could be connected to the veteran's family history, but I don't know why you'd need both for any spell. At least not that much of it. They took the ground as well as the wall.

"Why? I think we're letting one case get into our heads. We need to remain more objective," Sacha argues.

"You think someone else did this?" I ask skeptically.

"Maybe. We'll never know if we attribute every single thing we came across to one case. Our business is dealing with the strange. Why should we be shocked when we encounter it?" Sacha throws her hands up in the air.

Have I been compromised? My gut says no. I clamp my mouth shut and gesture forward in a sweeping motion with my arms. "You take point, Sach. We'll follow your lead on this one. You're right. I'm not able to remain impartial right now."

Sacha stalks forward, Artemis reborn with her confident strides, intensity, and strength. I trail behind her at a slower slip, observing the area for anything of note. The lack of evidence is sobering.

"What are the locals saying?" Fel asks.

"They're not saying it's aliens. But they're not saying it isn't."

Fel laughs. "When in doubt, blame the spacemen who probably have far better things to do than be bothered with us."

"Come on, cousin. You know humans are the most precious snowflakes in all the universe. We're the pinnacle in the circle of life," I say somberly.

"God, I hope not, or we're screwed." She draws out the last syllable and rolls her eyes.

The area has been hastily roped off with caution tape, but it's plainly been explored. Closed in two thousand and twelve after Hurricane Isaac, the state park has been all but abandoned.

"Do we have any clue how long it's been like this?" Fel asks.

Sacha shrugs. "People come out here so infrequently since it's been closed to the public, it's impossible to say."

"Who called it in?" I ask as we walk toward the opening, and I wonder what's keeping the rest of the structure from falling in on itself.

"A park worker who patrols here and happens to be a witch."

"Luckily for us."

"He said when he first discovered it, the place was swamped with bad juju. His words, not mine." Sacha raises her hands when we eyeball her.

"Do you feel anything now?" I ask. We pause and tune into our environment. There's an unsettling sensation that lingers in the air. A disturbance to nature has left a bitter taste in the wind. Chill bumps cover my arm.

"Did the temperature just drop or is it me?" Fel whispers.

"I feel it," I say.

"Me too," Sacha adds.

I can feel eyes on me. I slowly turn in a circle, trying to find the source. I rub my arms to ward off the chill. The stench of rotten meat burns the hairs of my nostrils. Fel gags.

"What the hell is that?" Sacha's voice is muffled by the hand covering her nose and mouth.

"I don't know." A shushing noise breaks the cloying silence. I turn my head and freeze as I spot a writhing black mass of slithering bodies making their way across the grass.

"Lou, please tell me this is some mating ritual," Fel whispers.

"Hell no. Nothing about this is normal," Sacha hisses as the snakes encircle us. We move to stand back to back. The wind kicks up, rattling the trees in the distance. A crack of thunder has us all jumping. A streak of lightning illuminates the gray clouds, blocking out the sun. Nausea hits me. Gray figures began to rise from the ground. Smoky, humanoid figures, they wait in the distance.

"Lou," Sacha screams over the roaring winds threatening to blow us over.

"I see them." I plant my legs and raise my hands in the air. I focus on creating a circle of blazing white light. The figures rush forward. The intense cold they bring burns hot. Pain explodes in my head. Metaphysical claws rip through my mental shield. I scream. Images of Fel and Sacha broken and bleeding fill my mind.

"No." I choke the words out as I force the foreign entity from my mind. Icy hands wrap around my throat. I'm yanked off my feet and tossed. I land on my back with am umph. With the wind knocked out of me, I'm unable to catch my breath. My vision blurs. I bury my fingers into the soil and pull energy from the ground. I wince as the remnants of the blood-soaked battleground buzz to life, disturbing sleeping ghosts.

This is more than a ghost. We're under a demonic attack. I roll onto my side and push myself into a sitting position. Weaving back and forth, I focus on my faith and block out the shrill screams of the others. *Ancestors, help me.*

A surge of strength flows in my veins. I feel the helping hands of ghosts, tired of bloodshed, supporting and lifting me to my feet. I raise shaky hands as the weak barrier I've gathered around me holds.

"The light of God surrounds us." The words come out loud, crisp, and sure. The exact opposite of how I feel. "The love of God enfolds us. The power of God protects us. The presence of God watches over us. Wherever we are, God is. And all is well." White waves of energy glisten above my head, like a living rainbow. The dome of protection surrounds us. The smoky creatures flicker into nothingness. Sacha sends a bolt of her power out, flinging the snakes back toward the wooded area.

"Let's get the hell out of here," Fel whispers. The girls come over and help me to my feet. Their clothes are ripped, soiled with dirt, and their eyes are dilated with fear, but they seem relatively whole.

"You were right. It's all connected, and that fucker is more powerful than I imagined," Sacha says.

"It was after you. Why?" Fel asks

"I'm the one it saw at Hal's."

"Well, it's seen all of us now," Fel says dazedly.

"More reason to get the hell out of here," Sacha mutters. I grip my side as we quickly depart. We're battered, and bruised, but walking away. Next time we might not be so lucky.

"We need to learn how to protect ourselves," Sacha whispers.

"Then that's our next stop. I don't know how long it takes this thing to manifest or regain energy. We hurt it. It's going to be out for our blood." I swipe at the trickle running down from my split lip. "Or more of it."

We climb into the car, and I lean back against the leather, inhaling the earthy scent of sage Sacha continually keeps burning in the ashtray. I close my eyes and check in with a concerned Cristobal. *"Ran into a demon. Everyone's okay. Right now, I need to focus."*

"I'll be monitoring." The connection between us is muffled. He's there in the back of my mind, present, but not distracting. What once terrified me has become a comfort. I'm never truly alone. In a world full of enemies and sticky situations, that's a good thing.

"What do we know about this thing?" Fel asks.

"Nearly nothing. Other than the sigil there's been nothing we can link to it. I think the demon is old. The kind of power it's wielding isn't something that underlings possess. I don't know if it's being controlled, or controlling. "

"Because one is better than the other?" Sacha's voice drips with dark sarcasm.

"No, but it might change our approach to information gathering," Fel says.

I watch as she types furiously into her cellphone. Organization is the way she deals.

We continue to toss about theory as Sacha drives to a small parish in the middle of nowhere. We pull up in front of a tiny white church that couldn't hold more than a hundred people max. I arch an eyebrow. She steps from the car, and I'm shocked by the protection surrounding the building.

"These are powerful wards."

"Faith can work magic all its own, and the man who cares for this place has a deep belief." She smirks. "He also knows a thing or ten about magic." She leads us around the side of the steepled structure and knocks at the door. It opens to reveal a man in his late fifties to early sixties. His skin is tan from working in the sun, and his face is a road map of kindness from its crow's feet in the corner of his eyes to the laugh lines. His green eyes are warm, and his silver hair is threaded with the lingering memories of faded black strands.

"Ms. Sacha. You've come to see me again, and you've brought friends I see."

"Father Axson, this is Louella and Felicite Esçhete."

"The honor is mine, ladies." He gives a slight bow.

"It's a pleasure to meet you, Father."

"As much as I enjoy your visits, I get the impression from your clothing this is an urgent matter?"

"Yes, sir," Sacha says.

"Please, step into my office." He holds the door open as we step inside and leads us through the well-loved interior with wooden pews and floors shined to a high gloss. The building has aged beautifully. There's a warmth in here that newer churches often lack. I peer up the aisle at the altar and feel the desire to take a moment to pray and reflect. There's power here in these walls and the man we're following. We gather in the tiny office, pushing three chairs close together across from the small oak desk with neat stacks of paperwork, a cross, and a gold nameplate with F.R. Axson written on it.

The walls are full of official documents, and photos of him with his parishioners and fellow priests.

"What can I do for you young ladies?" Father Axson asks.

"We've got demonic troubles, Father."

He straightens. "I need to know everything." He sits quietly while we fill him.

"Do you have the sigil?" he asks.

"No, but I can draw it," Sacha says.

He opens a drawer in his desk, rustles through the papers, and hands her a blank sheet of loose leaf. She sketches the sigil. Hope blooms in my chest.

"I don't know this by heart, but I can search the archives. You'll be targeted now. You have to be dutiful in your faith."

"What can we do to protect ourselves, Father?" Sacha questions.

"Keep holy water and holy objects near you at all times. They'll bolster your faith and weaken the demon. The demonic try to break you down. Be aware of your surroundings and moods. They creep in a little at a time, chipping away at our reserves, isolating us, and ultimately devouring our souls."

"Do you have any idea why they might be collecting these particular items?" I ask.

Father Axon shakes his head. "It's impossible to say without knowing who we're dealing with. Many of these demons have their specialties. Certain things can add to their power. For instance, a lust demon will be drawn to places, items, and people centered on lust. Think of it as fuel and batteries."

The more we learn, the further we feel from solving this case. My head is crowded, and my soul is heavy.

"Thank you for looking into this, Father," Sacha says.

"As soon as I find anything, I'll contact you," he replies.

I'm on autopilot as he walks us to the front and fills three bottles of holy water. "May God be with you as you fight this evil. People like you give an old man past his prime hope."

"You're not that old, Padre," Sacha says.

"We need new blood. Evil is ageless and rampant."

"Witch for Hire is here to help, Father. If we can ever return the favor, please let us know," I say.

"I'll take you up on that, young lady."

Chapter Eleven

W ha?" I push the long bangs away from my face and stab at the brew button on the Keurig. I've yet to receive my morning jolt of caffeine, and conversation is out of the question. Luz apparently has yet to get that memo.

"You need to come outside and see this." The machine rumbles to life, pulling water from the reserves and firing up the heating mechanism.

"Huh?" I grunt, unable to give her more as I watch the brown liquid fill my Queen Bee mug with the golden handle. I scratch the swath of skin bared between my tank top and black, white, and pink sleeping shorts.

"Right now," she speaks slowly. "There's a solar eclipse occurring."

I frown. "Um, no there's not." As a witch, I make it my business to know major celestial events.

"What you mean is there shouldn't be. Yet, if you step outside," she points toward the foyer, "you'll see I'm right."

I rub my puffy eyes and zombie walk in the general direction of the front door. Fumbling with the lock, I step outside and squint up at the pink, purple, and orange sky. The sun is being swallowed little by little. *I'm going to need a bigger cup of coffee.*

"This is bad, right?" Luz asks from beside me.

I nod my head, unable to make my vocal cords work. My mouth is bone dry. The power necessary to pull this off is unfathomable. It requires altering the balance of nature. "Bad is a major understatement."

"Do you think it was done intentionally? I mean, how is that even possible? Is it probable?"

"Playing with the laws of nature are bound to have disastrous repercussions. It's likely whoever caused this did anticipate this side effect. If it was done deliberately …" I rub the back of my neck and trail off as my brain boots up. "Doing this so publicly proves they're no friend to any of us. Humans will notice and investigate a spontaneous eclipse."

My mind returns to Sebile and her worry about breaches. The Unseelie queen's suspicions weren't unfounded or false. The situation is dire when I'm wishing the Fae were actually playing tricks on me. I grimace thinking of the fall out about to happen. The sun has barely coasted into the horizon, and I'm looking at a crisis situation. We'll have to reschedule all our appointments. Every witch in driving distance is going to gather today.

"What are you going to do?"

"Finish my coffee. Brew more and start returning the calls I know will be coming in." I'm going to subscribe to the airplane safety method of reasoning. In case of a loss of cabin pressure, you have to put your own mask on before assisting others. You can't help anyone else if you're not okay. I retrace my steps inside the house and grab my mug of warm coffee. I lean against the kitchen counter and let the jolt of caffeine hit my system. The heated drink goes a long way toward kick-starting my brain and chasing away the chill that settled into my gut.

Luz hovers close, a dutiful daughter as she observes me silently. I can sense the unasked questions hovering on the lip of her tongue. I love her for the way she holds back her natural habit of plowing forward full speed. I prep a fresh cup of coffee with cream and sugar. I'm ready to talk.

"I know you have a lot of questions, but at the moment, I can't really answer them. There are too many variable factors. We'll all gather and try to narrow those down, so we can form a plan and move forward. The next few hours are going to be incredibly stressful while we try to mobilize, and not kill each other. It's a lot of egos in a small place under stress." I rub the bridge of my nose. "It's a recipe for disaster and a headache." My phone vibrates on the counter, and I grunt. It hasn't stopped buzzing. Mémé, Sacha, Fel, and Mom's numbers have flashed across my screen numerous times.

"Are you going to answer them?"

"After this cup, yeah. I'm going to need all the patience boosters I can handle. How did you know the eclipse wasn't supposed to happen?"

"I pay attention to things, too. Our senses are strong. There was a faux quality. It smells, looks, and on a visceral level *feels* wrong. We're not as connected to nature, but we have our own brand of magic. A sense that aligns us with things on this planet. There's a reason we've always been connected with the evening hours. The connection is tied to endings. We exist after we should the same way the moon ends the day."

I can understand the bond. Vampires are beings of darkness. They have to feed on life to remain alive. It makes sense.

"Is this similar to the way witches tap into nature?"

"Exactly so."

I store the fact away for later. My phone buzzes again. *Fel.* I answer.

"Have you looked outside?" she asks.

"Morning to you, too, sunshine. I have. We should clear the schedule for the week at W.F.H."

"I thought the same thing. Charlotte, your favorite client, is going to be pissed."

I snicker. "Bully for her."

"I'm scared, Lou. This eclipse isn't happening anywhere else. It's specific to Cypress and the surrounding areas."

"There goes any hope of this being a weird global anomaly. This is impossible." The sun governs us all; anything happening to it should be universal.

"I know. They're calling a council lead meeting with the heads of families and all the witches who can make it in."

"When and where?"

"That's still being haggled over. They're scrambling at this point, and the fear is making them snippy."

"I can't blame them. This is either a bold statement or a sign of something very wrong with our neck of the woods."

"I don't know how we can do damage control on such a vast audience," Fel says.

"It would take one hell of a spell."

"Manipulating that many minds is skating on the edge of ethical."

"The rules are always flexible when it comes to what's best for the greater good. It would take all of us working together to pull it off. That in itself might require a miracle."

A loud boom makes me jump. "What the hell is that?" I rush toward the front door. The wards are firmly in place. It can't be an attack. A line of vampires dart out the door in front of me.

Sizzling like bacon dancing in a skillet fills my ears. My jaw drops as flaming bits of circular objects hurtle from the sky. The fiery rain ranges in size from large to medium. The ground shakes with impact.

I grab for the doorframe to stay on my feet. Marcellus and Luz are in front of and behind me instantly, holding onto my arms to keep me steady as the ground continues to vibrate.

"What the hell are those?"

"Meteorites." Percival and Miles voices are synched.

"What the hell is going on with this town?" Luz asks.

"Nothing good," I answer honestly. We've just experienced darkness followed by fiery rain. It could be read as a mimicry of biblical plagues.

"So, who pissed off God?" Ruby whispers.

"Apparently the town of Cypress as a whole." Ada snarky tone adds to the tension.

The ground settles as the shower ends and the sun is returned to rule on its throne.

"Well, we have an answer about the spontaneous eclipse," Larkin says.

"Are you okay?" Marcellus steps away and studies me.

"Right as rain." My voice shakes betraying my lighthearted words.

"Liar," Marcellus replies.

"Okay… physically, I'm unharmed."

"Better," Marcellus nods.

"Cristobal is going to be so mad he's in the Middle East right now," Gil adds softly

I groan. "Oh, he's going to be livid. We need to call him right now."

"Is Mother Nature pissed off or what?" Renee asks, joining us.

"Every witch in town is asking that question right now. I need to shower and prepare for the meeting that will be arranged."

"Here," Marcellus declares smoothly.

"That's an option. I don't get to make the final call, though."

"You have it here, or we can accompany," Marcellus demands.

"Why?"

"Cristobal is away on business, that means he's not here to make you do the things you ought to," Marcellus replies.

"What he's saying is we're responsible for your well-being, and we take that very seriously," Larkin recants.

"No. This is witch business."

"And yet, you're not less ours to protect," Marcellus counters.

"I can't appear to be afraid of my own people. You don't get to intrude on tradition or do anything to hurt my leadership. It's a matter of respect. This isn't a vampire attack. It's a break down in the balance of nature."

"And if you go off and find yourself harmed, who do you think will suffer?" Percival asks.

"Danger comes with ruling. We all know it's a part of the job description. We knew dual roles would be tricky to navigate. Let's learn how to handle it together." I stand my ground and stare each of them down. "If I am to be the lady of this court, that means you obey me, not the other way around. We are bound. I promise to call for you if I ever have a need. You can even stay nearby, but you can't be a visible presence. Separation is crucial. When I act as the Esçhete matriarch, its hands off unless indicated otherwise. There are too many witches who continue to distrust vampires. If we hope to change that we have to take baby steps. Foisting you into their fold at a vulnerable moment like this will only lead to resentment."

The look at each other. I've won. I relax. "I'll offer up the mansion as a suggested place for the meeting, but I won't push." Kneeling, I pick up the telephone I dropped off the floor. "I'll let you know before I leave."

Marcellus scowls. "Stubborn witch."

"Pushy vampire," I toss back.

Rows of white wooden lawn chairs decorate the Blanchard's large backyard. The white gazebo surrounded by colorful blooms is straight out of a fairytale, along with the archway covered with pink azaleas, a black wrought iron bench, and a well-tended flower and herb garden on the opposite side of the yard. I wish we were gathered for a happy occasion. Seated between Mémé and my mother, I study the witches and wizards dressed in formal wear. Their faces are set in various stages of concern.

Quiet conversations rise around us. I lean forward and glance at Sacha who's seated with the Morel family. Sensing my gaze, she turns to look at me. I arch an eyebrow and glance at the family surrounding her. She shrugs and smiles. I grin. *Its official, she's back in her father's good graces.* Snubbing them publicly would undo the progress they had managed. Seeing them operating as a functional unit feels good.

The council members begin to move toward the front. Mémé rises and takes her place beside the others.

"We've all heard about the eclipse and meteorite shower. It's the reason we're all here," Meadow says. Her floor-length, floral patterned dress has a V-neck that shows off her slender collarbone and glowing skin. Her voice speaks peace with it's soft, melodic quality. Tall and poised, Meadow is the epitome of grace as she walks from one end of the audience to the other, making constant eye contact. When this woman speaks, we all listen. Despite her light and airy tone, the power she possesses is prevalent. "We've come together to discuss theories, share any knowledge we may possess, and decide how we shall proceed."

"Perhaps the ancestors are displeased with the unnatural events going on. Witches are consorting with vampires. There are heads of families with split alliances. It's not the way it was ever done. We stick with our own kind." Zephirin Dupeux's voice booms out over the crowd.

"There was a time when this sort of thinking nearly cost us all our lives and legacies. We survived the Reaping by striking up working relationships with all the species. Because to overcome enemies we need to act together. Now, when a new powerful threat shows up, you wish to work backward?" I challenge his bigotry with fact. Tilting my head, I peer down my nose at him. "Sounds to me like the sort of thing we should be avoiding, unless we want history to repeat itself. We lost too much during the Reaping. We can't afford to go down that road again. It's no mystery many families are in short supply of members."

"Your opinions are prejudiced at best," Zephirin says haughtily.

If that ain't the pot calling the kettle black.

"No, when they're rooted in historical facts, it's called accurate."

"Your thoughts have been noted, Zephirin," Meadow interjects. "Does anyone else wish to speak?"

"Due to the Esçhete's open-minded approach, we believe we have a lead on what's creating the upheaval in nature. I have invited someone who has more information to join us," Mémé says. She gestures with a sweep of her hand, and we turn to face the entrance. Vale Meadow is escorting the Queen of Winter court herself down the aisle. The champagne-colored tulle dress has a silver sequined bodice that trails down into thin lines spaced evenly apart. A cape falls down into a train that trails behind her. It moves and flows like a living thing with each step she takes. Its winter couture at its finest. Dark ringlets of hair are twined with fairy lights.

"What is the meaning of this?" Mr. Morel barks.

Sebile narrows her gaze and lowers her lashes.

"Sebile comes to us today in peace. Bound in accordance with the agreement made with Rosemond Esçhete, she is not seeking to harm any here. Our esteemed guest will be treated with the utmost respect and kindness. Lest someone forgets themselves, remember, she's not forced to show mercy to those who step out of line," Vale says. I spot her faithful servants, Cein and Kul, standing on either side of the flower arch. Even with good intentions, she wouldn't be caught unguarded.

Spine straight as an arrow, she looks down on the crowd, nose wrinkled as if she smells something bad. Her smirk is full of secrets we can't hope to know. Even out of her own kingdom, she acts as if we're beneath her.

"There has been tampering with the veil between worlds. Someone seeks to open a portal that would allow their entire world entrance onto this plane. This is the root of your problems."

"If you knew so much, why are we only now hearing about it?" Mr. Morel asks.

"The problems of humans concern me very little. I would not risk an upset to the balance in my kingdom for those who care none for me and mine. But I enjoy our *arrangement* enough to allow you to investigate on my lands where I first detected the anomaly."

Everyone begins to chatter at once.

"You expect us to trust you with one of our own?" Zephirin asks.

"One of yours? No?" She laughs. The bell-like sound is cruel and cold, like the season she rules.

"Who will you grant safe passage, wise one?" Meadow asks, smoothing the rough waters like a white-water rafting champion.

"I've chosen one to represent you. A person I believe understands the complexity of traversing my rules and my people. She has consented to carry your cause and agreed to my terms. I choose Louella Esçhete."

"Of course you choose her," someone shouts in the crowd.

Sebile snaps her finger. Choking begins. "I think you've forgotten who you address. I am Queen of the Winter Court and daughter of the Night. Your fragile human bodies would buckle at the mere thought of the things I've done to others for far less. Consider this your only warning." Large gulps for air come from the back.

The invisible barrier keeping the rain from falling in the space does nothing to block the muggy heat. The moisture only unleashes misery with no cooling qualities. I shift in my seat, uncomfortable under the stares and poor conditions.

Frost coats the ground, and the temperature drastically plunges. Snowflakes drift to the ground. The acrid scent of fear drifts to me on a frigid breeze. The wind picks up, blowing her hair behind her like a dark banner. Amber streaks flicker inside the living purple fire of her amethyst gaze. Cein and Kul stalk forward with eerie twin movements toward the offender.

"Apologize to our Queen." Hands on the hilt of their swords they stop by Everard Dupeux. Like ignorant father, like son.

Everard raises his chin. "I am allowed to have an opinion among my own people. This is my world."

The swords sing as they are pulled from their scabbard.

I rise. "Peace, brothers. I offer retribution." I walk over, back straight and eyes firmly fixed on the glitter black chips of ice that bore into me. I kneel before them and lift my hand, palm up.

Cein and Kul exchange a silent conversation with a look.

"Lady, are you sure?" Cein asks, deferring to my connection with the court. *It's a blood matter.*

"Please, let my blood be a tribute for this affront."

"Very well." The sharp blade bites into the flesh of my palm. I clench my jaw, ignoring the pain. The blood wells up a red river in my palm. I tilt it and let it color the grass.

"Blood is spilled, and the apology is accepted," Cein and Kul announce in tandem. Kul holds out his hand and helps me to my feet.

Sebile floats toward me, hovering over the ground. "This is the woman I've chosen. See how well she handles herself. With dignity, honor, and bravery. The courts of Summer, Fall, and Spring extend their welcome." With a flourish of her hand, she heals my cut. A trail of snowflakes spin around me. The enchanted pieces of fluffy white frozen water dance, glitter in the sun like a scene from a winter wonderland movie. They whirl faster and faster, becoming a miniature blizzard. *This is what it'd feel like to be inside a snow globe.*

"Hold out your hand," Sebile commands.

I do as she asks. A fat snowball lands in my palms. With a flash of blue light, it becomes an hourglass. Pure white sands and white wooden frame.

"You have twenty-four hours to prepare for your journey. We shall come to retrieve you when the final sand drops. I'll take my leave. Interactions with humans are so very tedious." She takes to the sky, becoming a swirling fluid white. Her twin protectors follow at her side, dark splashes of black that flank her in a stunning display of black and white.

"Well, that's one way to make an exit," Meadow cracks the joke.

Nervous laughter sweeps over the group like mass hysteria.

"Are we trusting our future to this slip of a girl who only recently rejoined our community?" Zephirin asks.

"Well, you made certain it wouldn't be your lot once you opened your mouth, didn't you?" Mémé snaps.

An older witch rises in the back. Her gray hair is slicked back and wound tightly in a bun that makes her slender, oval-shaped face almost gaunt. Her high cheekbones are dusted with blush, her thin lips have a touch of color, and her wide-set brown eyes are full of intensity. "She's proven herself capable of navigating choppy waters. How many of us made foolish decisions growing up? Are we going to hold her to that forever?"

I finally place her. *Tangela Bishop.*

"I will question anyone who's in charge of representing us as a whole. This entire thing should've been vetted through the council. We decide who's worthy of such monumental tasks."

"Here! Here!" The cry rises among his cronies.

Is that what this is about? His pride is wounded because the council was skipped over?

"May I remind everyone that this is Sebile's call to make?" Meadow says.

I stand. "If you plan to insult my character and capabilities, you'll damn well do it to my face. I did leave. I had soul searching to do. If you expect me to apologize for that, you'll be waiting for eternity. I questioned what I believed in and why. I hope I'm always able to do that because there's nothing worse than going through the motions simply for the sake of it. We must always explore, expand, and prog-ress. That's what my time away did for me. I returned because I was one-hundred percent sure it was where I belonged. I am dedicated to my family, our people, and my responsibilities. The Esçhetes have never let the magical community down when it counted. We won't start with this generation." How quickly people forget all we've sacrificed, and how hard we fought beside them.

"Soon we'll see if all of this is more than lip service." Zephirin sneers.

I stare him down. "You will." *I'm going to make you choke on every vile thing you've spewed here.* With titles come the need to save face, be treated with respect, and stand your ground. I can no longer afford to live a turn-the-other-cheek lifestyle. If I'm honest, the fire in my belly is proof I no longer want to.

Chapter Twelve

Silence falls over our group as the final sand falls in the hourglass. Larkin, Marcellus, Percival, and Ada form a semi-protective circle around Sacha and I as we await our fate. With Fel acting as our eyes and ears with the council, we're free to try to tackle the task at hand. The wards scream as Sebile demands entrance. I lower them. Snowfall announces her arrival. I watch, amazed as snowflakes form into a silhouette that becomes the Unseelie-born Faerie. Dressed in a white fur cape with a muff on her hands, all she needs is a sleigh to complete the look. Shiny strands of bone straight hair stand out against the blinding white of her outfit.

She removes the full hood obscuring a part of her face and surveys our group. "Prompt and ready. I like it. It's never good to keep a queen waiting." She eyes us critically. It's a struggle not to squirm under her thorough inspection. Unsure what to take on a visit for an undetermined amount of time, we all packed one small suitcase. "Those rags will never do where we're going." Clucking her tongue, she waves her hands in the air, becoming our fairy godmother. Tingles run up my nerve endings as my chic black dress pants and blouse are transformed into a stunning velvet emerald gown that hugs my body, nips in at the waist, and bells down over old-fashioned, button-up, black boots with a slight heel. A dark brown fur cloak with a hood is wrapped around me.

Sacha has been dressed similarly in a velvet blue gown and a sable fur cape, and Ada in a soft rose-colored dress with a light brown cape. The men look like something out of a British period piece with dark pants, vests of various gray tones, mid-length coats, capes, and cravats. Their Victorian style reminds of a Jane Austen novel. Mix in their innate arrogance, and you've got dead ringers for Mr. Darcy.

"Better. You're decent enough to enter my realm." *Careful you don't compliment us too much, we'll think you're up to something.* "Remember to mind your manners. You're my guests, and while I wouldn't want anything to happen to you, there are rules you must abide by. Harm none, offend none, and be wary of tricks and deals."

I open my mouth to ask her what kind of protection she *is* lending us when the bottom drops out of my stomach. Air rushes past my face. I close my eyes tightly to help with vertigo and keep my stomach from rebelling. The disorienting trip ends abruptly in the middle of a snowy clearing. Despite the depth of the snow, I don't feel the cold or wetness on my dress. *Is the clothing charmed or is it their world?* The sky above is a pearly gray with clouds fit to burst with snow at any moment. The snow-covered trees and hills are a postcard perfection. Plump red berries stand out on the branches. My mouth waters. I can imagine their sweet flavor melting onto my tongue.

"Careful, Lou." Sacha touches my arm.

"Thank you." I shake my head to clear it. The land comes with built-in temptations. There's no telling what the berries would do to me. There are reasons humans who cross the barrier stay so long. In the distance, an elegant gray stone castle rises up toward the heavens. An icy pond rests to the far right, and a massive maze stands in front of the structure. The lush green walls lend a mysterious vibe to the building. A coach drawn by cream-colored Clydesdales with black roses wove into their magnificent manes, and feathered hairpieces, roll toward us.

The black coach is royalty ready with its gold filigree along the side, large golden wheels, and a golden crown of thrones rests in the dead center of the roof. As it gets closer, I see the galley along the edge of the roof is composed off intricately connected snowflakes

The horses whiny as the carriage comes to a halt, and a coachman in a black suit hops down. Long white hair tumbles down his back, framing his angular face. The pointed chin, thin pink lips, and large, bright purple eyes fringed with long white lashes give him an elfin appearance.

He bows. "My Queen." Opening the carriage door, he offers his hand. She takes it and floats up and inside the coach. Seated on the blood-red cushioned bench, she's every inch a royal ruler.

"Alston, gather their things." He removes a stool from inside the carriage and begins to load our bags onto an invisible luggage rack. I can't see the apparatus, but the suitcases are staying.

"Are you going to join me, or do you plan to walk to the manor?"

Her words spur us into motion. Larkin and Marcellus move into position, helping us up into the coach.

"There will be a feast to celebrate your arrival. Tomorrow I will take you to the hall of mirrors."

I study the landscape as the horses plod along proudly. White rabbits dart along the hills. Fae magic vibrates on a much higher level. It's unlike anything I've ever experienced. The powerful connection turns the surrounding environment into a sentient being. I can feel its awareness. I admire the woman across from us for being powerful enough to command it.

"You sense the magic, witch?" Sebile directs the question toward me.

"Yes."

She hums. "You're more powerful than I ever anticipated. I thought your line had seen the best of its day. Perhaps I judged too quickly."

I exchange a confused look with Sacha. I know she's baiting me. What I'm uncertain about is her motive. What is she searching for? Sandwiched between Marcellus and Ada, I'm aware of the additional shielding of my mind that keeps my thoughts private. I don't feel an attempt to tamper with my mental space. "*Is she trying to get into my mind?*" I send the question through the link, carefully studying Sebile. If she's aware of the communication, she's not letting it show.

"*No, we're precautionary. The best defense is a good offense,*" Marcellus says. I can't fault his logic. Cristobal sends him with me for a reason.

As we ride onto the property, I admire the ice sculptures of Faeries, wings open as if they're ready to take flight. Their flowing gowns and tunic and breeches are a throwback to a different time. The detail of each face is exquisite.

We finally come to a stop across from a grand stone staircase that reminds me of an entrance to a cathedral. The thick railing is covered with a glittery layer of fresh snow.

"Alston will bring your bags up to your rooms," Sebile says as he helps her down. We follow suit, and I take everything in as we ascend the stairs. A heavy, rounded, wooden door is decorated with elaborate carvings and words in a language I don't recognize. It swings open for its mistress. The sound of laughter, orchestral music, and conversation spill out to greet us. Crossing the threshold, I'm immediately swallowed by merriment. Servants walk by carrying trays of frosted glasses with purple, pink, blue, and green drinks, and an assortment of hors-d'oeuvres. The scene mimics an elite cocktail hour, except the guests aren't human. I try not to gawk at the beautiful range of skin tones and humanoid forms. Tree Fae with bark-like skin and leaves for hair, blue water Fae with white hair, and red-skinned Fae with hair the colors of a sunset are just a few of the unique beings mingling in the crowd. I knew Faeries were inhumanly beautiful, but this is a sensory overload.

"May I present Louella Esçhete and her esteemed entourage. Once they have a moment to freshen up, the feast will begin in the dining hall." She's brilliant as she rules over her subjects, and lords the *honor* of hosting us over the other courts. I can spot the stillness among the flurry of activity. Power radiates from certain individuals in visible waves. I know instinctively these are the rulers of the other three courts.

Sebile stops a young, dark-haired Faerie with a pixie haircut and over-sized amber eyes.

"Magena, escort our guests to their rooms, and guide them back down when they're ready."

It's a whirlwind of faces, hallways, and rooms that are fit for royalty. I'm sharing a suite with the other three girls done in gold and emerald with ornate four-poster canopy beds, high ceilings with crown moldings, and furniture older than the three of us put together. Our luggage is waiting outside each assigned room. I want to explore, but it's not polite to keep people waiting.

"She's not letting us have time to gather our thoughts at all, is she?" Sacha asks as we meet in the main room.

"No. I'm sure it's a tactic," Ada says softly.

"If she wanted to keep me off-kilter, she's succeeded."

"Be careful what you eat and drink," Ada cautions.

"We'll be checking everything with our magic," I assure her.

"Two or three times," Sacha adds.

A knock sounds at the massive double doors.

"Come in," I call.

"If you ladies are ready, I'll lead you to the dining room. The men are waiting." Magena clasps her hands in front of her as if she's praying. Back ramrod straight, and eyes trained on the floor, you can tell she's been doing her job for some time.

"Lead on, Magena." I smile.

We follow her outside where Marcellus, Larkin, and Percival are waiting.

"Are your rooms as luxurious as ours?" Marcellus asked.

"Yes. I'm thinking of asking for upgrades to the mansion now," Ada says.

I roll my eyes. "Snobs."

"Privileged is the word we prefer," Marcellus drawls.

"Children, can we get along, please?" Percival asks dryly.

Larkin smirks. It's all bravado. We're using the familiar banter to settle our nerves. What once showed animosity had become a sign of genuine affection. By the time we reach the main hall where people are gathered with drinks and curious gazes, I'm rock steady. Sebile slinks over with a wicked smile.

"May I present the soon to be Lady of the Cortez Court, and the matriarch to be of the Esçhete family, Louella Esçhete." All eyes are on me. I hold onto my skirts and curtsy, grateful for the stringent training from the court of courtesy rituals long past.

"This one has manners," Sebile purrs.

Laughter fills the space. I've passed my first test.

"One never knows what you'll get when dealing with humans. Perhaps this one will be tolerable."

Perhaps I should bite my tongue, but being meek won't win me any points with this lot, and I have to stand up for my stations. "*She* is right here, and sufficiently trained to rub shoulders with royalty like those who are now before me."

"Oh, this one will be amusing," a tall Faerie with long, black hair, and golden-eyes all but purrs. His voice is reminiscent of Alan Rickman in the role of Severus Snape.

"Artagan. Always a troublemaker," Sebile says with a laugh. The woman beside *Artagan* has wild chestnut curls, olive skin and high cheekbones, and full red lips that stand out in her heart-shaped face. The same startling gold eyes are full of amusement and kindness. It's not what I expected from any of them.

"It's been so long since we've had proper visitors. Can you blame us for being excited?" Her voice is a soft as the velvet of my dress, and full of warmth and mischief.

"Morag, taking up for your troublemaking mate again, I see? I should stop expecting better from you, sister."

"Bitter because the Fall Court likes to have fun?" Morag taunts.

I glance at the Faeries. I'd never say it out loud, but they're two sides of the same coin. They're darkness at different stages. I can see the family resemblance, but it's clear they're twilight and night.

"You forget which court you belong to."

Morag's eyes spark, burning a molten gold. "Believe me, sister, I know I'm a member of the Unseelie. You'd do well to remember it doesn't mean you have to be an utter bitch."

"Ladies, save the family disagreements for later," Artagan scolds, stroking his wife's wild hair.

"Introductions would be most prudent," a man with a full-bodied voice says. He's the very definition of a good-looking man. Golden-blond hair ends at his collar, and he has a masculine, square face with a dimpled chin. His light green, almond-shaped eyes are full of disdain.

Sebile's violet eyes flicker with annoyance.

"Louella, meet Tarinde, King of the Spring Court, and his wife, Friesal." The petite woman with delicate features, grass green eyes, and bee-stung, pale pink lips smiles. She seems like a strong wind could blow her over, but I know better. Her white-blonde hair is baby fine and cascades to her waist in an impressive waterfall of shininess.

"Your Highnesses, it's a pleasure to make your acquaintances." I curtsy and they greet me with a small regal bow.

"You've already heard from Artagan and Morag, King and Queen of the Fall Court."

I repeat the motions. "Your Highnesses honor me with your presences and invitation. I thank you."

Morag chuckles. "Oh, she's good."

"You may survive us unscathed," Artagan says jovially. The muscles at the base of my back tense. Is that a warning or a joke? I sense irritation coming from Sebile. If it's related to her sister, or the fact that she's yet to trip me up, I can't say. I came into this game playing to win. I refuse to fall into the trap of owing a Faerie.

My court presses in close to me. The brush of their psyches against mine brings me comfort. I draw strength from their nearness, keeping the faux smile plastered on my face and my eyes blank.

"King and Queen of the Summer Court, Oighrig and Evander." Tall and sleek with sky blue eyes, thick, red hair, their sun-kissed skin glows. Oighrig is broad-shouldered and muscular, with hair the color of blood he's pulled back into a low ponytail. He peers down at me with a curious expression. His wife is willowy with wavy, auburn locks that scream beach hair, and a perfect up-turned nose. They stand out against the most against the wintery environment.

"It's an honor to be in the presence of the honorable Summer Court."

They give small nods of acknowledgment.

"Tell us who you've brought with you," Oighrig instructs.

"This is Larkin, Marcellus, Percival, and Ada. They are members of the Cortez Court. Sacha Morel is a member of my witch community."

"How interesting that you should hold two conflicting roles," Evande says. "It's light and darkness."

I nod my head. "Yes. But we are all creatures with the aptitude for dual qualities, are we not? No one is truly one thing or the other."

"Fascinating," Oighrig says. I can feel him press against the barrier of my mind. I keep my walls high.

His eyes widen. I don't like his interest.

"Tomorrow we will conduct our business. Tonight is for celebration." Sebile claps her hands. The doors swing open to the dining hall. "Now we dine."

I curse the heavy black velvet skirts that skim the snow as we trail behind Sebile. A scarlet dress hugs her curvaceous frame, and dips low in the back, showing flashes of her back when her hair sways. An ornate crystalline crown rests on top of her head. She appears to glide as she leads us up the path toward a snow-capped mountain. A woman on a mission, her pace is relentless. We reach the top of the trail that dead ends into a mountainside.

Sebile waves her hand. An opening appears carved into the rock.

"This is as far as I can allow anyone other than Louella to go. What's beneath this mountain has been revealed to a select few. Each must prove their worth. Should you agree to enter, it must be of your own free will with this knowledge."

"Wait, you expect us to allow her to go in there alone?" Marcellus asks.

"Are you questioning my integrity?" Sebile counters.

"When it comes to my lady there is nothing I won't do to guarantee her safety. Since we've been here, you've spoken no words defining our protection in your kingdom."

"You want an oath then?" she asks slowly.

"I do. That she will be unharmed by you or anything else you encounter while you're inside that mountain."

Sebile tilts her head to the side. "That's a lot to ask."

"Only if you're planning on doing something less than honorable," Larkin says.

"Clever vampires," Sebile crows. We're sport to her. A fun interruption of the monotony that is immortality. "I swear that no harm that befalls her inside will be due to me. I refuse to take responsibility for actions she takes which may bring things upon herself." It's as good as promise as we're going to get from her.

Marcellus' clenches his jaw. "Fine. Lady, proceed."

"I agree," I say solemnly.

"The mountain is alive. It chooses who shares its secrets." She steps into the cave. Shrouded in shadows, she could be death's handmaiden. I follow quickly before I give myself a chance to overthink things.

"Oh." Ice coats every inch of the stone. Icicles hang down like fringe.

"Beautiful, isn't it?" she asks.

"Yes." I pull my cloak closer to my body, relishing the warmth as the temperature drops. My heels click over the cobbled stone.

"Not many can see the beauty in the darkness." Purple Faerie lights hover in the air, illuminating the area. There's an inviting quality to the darkness. Black roses grow out of the ice—large, vibrant, and fragrant. The sultry smell of dark spices and orchids. Here there are no limitations to what can exist.

The tunnels branch off into three separate entrances. We veer to the far left. Passing through the rounded arch, we enter a forest. Trees sprout up tall and curve inward on either side of the narrow path, covered with silvery snow. The light from the full moon in the night sky above us is brighter than the one on earth. Tilting my head back, I study the differences. The stars are so much closer and crisper here. As we move deeper into the forest, the trees close in around us, and the path becomes a thin ribbon of stone. The sound of running water reaches my ears.

"Is their water ahead?"

"Yes, we're coming to a stream. Here you'll face your first test."

"Test?"

"I told you, the mountain judges who's worthy or not."

It's not an outright lie, but the omission is splitting hairs. We wind our way around a bend, and I see the stream in the distance. A stone bridge leads to the other side.

"Peer into the water and tell me what you see."

I kneel cautiously, never feeling the cold. Bending over hesitantly, I hold my breath. My reflection stares back, warped by the flowing water. I relax. A movement beneath the surface and a flash of white and blue catches me off guard. Aquamarine-skinned water sprites with long, white hair swim on their back. Their frosted white eyes latch onto my gaze. The glint of metal catches the moonlight. I lean in closer, narrowing my gaze. The water is lit from within, a soft blue that's easy on the eyes. A rusted copper key rests on a pile of large gray stones. The top of the key has a Celtic knot woven into its design.

"What do you see?" Sebile asks.

"Water sprites. And a key."

"They're the guardians of this waterway. If your intentions are as pure as you claim, they'll allow you to remove the key. Providing they find you fit to wield it." Her tone lacks certain confidence.

"And when was the last time that happened?"

"The years all blur after so long."

I lower the cloak and push up the sleeve of my dress. Waiting won't change the outcome. My hand trembles as I sink it into the icy deeps. The cold sinks bone deep. My teeth chatter. The sprites circle my hand. Their hair brushes against my skin. Like synchronized swimmers, their tiny legs work in tandem, keeping them moving in a hypnotic display of graceful shapes and formations. My fingers brush the key. They tighten their ranks. My throat dries out. *Are they going to attack?*

I pick up the key, ready to fend off an attack. Their tiny hands brush up against my skin as they wrap their bodies around me. I lift my arm out carefully. I clear the water, uncertain if a battle with them will anger Sebile. The minute they feel the air, the sprites let go. Their wings are iridescent, glowing in the moonlight. They move in to caress my face as they pull my hair gently. I don't understand the significance, but it's a far sight better than the tiny teeth ripping into my flesh as I'd imagined they might.

"They're giving you their blessing and thanking you for their freedom. They're bound to protect the key, but while it's in use, they can do as they please."

"Thank you," I whisper. I smile as they flit away, skimming the top of the water while they disappear from view.

"You've passed the first test. Come."

Clutching the key like a talisman, I trail behind her over the bridge. The trees grow larger and flesh out. A trail turns to the right. The light lessens as the trees grow together above us. My stomach knots. Glowing yellow eyes watch us from deeper in the forest. I imagine the hungry beasts that possess those luminous gazes. Branches rustle. My instincts kick in, adrenaline pumping. I'm in fight or flight. There are things stalking us. Plenty of lore describes the being with teeth, claws, and ill intentions among the Unseelie.

I glance over my shoulder and catch wispy white apparitions trailing behind us. Spindly fingers appear on the edge of the walkway. *Goblins?* I'm grateful when we enter a clearing. Three tall oak trees reach for the evening sky. Their branches like fingers spread as they worship its majesty. In the center of each thick trunk are doors. I study the key. It gives no indication which door it will unlock. The door in the middle is made of pale wood, lovingly sculpted into a giant owl. Its eyes are carved deep and seem to follow you. A navy-blue door, which has a rounded top with an embossed pattern of swirls, is at the right. On the far left is an ornate black door with a gold frame with an odd cutout design.

"What am I supposed to do?" I ask.

"Each door leads somewhere. But only one will take you to the hall of mirrors."

"What keeps me from opening every door?"

"You may only use the key once." She smirks. It felt too straight-forward. I want to ask, 'Where's the catch?'

"May I touch the doors?"

She nods. "You may. Take as long as you like to make your decision." There's no kindness in her words, only a blatant arrogance, and mockery. Her high-handed attitude presses my buttons. I move to the black door, close my eyes, and place my hand on its cool surface, opening all of my senses. Dread forms in the pit of my stomach. Fear, anger, and darkness fill me until I'm ready to explode. Images of curved nails, and bared teeth dripping with bloody saliva, fill my head. There's nothing but pain and suffering behind the pretty packaging of that door. I snatch my hand back, shaken by all I've experienced. My body trembles. I wrap my arms around my waist. "What is that place?"

"The forgotten place." She frowns. "Most are fooled by its exterior."

"You shouldn't mistake witches with humans." I smile. Her lips press together in a thin line. I move on to the owl. I brush it tentatively with my fingertips. Nothing. I press my palm flush against the wood. It's warm to the touch. Feelings of well-being and joy wash over me. I want to experience more of what the entrance is offering. I caress the notches in the wood and lift the key. A shrill cry snatches me from my trance. I stumble back. Any door that begs to be opened this way shouldn't be.

"Not this one."

"Are you sure?" Sebile purrs.

More than ever. "Positive." I walk over and touch the final door. It's a breath of fresh air. Cool like a refreshing dip in a hot day, it eases my apprehension. "This is the one."

"Use the key if you dare."

I place the key in the lock and turn. The door swings open. High arched, brick ceilings curve with the majestic architecture of the medieval time period. Mirrors of every shape, size, and varnish are attached to the walls.

"It appears you're determined to live up to the hype, Louella Esçhete."

"We all want the same thing, don't we? Neutralization of a threatening force?"

"Hmm. This time." She waves a hand. "After you."

Ignoring her unsettling games, I step inside. Mixed vibrations clash. My stomach swirls in the vortex I swear has been opened up inside of this space. I slowly rotate as I struggle to get my bearings.

"Why does it feel like this?"

"Every mirror is a portal to another realm. When you put them all in one space, the energy can be chaotic."

My jaw drops. It adds an entirely new meaning to the phrase 'Into the looking glass'. Perhaps Alice in Wonderland wasn't a fictional work after all.

The corridor stretches out beyond my eyesight. "There are so many."

"Silly humans. Always thinking they're all there is to existence."

"More like praying we aren't," I say honestly.

She sneers. "I'll believe that when I see it. For centuries I've watched your kind destroy what you can't understand."

"Witches worship nature and do what we can to keep the balance of things. How easily you forget I'm not human." I let the fire in my eyes come through. I'm not above using my newly gained gifts from the bond to flex some muscle.

"It's close enough."

"If you truly believed that, I would not be here." I'm bluffing, but the confidence I'm faking will never alert her to the truth. I focus on keeping my breathing steady, my muscles loose, and my mannerisms lax. On the inside, I'm close to a mental meltdown. She could laugh as easily as she could lash out.

"Smart girl. I need you to help me decide my position on this matter. Don't mistake this arrangement for anything more than that."

"I wouldn't dream of it," I say honestly.

"Familiarize yourself with the hall and explore. You'll feel the fracture."

No pressure. I walk the space arms out. Each mirror has a distinct signature of energy. It's like being in the center of a large airport with an infinite amount of potential gates that lead to different destinations. I feel a tug at my magical core as I approach each one. An oval-shaped, silver-gilded antique runs up a wall, dwarfing me. There's an old feeling of nobility to this one. I stop a few feet down in front of a small, circular mirror surrounded by metal roses. The impression of light-hearted fun and whimsy bring a smile. I trail my fingertips over the glass. They sink in slightly. Startled, I pull them back.

"Careful you don't take an accidental journey," Sebile cautions with a throaty laugh.

I continue my walk. After a time, I feel the sour note playing among the beautiful symphony. I retrace my steps and stop at in front of a mirror with Middle-Eastern roots. The pointed apex rounds out to a curved that smooths into a rectangular shape. Intricate floral designs and interlocking squares line the double border. I run my finger along the edge. The power here isn't contained. It's leaking out. I sense a fracture. I use my magical vision and find a crack that's beginning to form a spider web of smaller imperfections. I'm certain Sebile saw this. Why didn't she act?

"What's on the other side of this one?"

"Look for yourself."

I frown. "When you cross the threshold, do the inhabitants see you?"

"Not if you shield yourself and keep the visit short."

With a quickly whispered invisibility spell, I push my head inside. The stench of brimstone chokes me. Smoke burns my eyes. I swipe away the saline as I try to take in my surroundings. It's complete desolation—a ruined landscape of scorched earth dotted with small fires, and an active volcano. Heat engulfs my face. A shiny object flies up into the air, hopping around as if it's alive. The lid rattles, and as it pops off, I realize it's a lamp. A smoky figure explodes out of the spout. The gangly creature with pale green skin and ghoulish features is instantly recognizable despite the sinister tone rarely associated with its kind. *Djinn. Holy shit.* The Djinn turns its head toward me, and I pull out of the mirror.

"Genie."

"Yes. It appears after a few millennia they've found a way to make their move on claiming the earth as their own."

"Why? How?"

"They are not benevolent mystical beings who live to grant wishes. Djinn are fallen angels who want to not only return but rule and destroy the human race in the process. If they manage to breach the barrier, life as you know it will end. They live for death and destruction and hate … the creation they feel their father revered over all others."

"You knew. Why do all of this?" I throw my hands up in the air.

"I always choose the winning side, Louella. Right now, I'm not convinced you'll be the ones who come out on top."

"Self-preservation?"

"Wars take time, cause casualties, and quite frankly, they bore me. I won't put my people in the position for petty humans."

"Why contact us?"

"To tip the scales in the favor I want them."

I know next to nothing about Djinn. That needs to change immediately.

"We have to go home and prepare."

"Be sure you win. You don't want me for an enemy."

Chapter Thirteen

Dumped unceremoniously outside the wards of the court mansion, Marcellus grumbles loudly about our rushed exit.

"What the hell—"

I hold my finger up to my lips and cross through the wards.

"I don't put it past Sebile to linger. Once we're inside the house, I'll explain more."

The minute we open the door, Luz and Ruby greet us.

"Where's Miles? I need all hands on deck in the library."

"Welcome back …" Luz trails off.

We dump our luggage by the front door, and I hug her before continuing to the library. "I know what we're dealing with now, a Djinn."

"A genie? Like Aladdin rubbed a lamp?" Luz asks skeptically.

"Yeah, the actual thing is nothing like the Robin William's Disney version." I snort. The concept is a ridiculous one now that I've seen the real thing.

"What happened with Sebile?" Marcellus asks, bringing us back to task.

"She took me to a place where dimensional portals exist. I saw with my own eyes where the Djinn lie. I watched one come out of a lamp. It's the only thing the legend got right. Their land looked like hell. Fires, volcanic explosions, and destruction as far as the eye can see. I'm not shocked they want to get out of there. There wasn't a hint of anything living."

"What are we going to do?" Sacha asks.

"Wait, you're going to trust what you experienced in the Fae realm?" Ruby asks.

"No, we're trusting my senses. I have never experienced an environment so devoid of hope, light, or love. I'll die before I let that be the Earth's future. Sebile said they wanted to conquer and reign. I believe that."

"The first thing we need to do is learn everything we can about our enemy," Marcellus states. This is the man charged with keeping members of the court safe.

"That's why we're here." I gesture to the rows of books stacked neatly in the library and long for Cristobal once more. He's meeting with an expert in the Middle East about the sigil. Communication has been sparse.

"Given the recent development, do you still believe the murders and strange occurrences are connected? It doesn't seem like anything a Djinn would do," Sacha says.

"Yes. I don't know how though. I feel like it's a huge piece of the puzzle we're missing."

"What do any of us know about them?" Ruby questions.

"Only the myths which are always a mix of fact and fiction and not helpful at all," I admit.

"I know the basics." Percival gestures for us to sit before continuing. "They were a branch of the fallen angels cast down after the war. Angry and bitter, they live to bring down the humans they envied and despised. Their wish giving abilities are linked to the leader of their rebellion. Much like demons make deals for souls, so do the Djinn. The major difference is their approach. The three wishes are the free sample plan."

"Damn, it's manically genius," I whisper.

"Wait. Can you extend your wish quota? I thought that was against the rule, wishing for more wishes." Sacha's brow furrows.

"Oh, it's allowed. For a fee," Percival reminds her.

"It's like a drug trade. You give 'em a taste to get them hooked, and then there's no price too high," Luz marvels. "And people think vamps are fucked up." Luz snorts.

"Do you have any idea how to stop them, Perc?" I ask.

He shakes his head. "I wish I had better news for you, my Lady. They're a vastly unknown subject matter."

"Well, kids, let's break out the books and dig in." Marcellus twines his fingers and cracks them. "It's time to get the research ball rolling on all fronts." His pointed stare makes me roll my eyes.

"Okay, daddy. I'll contact the witches. I'll need to call another council meeting anyway."

"Tread carefully. Zephirin's itching to nail your ass after the stunt you pulled with Cein and Kul."

"Please." I roll my eyes. "I saved his son's ass. It's not my fault his stupidity overrides his survival instincts."

"Clearly, it's a family trait he inherited from his father," Sacha says drolly.

I snicker. "Too right you are there."

"You bled for the bastard. He owes you, and everyone who witnessed it knows that. Use that to your advantage when the time is right," Sacha suggests.

The vampires hiss. Blood matters are a big deal.

"When the time is right, I'll call in my marker." I soothe them through our link. *"At the time it was the easiest way to handle a potentially dangerous situation. I don't regret my actions. Uniting against a common enemy outweighs any lingering prejudices."*

"I'd pay money to see his face when he realized the family is now in your debt," Sacha says as we move to the bookshelf.

"Like he's sucking on a sour lemon, I'm sure."

Sacha wrinkles her face and squints her eyes. I can't hold back the laughter that wells up at her imitation. The oppression lifts, as we dive into the leather-bound tomes. The smell of parchment, the careful turn of pages, and the ingestion of information whittle away the hours. I slowly surface when my stomach growls loudly.

"Okay. The humans need food and sunlight. I'm stealing your Queen. We have to touch base with our people anyway," Sacha says.

I close the book, *Middle Eastern Monsters and Myths*, and stand. My legs protest my inactivity. I roll my stiff shoulders and neck.

"Call me if you find anything?"

"Of course," Luz says.

Sacha and I link arms as we make our way out of the library. The moment we're outside she turns to me.

"Tell me really, are you okay?"

"I feel like we're on a time limit. I can't shake the image of an invisible doom's day clock loudly ticking down the seconds until total destruction. There's so much we don't know. It unsettles me. Every new death reported feels like a direct result of our failure."

"You can't think like that, Lou. You'll go insane."

"I know." I sigh. "I hate to go to sleep at night because I'm not sure what horrors await me upon waking. People are starting to take notice of the strange things occurring, and the council is expecting me to make it all go away. I didn't even know what the hell we were dealing with until today. A few hours ago, genies were ancient lore, not history."

"There are people desperate to discredit you right now, and others looking on to see if you can prove you can handle yourself against their attacks. No one believes what's been dumped on you was caused by anything you did. What do you think Sebile's angle is?"

"She's hedging her bets while helping us under the table, so she can keep her hands clean. Just in case the Djinn come out on top. Fae forbid she has a war waged on her over humans."

Sacha laughs as we make it to her car. "We're going to gorge ourselves on Mama's Soul Kitchen and put everything else on hold. After our bellies are full, I'm going to keep the council at bay for the next twenty-four hours, and you, my brilliant bestie, will have something for them when they approach you after that time."

"Don't ask me what," I say sarcastically.

"That's the spirit. Polish the turd. Make it pleasant to the ear and give them a call to action that makes them feel important. I've watched my father kiss enough influential ass to know how it works."

Climbing into the teal beast, I lay my burdens down momentarily.

"You look to be in one piece, but I'm not so easily fooled. If there's one thing I know about witches, it's that they hate to lose face."

I turn in the garden and smile up at Percival. I slipped to my sanctuary to think after lunch. Hands shoved into his black slacks, the dark-haired man is studying me carefully. I wonder who elected him to come out and check on me.

"And you know this from experience, do you?"

"Firsthand with Rosemond. But I think you knew that, didn't you?"

I shrug, uncertain how to respond. It's a bold admission coming from the usually private man.

"I sensed the change. You paid close attention to me and gained a softness in your demeanor toward me that hadn't been there previously. It made it easy to put two and two together. For the record, I don't mind you knowing. I'm not ashamed. I loved her. The timing killed any chance we might've had. The world wasn't ready for a union like ours. Not even after the collaboration necessary to end the Reaping. No one likes to mention how we banded together to defeat our foe these days. It's akin to a dirty secret we all try to keep shoved in the back of our closets." I remain silent, afraid he'll stop talking if I interrupt. "Those were desperate dark days. Bloody battles and blood magic were part of the sacrifices."

"What?" The word is out before I can bite my tongue.

He looks up at me. "I could never deny Rosemond much. The power she needed to harness with the loss of so many in her family required more than she could attain on her own. Your ancestors were silent in those days, dismayed with the actions of their future generation."

Excommunicating family members for no damn reason would piss them off all right.

"What did you do?" I ask, silently willing him to continue opening up.

"I bound myself to your line, pledging my power to her cause."

"You drank from each other?" I ask, stunned.

"Yes."

"A-Are you still bound?"

He shakes his head. "No, what we did was temporary."

"You still love her?"

"There will always be a special place for her in my heart. Love is not so easily carved from us, is it?"

"No. Why are you telling me this?"

"Because I think it's time for you to hear it. You doubt yourself and your choices. Yet you've already made calls your predecessor couldn't. They let fear rule them. In this way, you are fearless. Witches like to pretend they're above pettiness and all-powerful, but they too have their secrets and reach out for help. The only thing you did was be transparent about it. It's earned you the respect those who came before you never had."

His words are enlightening and needed at the moment.

"You are about to take two thrones for a reason."

"Yes. Which means every decision I make affects twice as many people."

He smiles kindly. "There are too many good people around to allow you to cause irrevocable damage. You've yet to realize the superpower you're assembling. This community has long needed an individual like you. One who can remain fair and just because they're able to see both sides. The Cortez Court is on the cusp of another power level up. It makes us more noticeable to others, and therefore a target. It's made it harder to touch us. Thank you."

"It wasn't intentional—" I refuse to accept his gratitude.

"Doesn't matter. Others have ignored the bond. Whatever this family needs to do to keep you safe we will. You're one of us now. So, if that means spending a day buried in dusty old books to fight your latest enemy we will." He wraps an arm around my shoulders. I surprise myself by allowing it to remain. "Come on, Cristobal will return tomorrow with the one he's searched for."

Hope springs up inside of me. We may pull this off yet.

Eyes burning and stomach growling, I stumble to the car with a sixty-four-ounce mug full of mocha coffee. Three hours isn't enough time to feel human. I curse Charlotte as I drag my weary body into the car. If her idea of an emergency doesn't coincide with mine, she won't need to worry about a haunting 'cause I'll kill her myself. I shove half a breakfast bar into my mouth and chew, ignoring the way my cheeks balloon out like a chipmunk. I'm never good company when I'm hangry, and I need to approach this situation professionally.

The frantic woman wringing her hands as she paces the length of the front porch is a far cry from the woman who crept into our office weeks earlier. Frizzy hair, pale skin and manic behavior have taken over. In her long, white nightgown, with a clearly disturbed psyche, she looks set to play Othello's madness scene.

A malevolent force shrouds the plantation in the form of darkness that can only be felt. The oppression is heavy. I pull up beside the Studi Baker, grateful they waited for me before they proceeded beyond the tall iron gates.

Sacha rolls down her window and presses the gray button on the intercom. The speaker box buzzes loudly, and the gates slowly swing inward. Charlotte leaps from the porch like a gazelle, bounding the stairs two at a time as she races toward us. My car has barely come to a complete stop when she slams her body into the teal beast. The thud makes me jump.

Fel exits the passenger door. "Charlotte, are you okay?" she asks quietly.

Charlotte turns her head toward Fel, but her expression is blank. Dark circles make the skin under her eyes appear bruised. It could be lack of sleep making her slow to respond, but the dead-eyed stare gives me the chills. Fel places a hand on her shoulder. "Charlotte?" she whispers softly. Her body shakes like a car in desperate need of an alignment driving on cobbled roads.

"Mrs. Addington," I say sternly.

She blinks. Awareness floods into her expression. "What happened?" I ask.

"I-I woke up to the smell of smoke and the shriek of smoke detectors. There were wads of tissue all over the hallway. A few were still smoldering, and others had burnt edges. The shadow people have moved from rattling doors to lighting fires." Her voice cracks. She tugs at the neck of her gown, scratching the red, irritated skin.

"Why are you still here? This house isn't worth your life," Sacha says incredulously. "You should've left."

"They won't let me," she whispers.

What? We all stare, confused.

She's lifted off her feet and pulled toward the front door. It slams open just in time for her to disappear through the dark entryway before it closes. It's a blatant challenge. I ball my fists.

"I think we've just been called out," Fel says.

"It'd be rude of us not to properly respond." I stalk to the back of my car and pop the trunk. My mind is focused on retrieval as I gather crosses, holy water, and a *Bible*.

"Who's ready to put everything we've learned to good use in a crash course in demonology?" Sacha asks in a snarky video game host impression.

"I'll take us for a thousand, Morel," I reply.

The house is an enemy ready to engage in battle. We walk toward is it side-by-side, united. I wave my hand, ripping the door open. Flickering lights cast odd shadows in the foyer. My eyes struggle to take in the information they're rapidly receiving with every befuddling flash. We step inside cautiously. The chandelier rattles above our head. Skirting the potential death trap, we quickly move to the left.

Curtains ripple from an invisible source in the room to the right. The door shuts behind us. A creature scurries across the ceiling. Debris rains down on our head. Fel cups her mouth to call for Charlotte. I slap her hands down. "Try not to turn us into the stereotypical first girls to die in the horror movie, please."

"How do you think we should find her?" Fel asks.

"I don't think that's going to be a problem," Sacha whispers. "Look." She gestures her head toward the stairs. Charlotte is crouched at the top of the stairs, foaming at the mouth like a rabid animal. Her head moves jerkily to the left and right, like a nervous tick. An inhuman growl leaves her lips.

"I think it's safe to assume she's possessed," Sacha mumbles.

"This one is mine." I step forward, planting my feet. "Who are you?"

Charlotte stands. Her dry laughter explodes, echoing off the walls. The smell of rotting flesh fills the air. An icy wind tugs hair from my ponytail. Chill bumps raise on my skin.

"Come and join me. I can grant your every wish."

"There's nothing worth your fee, Djinn," I yell to be heard over the wind.

Charlotte blinks, stunned. "You know me." Charlotte smiles. "Let me show you my power. I can offer you your heart's desire." Charlotte beams.

"We don't want what you're selling," Sacha shouts.

"Are you so sure? How would you like to have your father eating out of the palm of your hand? Deep down, you've always longed to be a Daddy's girl, but he never saw you as more than a political pawn." Her voice is infused with false sympathy. "I can change that." An image flickers on the wall across from the stairwell, like a projector movie. "I can change it all … past, present, future." He shows her images of her father, lovingly playing tea party, and helping her build a lemonade stand. She's glued to the images that I know never happened. "You know he'll never come around on his own. Why deprive yourself of true happiness?" The Djinn's deep voice is off-putting coming from the disheveled blonde-haired woman.

I reach inside my jacket for the bottle of holy water, push the tab, and send it hurtling toward her with a flick of my wrist. "We're not interested in your lies, deceiver."

She hisses like an angry snake. I send another blast of holy water hurtling toward it with my powers. I won't give it a chance to ensnare any of us again. Charlotte's mouth opens wide. Projectile vomit rockets through the air, staining the stairs a sickly green hue. Dropping to all fours, she crawls down the stairs through her own sick.

"We rebuke you, unclean spirit," Sacha says shakily. She holds out a cross, and Fel joins us. Steam pours off Charlotte's skin as the water makes direct contact with her face and sizzles. She scuttles away in a crab walk that has me wishing we were trying to kill her with fire instead of trying to take her alive and exorcise her.

"We can't let it get away." I give chase. Lights burst in our wake, showering us with glass. Tiny slivers bite into my skin. I ignore the stinging pain as we slide around the corner. Black figures spring up around us. I jump to the left to avoid one, only to scream when two more appear and run through me. Frozen from the inside out, my legs are kicked out from underneath me. I hit the floor at an awkward angle. Pain shoots through my upper body and my shoulder as it pops out of the socket.

I roll to my side and struggle to my feet like a turtle flipped on to its shell. My left arm dangles uselessly at my side. More shadow beings crowd in around us, rising from the floor. Fel screams. Three claw marks appear down her neck. Sacha gags, scratching at her throat. Her face turns red.

"Cristo," Fel barks. The attack wavers long enough for the girls to pull their crosses. We may not be ready to perform a full exorcism on our own, but we can protect ourselves. The floor shakes. A sound like cloth ripping rings in my ears. The floor splits beneath us. I flail as I drop and slam into a dirty floor. Dust flies around us. I cough when it enters my nose and lungs.

"Oh God. They're trying to break through," Sacha groans.

"We need to hold the veil together." Suddenly the ripping noise makes sense.

"It's not a long-term—" Fel begins.

"We need to buy time." I cradle my arm to my body. Hooves click on the floor overhead.

"It's going to take more power than we have," Sacha says.

I find the crack in the barrier they're squeezing themselves through like mice. Envisioning a seal over the tear, I thrust my power into mending it. I hold the pieces together, magically sewing it back together. They're sucked back through as the magic takes hold. Sacha and Fel lend me their power to channel into my task. My body aches and protests the amounts of energy being run through it. I taste the coppery flavor of blood in my mouth. My nose is gushing red, and my eyesight is fading. I sway on my knees, struggling to breathe as my lungs burn.

A wet cough rattles in my chest. Blood blossom. The tug on the other end of the veil lessens. I feel their tenuous hold give. The banishing is done, for now. With the danger passed, I let go. Light explode beneath my lids, blinding me before my consciousness fails me.

Chapter Fourteen

"Are you sure you're up for this meeting?" Fel asks.

A few days after the attack, I'm still babying my shoulder and taking antibiotics for an acute case of bacterial infection that set in my lungs. Forty-eight hours in the hospital being pumped with powerful meds, and a shoulder popped into socket later, I'm dragging myself to a council meeting. I could use a week of recovery at the least, but the Djinn aren't going to wait, so we can't afford to either.

"I'm a fast healer, and we don't have the luxury of time on our side."

"Where's your jailer? This is the farthest away I've seen him since you were in the hospital," Sacha says.

"I think it's sweet," Fel states.

"More like terrifying if you try to get between the two of you," Sacha argues.

My face heats. Things between Cristobal and I had been shaky at best since I woke up in the hospital.

"Trust me, he's around, and there's a reason the meeting is being held here at the mansion."

"I can't blame the guy. Things could've been so much worse," Fel says.

"Are you fully riding the Team Cristobal train, or what?" I give a weak laugh.

"I'm all for anyone who puts your first. Because you never will. Haven't you ever wondered why I was never upset you left?" Fel replies.

"Yes," I admit.

"It was the one completely selfish act you'd ever allowed yourself. Even back then, you felt the weight of the future. We all knew you'd be named a successor. Mémé pushed you harder, forced you to take on more responsibilities sooner, and judged you on a completely different scale than everyone else in the family. I watched you lose a lot of who you were after we graduated high school. Then you met Cristobal, and I saw the old Lou."

I look to Sacha. "Is this true?"

Sacha clears her throat. "I'm the last person to talk about letting family expectations color who you are. I was in the same boat. I always thought we remained so close because of that factor. When you left, it felt like I'd been betrayed and left to atrophy alone. It also sparked a fire inside of me that grew. So … Thank you for being brave enough to venture out into the world and see what else was there."

"Do you mean that?" Hurting her has always been one of my biggest regrets.

"Positive."

I smile. "Thank you."

"Now that we have the after-school special moment out of the way … Fel's right. You always put yourself last when you're placed in charge of people. Without Cristobal, you'd run yourself into the ground, and continue to be self-sacrificing."

"That's not what I'm being at all."

"Yes you are," they say in unison.

Caw. I glare at the trees where a Raven I know to be Cristobal is perched, keeping an eye on our visiting guests incognito. The sound draws me back to my time in the Fae lands when I'd almost chosen the wrong door. Was he there even then? *"You've got some explaining to do, Cortez. As soon as we get out the boiling water threatening to cook us."*

"Even the animals here agree with us, Lou. Stop being so stubborn and realize we only want to help," Sacha says.

"I refuse to change who I am. I tried that once, and it didn't mesh well. I ended up running for the hills, remember? This time they get me warts and all."

"No one expects that. But you can change the way you approach things," Fel responds quickly.

"How so?"

"Look before you leap, and let someone else take the lead when there's danger. You're not indestructible or so easily replaced," she says gently.

Her worry echoes Cristobal's.

"I was never meant to be a princess in a tower."

"No, but there's got to be a medium between first on the frontline and hidden away in the castle."

Her words strike a chord. "I'll try my best to find that place." It's the best I can give her. She smiles, and I know, for now, it's enough. I feel Cristobal's contentment through our link. It hits a nerve. He has an annoying habit of constantly getting what he wants. I sniff indignantly and put a wall up between us in the bond. I'm not above being petty or keeping him off kilter. The lord is too used to getting his way. I'm his partner, not another member of the court who must obey his every command. The conversation from the hospital remains in the front of my mind as we move into the house to prepare for the meeting.

Two Days Prior

"I'm going to get a complex if you keep getting injured while I'm away."

I swim up through the layers, toward the voice. My fingers twitch, and I fight against the urge to return to slumber. My lids seem to have weights on them as I struggle to peel them up. Cristobal's face comes into view, and my soul rejoices.

"Hi," I croak.

He bends over me, kissing my forehead. "Let me get you some

water." He disappears momentarily and returns with a large pink cup with a straw. Using the button on the side of my bed, he helps me sit up and holds the cup to my lips.

I take a drink. The cool water coats my mouth and throat. I moan my approval.

"Thank you. What happened?"

"I should be asking you that. Why would you take on such a tremendous task by yourself?"

"I had help." I regret the white lie immediately.

"The sorry state you arrived in says otherwise. What were you thinking using that much of your magic."

"If I hadn't neither of us would be here because we'd be fighting a war."

"You can't protect everyone—"

"I know you aren't insinuating I should've left the girls out to dry."

"No, I'm telling you I'm not fooled by your martyrdom. You used them as a vehicle to help you channel, but you left their power untapped."

"Because they were the second line of defense had I failed."

"You cannot continue to take risks like that."

"Why am I more important than anyone else?"

"A queen is meant to be protected. Not because she is weak, but because she's far too valuable to risk."

"Pretty words that mean nothing. I was raised to fight for what I believe in, and my people."

"And you have. Now let them return the favor."

I grunt and wince, immediately regretting it.

His look screams, '*See.*'

"It's poor manners, kicking a girl when she's down," I croak.

"I'm not kicking you. I'm trying to make you see reason."

"I'm not conceding this time. You've gotten most of what you've wanted since I came back—"

"And you haven't?"

"No," I say firmly.

Shock reaches us.

"I've met you halfway and compromised left and right with the understanding that we are literally two different species who think in different ways. You've asked me countless times to keep this in mind. Can you honestly say you do the same? This is who I am. I won't spend the rest of our time together biting my tongue and feeling encroached upon. I protect the people I love. That means putting myself in the line of danger. It can't be helped. Stepping in as Lady and Matriarch are going to exacerbate that fact, not lessen it. I ask you to give me the same respect I give you. For a modern man, you have some archaic inclinations when it comes to love and relationships. "

He looks offended. "I'm a gentleman with decorum."

"No one would deny that." I can feel the wheels in his head turn. After a quick knock, the nurse enters.

"It's good to see you awake, Ms. Esçhete." Her presence ends the awkward conversation. Worn out from the emotions, I welcome the reprieve. This is far from over.

PRESENT

I take my time finishing my tea, making the council wait for me to begin my speech. It's a trick I've learned from the court. No one does polite insults the way they can. This might be their show, but we're in my territory, and that gives me some home court advantage. I set the empty cup on its saucer and clear my throat.

"As Felicite shared with you briefly, we're dealing with a Djinn. For eons, they've searched for a way to break through the veil between our worlds. It seems they've finally succeeded."

"What do you they want?" Vale asks.

"To make us suffer and take over. I was able to hold off the inevitable by resealing the tears, but it's a temporary solution. The recent rashes of disturbances are connected to the breach, but we're not sure how or why. Information on the Djinn is few and far between. Thanks to Cristobal, we've found an expert on the subject, Baal Shem Issur Shafir."

"A what, my dear?" Meadow asks.

"A Baal Shem, a Jewish holy man, similar to a rabbi who specializes in history. He's agreed to educate and assist us."

"Wait, are we talking about a Jewish exorcist?" Zephirin snorts.

"Issur is much more than that. An expert on the Djinn with access to rare and accurate documentation, he's the best chance we have. He's come up with an interesting theory I'd like you to allow him to share." I grab a scone from the three-tier tray and wait as they talk among themselves. The high-tea setting is informal, but the decisions are life-altering. After a time, Mémé turns to me.

"We'll hear him out," Vale says, speaking for the rest of the group.

"Thank you."

"Please send Baal Shem into the parlor." A few moments later the pocket doors slide open. The expressions range from shocked to uncomfortable when they realize I've summoned him without saying a word. It's almost comical. At five-foot-five-inches, the thin man with a shock of white hair under his wide-brim, black hat should seem frail. Two mid-length payots curl along either side of his long, thin face. His black suit is modest. If one passed him on the street, they wouldn't look twice.

It's in direct contrast with the aura of power that surrounds him. The intensity in his dark gaze labels him a man not to be trifled with.

I stand. "Baal Shem Issur thank you for joining us today."

"We must all join together in the pursuit of vanquishing this evil. I've spent my entire life battling the devil and his offspring, but at no time have they been closer to prevailing. They have one goal, conquering the Earth, and always they are seeking a way to achieve this."

"Please sit." I steer him to an over-sized brown leather chair.

"How do you think this happened?" Vale asks.

"Sealed places by Yahweh keep most demons below. However, Djinn are different. They have their own universe. Yaweh knew they needed more to contain them. I make it my business to know the state of the seals at all times. They remain unbroken. Which is puzzling."

"How is this happening, then?" Fel asks.

"They've found a shortcut if you will. There are demonic artifacts capable of attacking the veil. It would take time and immense negative energy, but for them, waiting is what they do best."

"Negative energy?" Mémé tilts her head slightly.

"Human corruption is fuel for them. The three wishes are a way into a person's life and ultimately their soul. They offer a chance for more in exchange for favors. They start small, allowing them to build trust. Then the depravity grows. The Djinn will claim he requires more personal sacrifice to generate the power needed to achieve their desires. What people are capable of doing to get what they want would shock you. It turns good people into vile, unrecognizable strangers. Ask yourself this question: what wouldn't you do to get everything you ever wanted?"

"A hell of a lot," someone mumbles.

"How can we figure out what this artifact is?" Mémé asks, getting straight to the point.

"I have access to texts, outlining them." He pauses and twines his fingers. "I believe it's best to go straight to the source in this matter. We must learn the name of the Djinn, and summon him to get more information and narrow our search. I fear what may happen if we leave it too long—"

"Wait. This thing put Lou in the hospital after a short encounter and yet you want to face it head on?" Zephirin says slowly.

"Yes. Yahweh has provided us with a clue. The woman who was possessed is currently in the hospital. A deliverance would allow us to free her from entrapment and discover the name." Charlotte was rushed to the hospital with a case of *exhaustion, dehydration, and shock* after a freak low-level earthquake caused a house to shift, due to a fault that had lain dormant for years. People will go to great lengths to explain impossible things, in what they believe is a logical manner.

"Baal Shem. With all due respect, I highly doubt her high profile husband would—" Sacha begins.

He holds up a hand, silencing her in mid-sentence. "Yahweh will smooth the way. We must act quickly. Today. Father Axson will be assisting me locally."

"What do you need from us?" Mémé asks.

"Your support when it comes time to repair what's been damaged in the barrier between our worlds," he says.

"I take it you have a plan, Mr. Issur?" Meadow says.

"Yes. One I'm ready to set into motion immediately."

"I believe I speak for the majority of us when I say let us proceed. Those opposed?"

"Nay." Zephirin's objection is expected.

"Those in agreement?"

"Yay."

"The yays have it. Tell us what we can do to help, Baal Shem," I say.

Wooden bowls line the food tray which serves as a makeshift altar. Charlotte's still form rests on the bed. The rise and fall of her chest and the steady beep of her monitors are the only indications she's alive. It's a crime to see a woman so full of a life cut low. With severely chapped lips, mottled skin, and sunken in cheeks, she's ravaged. Even if she gained her new husband and wealth with wishes, she doesn't deserve this. Baal Shem prays quietly in Hebrew as he anoints himself with oil. He picks up the white tallit with fringed edges, and a blue and gray striped design, kisses the prayer shawl, and bows. I wonder at the symbolism as he wraps it around his shoulders.

This is a glimpse into a world I've never been a part of. Father Axson steps inside and closes the door behind him.

"The staff is used to me being here to visit with the patients. The nurses usually make their rounds on this floor about every hour. Between the distraction spell and our lookouts, we're fine to begin." Father Axson turns his attention to Sacha, Fel, and I. "Are you ready to hold her in place?" He insists using our powers to keep her immobile is more humane than the usual method of tying her to the bed. It still feels wrong to restrict someone this way. I double check the silencing spell before nodding.

"We are."

Father places his brown leather case on a chair and removes his purple stole. He kisses the strip of fabric before placing it around his neck, removes his cross, and a bottle of holy water. I watch as his face becomes serious. The sparkle in his eyes is replaced with determination as he prepares himself for the battle to come. He pulls out his *Bible*, as Baal Shem begins to sing, rocking back in forth in a continuous bow.

Charlotte sits up so fast I'm surprised she doesn't get whiplash. Her eyes pop open.

"What are you doing in here?" She clutches the sheet up to her chest, sounding like a lost child.

"Do you remember me, Charlotte?" Father Axon steps forward. "We've talked before."

"No." She shakes her head. "None of you should be in here. This is my room. I want you all gone." Her voice turns shrill.

"Your tricks won't work on us. No one is coming in here," Father Axson says calmly.

"You're crazy," she whispers, shaking her head. Her lower lip trembles. Her knuckles turn white where she clutches the thin sheet. She plays the victim well. If I hadn't seen her reenact a scene from a few days ago, I'd be inclined to help her.

"We are speaking with the entity inside of Charlotte now," Father Axson says. His deep baritone is clear and commanding.

Baal Shem lights a stick of incense. The sharp scent of sulfur fills the room. Charlotte's lip twitches as he waves the smoke around her bed, fumigating. The process is meant to coax the spirit out of hiding. We received a crash course on Jewish Exorcism on the way over. It differs from the traditional Christian practice in a number of ways.

Her eyes bleed black, and she growls, gnashing her teeth. "You can't stop what's put into motion, holy men," she says in a deep, gravelly voice.

"Speak your name, and leave this child of God," Father commands. Charlotte jerks. We focus on keeping her arms and legs pressed into the mattress. The bed rattles. A crack forms the length of the ceiling to the floor.

"She's mine. She made the deal and asked for this. They all do."

"We will break your hold." Father ignores his comments and begins to read the *Bible*.

Charlotte begins to speak in a harsh language. She jerks her head to the left and right, fighting our grip.

"I command you to tell us your name." A lump forms in Charlotte's throat. An unholy snarl vibrates in her chest. She snaps her teeth. The bed comes off the floor and slams down in a rhythmic pattern. The overhead lights flicker and the blinds open and close.

"Ah. Aaaah." The sound is violently ripped from Charlotte's throat.

Baal Shem flicks holy water onto her. Steam rises off her body like dry ice has been dropped into water. Her skin sizzles and blisters.

"Ag. Ag." She chokes on the sounds. "Agares."

Baal Shem begins a haunting wailing of the Djinn's name. He bows repeatedly. Her body convulses. Windows shatter inward, coating us with glass. We scream as the glass knicks us. The Djinn sends out a jolt of power that slams the three of us to the wall, breaking our hold. Charlotte dashes to the large window, pausing briefly. She peers over her shoulder at us with sorrow-filled eyes.

"It wasn't worth it. You have to destroy the box." She turns mechanically and steps out the window as if she expected to walk on air.

The loud thud as her body hits the ground is quickly followed by screams that set us into motion. I push myself off the floor and stumble across the room on Bambi's legs. No one can know we were here for this. I'm numb as I repair the damage and help the men collect their equipment. Tears blind me as we leave the room under a veil of spells. Self-preservation wars with self-loathing as I force one foot in front of the other. We'd killed her as surely as if we'd thrown her out the window.

Silence remains as we wait for the elevator. I fight the urge to give in to tears. I didn't like her, but life is precious, and hers ended badly. An alarm sounds as nurses rush into the room and panic begins. The elevator door opens with a ding. We step inside. I'm a Cyberman from a *Doctor Who* episode. Emotionally bankrupt, running on instincts, and focused on the mission. Whatever my personal feelings, this is about preventing the end of the world. It trumps everything else, right? It's hard to tell when my brain is on overload. The gentle caress of Renee's consciousness against my own makes me smile. He's letting me know he's here. Able to blend in and charm, he was the perfect choice for our lookout.

We walk out to the insanity of police sirens, crowds, and security rushing in to provide order. We were the stone in the pond that caused these ripples.

"If that was the right thing, why do I feel like a murderer?"

"Do not let the enemy weaken you. He wants to distract you from your purpose. Always remember, he's the one who caused this. We will end this. Do not let Charlotte's last gift be in vain."

"What gift was that, Father? All I saw as pain and despair."

"Hope. With the name and the clue, she gave us the most powerful gift of all next to love."

"He is right. I believe I know the artifact of which she spoke," Baal Shem says as we walk across the road to the parking lot. "It is a puzzle box. Fitting for a Djinn, isn't it? It's an intricate creation made up of tiny pieces that must've been gathered over the ages."

"Demons have nothing but time. That's what makes them so dangerous. They never forgive, and they'll wait for the perfect moment to strike every time," Father added. "What you're all feeling right now is the aftereffect of being exposed to the demonic. This will pass in time. Keep your faith close."

"How do we find the box, and what do after we get our hands on it?" I ask.

"We must consult the books," Baal Shem replies.

Two steps forward and a million back. No one speaks as we make our way to the church van and climb inside. I'm grateful that Father is driving. I tune out as we pull onto the road and I watch the scenery go by. The sun sets in a beautiful display of peach, lavender, royal purple, and blush, yet all I feel is cold. Resting my head against the cool window, I welcome the night. A thump on the windshield draws my attention from the safe cloud of nothingness I'd allowed my brain to sink into.

"Suicidal bug," Sacha mumbles.

I snicker.

Three more splats make me tense. Insects begin to pelt the car like hail. The wipers swish furiously, but they're no match for the carnage of carcasses. Fog rushes toward us, effectively cutting us off from the rest of the world as visibility shrinks to less than a foot in front of us. A body appears in the middle of the road. Flying into the air, it slams down onto the hood. We veer off the road. The long-limbed creature's claws clack over the windshield. It offers us a jagged, rotting-tooth grin. It disappears from view. Pop. The front tires blow. The van swerves as Father fights to gain control.

We rumbled to a stop in the grass on the side of the road.

"Is everyone okay?" Fel asks.

A chorus of 'yes' comes back to her.

"It's trying to stop us. It's frightened," Father marvels.

"This means we're on the right path," Baal Shem replies.

"We have to get out of the car." I fumble with my seatbelt and shove the door open as my instincts scream at me to move faster. The thick fog keeps us close together while we move away from the van. A semi slams into the side, dragging the vehicle away into the dense white. I scream, jerking back. If we'd been slower …

I can feel the court racing toward us.

"The others will be here soon," I say. *We just have to make it until then.*

An eerie howl goes up in the distance. Others join. We shrink back. In the distance, I make out vague shapes moving toward us.

"Do you see them?" Sacha asks.

"Yes."

"Hell Hounds," Father whispers.

Close enough to view, the black dogs crouch, baring their fangs. Saliva drips from the pointed tips like venom, and their red eyes pierce the darkness. Without the holy men, we're lost. Their safety comes before mine. The adrenaline coursing through my veins tricks me into believing I have energy. Prepared to take advantage of the pain blockers, I come up with a tentative plan. Planting my feet, I erect a barrier between us and the dogs from hell.

"On three, I want you to run. The others are close. We just have to make it until they arrive. Fel, stay with them. Sacha and I will lead them away."

"What? I'm not leaving you."

"Felicite. Please."

She sneers. "Fine."

"One. Two. Three." I shove the barrier forward, sending them fly-ing back like bowling pins. The sickening smack upon impact gives me a moment of happiness.

"Feu!" Sacha calls. A wall of wire leaps up, putting a physical bar-rier between them and us. We dart off in opposite directions. I can hear their massive paws pounding the ground as they resume the chase.

"Terre!" A wall of dirt rises. Loud yelps tell me I've hit my target. Still, more panting remains too close for comfort.

Archangel Michael, defend us. I pray like I never have before as my lungs burn, my legs shake, and fear rises up inside of me. A brilliant light flashes. I stumble and throw my arm up to shield my eyes from further damage. A large, flaming sword slices down, cutting a path through the fog. Stunned, I turn to Sacha. She grabs my hand, and we run full tilt down the cleared space. I glance back to see a form made of pure light wielding the weapon once more. The winged figure cuts the dogs down with a few quick blows.

"Dove."

I'm swept into Cristobal's arms. Eye ablaze and fangs distended, my court is a formidable wall between us and danger.

"We felt your distress, but I had to use magic to get here to you. There was a powerful barrier." He cups the back of my head, and I bury my face in his neck, allowing myself a moment to enjoy being alive.

"The others?"

"Safe. I already had Larkin, Percival, and Miles carry them off."

I relax. "Thank you. All of you." My voice shakes.

"You're dead on your feet," Cristobal remarks.

"It's been a rough week," I say sarcastically.

He moves to bite his wrist, and I shake my head and wiggle. He lowers me to the ground.

"We should go. I'll be fine. I just need rest."

"Blood will help boost your energy." Cristobal holds out his wrist.

I turn my head away. "It's not a V-8, Cristobal. I don't need it that bad."

"Because you have to be at death's door to drink from me?" Cristobal glowers down at me. He's not used to being opposed.

"I didn't say that. You're overreacting." I refuse to let drinking blood become a crutch I constantly lean on.

"No. You are clinging to outdated beliefs."

"Let me. You're carrying around some long gone practices yourself." His anger is a hot wave. He's shaken by the close call. So am I.

Marcellus clears his throat. "We should go."

"We'll send someone to retrieve the van and replace it for them," Cristobal says banking the fire in his voice.

"I've got Sacha," Renee offers, turning his bright grin her way. "It's like a piggyback ride at warp speed."

She laughs. "I guess there's a first time for everything. We'll see you back at the house."

She's gone with Ruby and Ada trailing them before I can comment. As the rest of the court disperses, Cristobal scoops me up under my knees. He's far too dignified for a piggyback ride. I giggle. He smiles down at me. "Hold on." He takes off like a bullet from the gun. I close my eyes as the world rushes by in a rush of air.

We end up in the gardens.

"Do we have to finish this now?"

"Yes, we've already left it too long."

"We're bonded. I'm becoming Lady of your Court. Do you really need more from me right now?"

"Don't you see you're only delaying the inevitable?"

"How do you figure that?"

"Living in our home, attending our celebrations and following our customs, you'll be one of us. Blood exchanges will be commonplace."

"To you and the others because you're a vampire. I am a witch."

"No. You were. What you are now is more. This bond changed us both in ways we've still yet to comprehend. I need to know you can handle what might come with that."

"It's a little late to question my ability to keep it together, don't you think?"

The elephant in the room resurfaces. We may be adjusting now, but it doesn't erase the fact that he bonded us without my permission. It's not a choice so easily forgiven, forgotten, or moved on from.

"Are you going to bring that up every time we disagree?"

"When you forget I didn't choose this situation for myself or come into it with all the facts and my eyes open, yes."

"I expect you to see the big picture."

"I do. Mine just happens to look otherwise."

"It's my job to keep you safe. How can I do that when you fight me constantly?"

"I can take care of myself. We face things together. You linked yourself to a modern woman who rules in her own right. You have to make adjustments for me, too."

I will not lose myself for anyone. I worked too damn hard to figure myself out.

"We should go back inside. They'll be waiting." His voice is soft. He's dropping it for now. I'm smart enough to know it's been shelved temporarily. I can't help but wonder if the price of ruling will be our love.

Chapter Fifteen

The sky let loose with a thunderous boom hours ago, and it hasn't let up since. Even with the wards, sleep was sparing. It's the calm before the storm as we scramble to secure everything necessary to send the Djinn back where he came from and learn more about the puzzle box. My dry eyes burn as I pour over the translations Baal Shem has written out. Unable to remove the ancient text from its heavily guarded location beneath a synagogue, we're left with this and copies. Not that I could read Hebrew.

The picture of the box is breathtaking. The wooden box is a mixture of smooth dark wood, overlayed with gold molded in intricate shapes with distinctive Middle Eastern flare. The pointed domes resemble the ornate buildings of the Taj Mahal. Every wish granted after the initial three wishes cost a bit of the wisher's soul. The acts required to gain a piece of the box are ghastly.

I scan the cross-referenced events Baal Shem has discovered in the book. The skull of the astronomer, the bones of a righteous woman, and blood-soaked battleground. I can't imagine what else the text lists. What's been collected and what hasn't? What could be worth taking the life of another or bargaining away chips of your soul?

"Well, we know how all the cases are linked." Sacha runs her hand through her hair. "This is a lot to take in, I get that. It's important to know what we're up against. I don't see how it can help us track the wishers down."

"I think what the summoning is for. Once they capture the Djinn they can make it talk," I say. "We'll have to trust the holy men for that. We're here to back their plays and learn everything we can."

"You seem calm about handing over this case. It's not like you." Sacha studies me with a curious gaze

"When we were trying to escape those hellhounds, something happened. I cried out to the Archangel Michael, and he answered."

Sacha furrows her brow. "What are you talking about?"

"I watched a fiery blade cut a path through the fog, and I saw wings. Not feathered, with a filmy shape outlined."

"You remember you'd just knocked your nogging on the window, right?" Sacha asks skeptically.

"Do I seem like the type to hallucinate about angels?" I glance from Fel to Sacha.

"Given the nature of this case, it wouldn't be far-fetched." Fel speaks softly like I'm a wounded animal.

"I know my mind. How else did we escape?" I challenge Sacha.

"We threw some nasty spells at them, Lou," Sacha says.

"Believe me or not, it made me realize there are other things at work in this case." I shrug, disappointed in their disbelief.

Gentle rapping comes at the door. It swings open.

Renee's grave face looks wrong. "You should look at the news."

I pull out my cell phone, and discover Tropical Odette in a tropical depression three-hundred miles outside of The Gulf of Mexico is forcing heavy rains in Louisiana and experts on high alert. Drenching Central America in a torrential downpour, this deadly storm has claimed fifty lives. Meteorologists are watching this Storm Front closely and issuing alerts. Fear of a repeat of Katrina as the depression appears has been mentioned.

I watch the newscast play on my phone. The name Katrina is not thrown around easily here in Louisiana. This means things have the potential to get bad fast. It's July … early for hurricane season. My gut tells me this is the Djinn.

"We can't take another storm like this. We're still trying to recover from Katrina in so many ways," Fel says.

"Nothing about this feels natural," Sacha growls.

"Because it's not. We need to make sure we force this storm to turn out." Picking up my phone, I call Mémé. "Mémé, have you seen the weather forecast?"

"I've seen it. I'm getting the council rallied. You know we try to let nature run its course, but nothing about this comes from Mother Nature."

"This is pushing up our timetable. The Djinn is getting desperate. We're going to need a multi-coven spell to combat it."

"I know. We haven't come together like that—"

"Since the Reaping."

"Yes."

"Perhaps that's why Alida wanted to us to remember. I know you don't like talking about it, Mémé, but if we don't, they'll find reasons to let their egos, pride, and personal feelings get in the way. We need to be reminded of what we can accomplish together, and how bad things can get when we don't. I'm going to send Fel to you. This is her job now. My place is on the front line."

"Be careful." Her easy acceptance is disarming.

"I always am." Putting my phone down, I turn to my cousin. "Fel?"

"I get it. I'm putting my politician cap on."

"Let's call the holy men and see where they're at on their end."

Twenty-minutes later I have the court gathered.

"They'll be summoning the Djinn tonight. Waiting for the storm threatening is too dangerous. They believe it's a last ditch effort to shed the blood of a thousand with the storm. Our goal is to stop that at any cast."

"What can we do?" Cristobal asks.

"Support me. This is a magical issue more than anything else."

They exchange looks, and Cristobal holds out his hands. Marcellus takes one, Luz takes the others, and they form a chain of held hands; Ruby and Renee close the circle. Cristobal bows his head and the air crackles. A smoky gray dome glimmers around them. Cristobal raises his burning amber eyes. A breeze circles them, ruffling their hair.

"We have magic of our own. This is what makes our line so unique."

"Holy shit," Sacha whispers.

"We can cast a simultaneous circle when the others cast. All the energy going toward the same goal is helpful."

They let go of each other's hands, and I feel the difference. Their magic is the opposite of what I've grown up with steeped in darkness, but not black—it has the same unnatural feel as a vampire. I want to explore and dissect it. Right now, I don't have the time.

"You want to lessen the storm's impact?" Cristobal asks.

"Or get it to turn and dissipate altogether. We have to wait to see what the council gets everyone to agree on." It's painful not being in the thick of things. This is the price paid for one foot in each world. Never fully belonging.

My phone rings. Carter's name on my phone display pushes me to the edge of sanity.

"Hello?"

"There's something I think you need to see."

"Can it wait, Carter?"

"It's time sensitive."

The tone of his voice conveys more. *What am I missing here?*

"When and where?"

"St. John's Hospital as soon as possible."

"The morgue?"

"No."

"Carter?"

"Remember the cases and the lack of evidence? Well, this incident has a very lively clue."

Is he telling me there's a witness?

"I'm on my way, Carter."

"Call me when you arrive."

"What happened?" Sacha asks.

"I think we got a break in the cases. It sounds like there might be a witness at the hospital." I look at Cristobal. "We have to follow this lead."

Things remain off between us. The critical situation hasn't allowed us time to talk anything out.

"Go with them, Marcellus."

I don't bother protesting. I've grown used to the vamp's presence, and there's no time to waste.

Driven by an intense sense of urgency, I rush for the front door with the duo behind me.

"I'll drive," Marcellus says. My phone chimes.

"Works for me."

He chops the thirty-minute drive in half, and I text Carter to meet us. I powerwalk my way over to the entrance when I spot the familiar redhead emerge. Carter observes Marcellus.

"Good, you brought back up. You'll need them to get inside."

"Are you going to fill me in?"

"Officers were called in on a case today. A body was dumped in a church. The man was flayed alive."

"Jesus Christ."

"He must've been involved because when they arrived on the scene, they discovered he wasn't quite dead. I don't need to tell you how improbable that is. The blood loss and the shock from having so many nerve endings essentially shredded should've killed him long before they got there."

"You suspect magic?"

"Has to be. I'm here unofficially, so my ability to help is slim to none today."

"The tip-off is plenty of help, Carter. Thank you."

"Anytime. The man's in Room 415."

I pat his shoulder. "We'll take it from here."

"If he's being kept alive by magic—"

"I'll put him out of his misery," I promise.

"That's good." He walks away, clearly disturbed by the case.

"I'm going to need your special skills of persuasion, Marcellus. I'll handle the blending in and not being noticed once you distract the woman at the front desk on the floor."

"Teamwork. Because there's no I in team."

His sarcasm makes me snicker. Before, I never got to see the humorous side of his personality.

Inside the elevator, I employ a glamour that makes me look like another nurse in scrubs before we step out onto the fourth floor.

"I'll keep the staff enthralled with my whit." He winks.

I follow the room numbers down the hall and slip into a dimly lit room. I let the glamour slip, conserving my energy as I place a ward on the door. It'll alert me if anyone gets close. I walk over to the side of the bed. Swathed in bandages, the victim looks like a mummy. He's tall with gangly limbs. Miles was correct in his deductions. An IV bag full of what I assume is medicine and antibiotics run into his arms. *Who skins a man alive?* It's the same thought I return to over and over again. The thought of skin sliced carefully an inch at a time is one of the most disturbing I've ever had to consider.

A low moan shocks me. I peer down and find a set of bloodshot pale blue eyes studying me. I can feel the dark magic pouring off him. It's a nasty hex, meant to prevent him from resting. No amount of medication will put him under. They meant to make him feel every ounce of pain until he expires. His pain filled whimpers lacerate my heart.

"I'm Lou, and I'm here to help you if I can. The people who did this are very dangerous. We want to catch them before they do this to another person. I know you're in an insane amount of pain, but if you'll allow me to, I believe I can help." He studies me warily. "Blink once for yes, and twice for no. Do you want me to help?"

He blinks once. I place my hands over his heart and concentrate. I can't remove the spell—it's blood magic shared between him and the Djinn. Tampering with it will only make things worse. What I can do is dull the pain. I cast a spell to block his pain receptors. The relief is visible. His eyes clear. He focuses on my face.

"Can you talk?" I ask gently.

"Yes." His voice is raw and rusted like metal left out in the rain.

"I know about the genie and the puzzle box. Is there anything you want to share with me?"

"I couldn't do it. Destroy the city again. Not even to save my wife from cancer."

My heart races. "Were you working with the Djinn?"

Tears spill from his eyes and onto his bandages. "It started small. Gathering information, stealing." He breathes heavily. "I got in over my head. I couldn't do it. Harvest the skin of a betrayer while they were alive." He chokes up.

"So they took yours instead."

"Yes."

"Why?"

"Storm." He's beginning to fade.

"How?"

"Seven skins to complete the box."

His body trembles. "Can you tell me their names?"

"Ernest Pattan. Wallace Brown."

"And your name?"

"Harold T-Tyler."

"You did a good thing today, Harold. I'm going to make sure the nurses know your name so they can contact your family."

His eyes turn up slightly at the corners.

"The pain blocking spell is my gift to you."

His eyes close. He may not be able to find true sleep, but now at least he can rest.

This entire time I've been picturing greedy monsters. He's human like the rest of us. Who's to say what we'd do to save the one we loved from such a painful death? What would a person risk to see all their dreams come true?

Too much. I'll make sure his family is contacted. He did the right thing in the end, and he's suffered greatly for it. He deserves respect.

Thirty minutes later, my eyes water as I watch an emaciated, balding woman be wheeled into the hospital room by an older daughter. The girl with a waist-length auburn mane and peaches and cream skin can't be more than sixteen. Her brother is older. Lanky, and tall with darker hair, he has the look of a youth who's had to grow up too fast. He's on the verge of losing his mother, and now his father will fall.

My vision wavers. I hold back the tears. I'll cry when this crisis has been averted. I may be tough, but I'm not a robot. The devastation that's occurred over the past few months is starting to get to me. I push on because it's what I do.

"It's time to hunt, Lady," Marcellus says from his position beside me.

"Yes, it is."

The lights of Festival of Freaks shine brightly at the edge of the forest. The year-round haunted house is the location the pendulum located during dousing. The worn wooden fence is loaded with the 50s themed posters advertising Lobster Boy, the Bearded Lady, Wolfman, and more. The once campy acts have been transformed into fanged, clawed, and bloody monsters.

"Cheery," Sacha drawls.

"Are you sure we can't have a bite to eat? No one would ever notice her," Ruby mutters.

"No, we're here to capture and contain," Cristobal says firmly.

"Wait. She was serious?" Sacha asks.

"Vampire," Ruby drawls sassily with an exaggerated brogue.

"Same team tonight," I remind.

The abandoned theme park for children has sat unused for years, rusting. Plant-covered and eerie, it's the perfect backdrop for a haunted house.

The small Ferris Wheel and roller coaster tracks are visible through the open gates. The rundown carousel slowly spins, playing warped and broken music. The happy jingle has become a jaded tune of terror since the sound mechanism broke down. Why pay to create a creepy atmosphere when you can buy it as is?

The clowns lurking by the entrance with garish makeup and neon blue and orange hair invite us in with a wave.

"I hate clowns," Larkin mumbles.

"A vampire is afraid of clowns?" I tease.

"Not afraid, distrustful. You never know what's lurking under all that makeup."

"How is that different from any other time?"

"Touché," Larkin smirks.

"We remain with our groups. Larkin, Sacha, and I, and Lou, Ruby, and Marcellus."

"Once we locate our targets, we wait to join each other before we move in," Cristobal says.

"Yes, sir." I salute. "Anything you say, sir."

He glowers at me, and I wink before we split and head in separately with our online tickets. A zombie clown with pale skin, balding head, and a dark suit shuffles toward us. This would be fun under different circumstances.

The pounded metal band I've charmed to react to the nearness to Wallace and Ernest is lukewarm on my wrist. I turn to the left and make my way through the crowd.

"Anything?" Marcellus asks.

"Not one change in temperature either way so far."

"Hmm. Then we can consider this the midway point. Not too close, not too far," he suggests.

"That's smart."

"Notice she sounds surprised," Ruby remarks.

"They have carnival games over this way. Maybe they're mingling with the crowd."

"Or working the games," Ruby says. "If you were a psycho killer, this place has to be the perfect gig." Ruby shrugs.

Even the games are themed. The workers are dressed to frighten. Pale-faced, stereotypical, widow-peaked vampires with fangs and blood drops in the corner of their mouth heckle the crowd into playing ring toss. Dead-eyed dolls, zombies, and ghouls entertain with ghoulish gimmicks and showmanship. It's a mixture of vaudeville and modernism.

I pause in front of the stacked milk bottles when my bracelet turns icy cold.

"All right, this is the dead zone. My wrist feels like it's going to get frostbite." I shake my hand to get the blood flowing and change my direction.

"We know it works then at least."

"We found them. They're working in the Fun House."

"How could he tell if they're in a uniform?" Ruby asks.

"Sacha's bracelet must be blazing."

"They're smart, hiding in public like this. Even if they're caught, they won't be easy to capture," Marcellus says.

"I'm going to pretend you aren't impressed by the madmen we're here to capture."

"I bet they're completely unaware that Harold is still alive, and they've been ratted out," I muse.

"You're right. I'm giving the humans too much credit."

I've grown used to their flippancy. I often wonder if humans are truly like cattle to him. With his abrasive attitude and grim humor, Marcellus is often hard to read. I take four steps to their two. If it wasn't for my training, I'd be winded by now. We join the fast-moving line. Groups of three and four are herded into the building. The small doll-like woman in a dingy red polka dot dress rises from her perch on a raised platform and silently stalks every group as they enter. Her movements are mechanical and awkward.

Larkin, Cristobal, and Sacha join us. Her glossy blank stare hits me in the gut.

"Sach, are you okay?"

She raises her head. Her lower lip trembles. "I'm not sure I ever will be again."

"What the hell happened in there?"

She shakes her head.

"Cristobal?"

"You have to see for yourself, reina. There are things that are beyond, even for me."

I study the three of them. They've all been rattled. My apprehension rises. We move forward, and I toy with my silver bracelet, running my fingers over the smooth textured surface hand hammered and spelled. The doll woman waves us forward. We step inside, and a high-pitched scream assaults my ears. I've never heard such realistic depiction of torture outside of a movie. A clown rushes forward, rattling the bars on the makeshift jail cell to our left. We continue down the hallway full of mirrors. Each one distorts our shapes, squashing our bodies, twisting our limbs, and enlarging our heads. We step onto clear tiles. The plastic gives, going squishy as it fills with blood red liquid.

The haunting screams continue to grow louder as we move forward. The black light section plunges us all into darkness. Neon green triangles and squares are mingled with orange ovals and pink circles. A black and white circle swirls in the background.

A black shadow jumps forward. I clench my fist to keep from reacting. We clear the hallway, and the path turns to the left. Scenes play out in a viewing area. A mad scientist pulls the lever on a machine. Sparks fly. Frankenstein twitches on the operating table. My bracelet burns. We move to the next scene. A puddle of blood darkens the white floor, floods the metal table and the doctors in surgical scrubs and masks. The body strapped down jerks as the scalpel slices into flesh and they slowly peel it back. *Oh my God! This is real!*

Yes, it is. Steady, reina. We don't want to alert them.

My body shakes. These people are being entertained by the torture and killing of a human being. Hoarse from screaming, and shifting into shock, the man on the table goes silent. Eyes wide, chest heaving, and mouth wide. His shallow pants are worse than the scream. That at least had fight behind it. This is surrender and acceptance. It's the silent prelude to the end. The surgical masks obscuring their faces does nothing to conceal the maniacal joy shining in their eyes. The line continues, and we move to the next station. Unseeing, I can't concentrate on anything but holding myself together.

"We can't let them get away with this."

"We won't," Cristobal says.

"How can we leave them here like this?"

"The panic we'd cause alerting everyone to the truth would create the perfect storm for them to escape."

"I know. The greater good theory is a real bitch."

He grips my neck, lending silent support.

"Are you guys doing that silent mind-meld thing?" Sacha touches her face in three places like Spock, and I burst out laughing.

"That's not how it works," I say between breaths.

"Well, I don't know. That's why I asked." She shrugs and smiles bashfully.

"The others are positioned at all the exits. We'll have them in custody tonight. I swear it to you."

Cristobal wraps an arm around my waist, and we blend into the crowd.

I don't like violence. I avoid it when at all possible. Still, I must admit to a sick sense of satisfaction watching Wallace and Ernest's heads snap back under the extraction techniques. Marcellus and Luz are masterful, causing pain without overwhelming their body with damage. The cocky bastards never saw us coming. They'd walked to their car cracking jokes. One minute they'd been congratulating each other on a job well done, and the next, there was only darkness as I knocked them unconscious. We loaded them into the car and brought them down to the root cellar.

The evening is progressing every bit as slow as their intricate knife cuts.

"Are you ready to share what you know about your master?" Cristobal asks as he studies his fingernails.

Wallace spits out blood. "I don't know what you're talking about."

"Don't you?" Cristobal gives a mocking laugh. "He's got you doing all his dirty work in exchange for what?"

"None of your business," Ernest growls.

Cristobal moves faster than the eye can track. "You made it mine a while back. You haven't cleaned behind yourself very well, gentleman."

"It won't matter when you see what's coming." Wallace scowls.

"Shut your gob," Ernest barks.

"No, please enlighten us." I walk over and place the toe of my boot onto the wooden chair he's lashed to with rope. "Spill words before I let them start spilling your guts." They remain stoic. I nod at Renee and Ruby. They rush forward; fangs extended, eyes on fire.

"You're bluffing, bitch. You need us," Ernest crows.

"Are you willing to bet on that?" I shove the edge of the chair hard and watch as he hits the ground. "You seem to think we won't kill you if you don't talk. I think the better question is, how will we kill you?" The blood drains from Ernest's swollen face. I smile. "I'm hoping you don't talk. 'Cause the last thing you deserve is an easy death."

Wallace begins to hyperventilate.

"Careful, my love, you're scaring the guests," Cristobal says.

I'm angry, but I don't feel rage. Outside of my emotions, I'm free to act however I see just. It's unnatural feeling so disconnected with one's self. Focused on the need to avenge the deaths of those I couldn't save, I walk over to the prone man and place his throat under the heel of my boot. "Give me one good reason why I shouldn't let them end your life."

"Lou." Sacha's shaky voice draws my attention. The fear in her eyes wounds me. *'You okay?'* she mouths.

I nod my head. It's a lie. She just kept me from committing a grave mistake. I forgot myself, lost in the bloodlust.

"What the hell was that?" I ask Cristobal.

"A glimpse of what it's like in our heads."

I store the information to examine later. Right now I'm back in control.

"I didn't hear an answer, Ernie."

"Keep your mouth sh—" Wallace chokes on the rag Luz shoves into his mouth.

"Yes. By all means, remain loyal to the man who had you flay your friend alive when he couldn't accomplish his task. I'm sure he's the forgiving type, who won't see your capture as a failure," Cristobal says.

"It's different," Ernest insists.

"How sad for you," I whisper. "You'll walk into death for one who feels no loyalty toward you, and you'll bring your friend with you." I latch on to the fear in Wallace's eyes and remove the rag from his mouth. "Final chance to speak."

"Wh-what do you want to know?"

Wallace licks his split lip and hisses. Cowards always break and jump off sinking ships.

In the blink of an eye, Cristobal has Ernest upright. "This is your last chance. Talk," Cristobal demands.

"He said he'd reward us for helping his people cross over into this world. We'd live like kings while others died. I'd get my family back. It'd be like the accident never happened. There's nothing I wouldn't do for my children. They never should've died." His voice cracks.

"You're going to live like kings with your family where? What you're doing is creating a storm that's going to do its damnedest to wipe this city of its map. Are their lives worth thousands of other ones?" Sacha asks.

"Yes," Ernest whispers.

"So, you what? Skin seven people?" I wrinkle my nose.

"Not people, betrayers."

It's like looking at someone who's been brainwashed.

"What happens afterward?" I ask.

"The box is complete," Ernest grumbles.

"And the Djinn take over the world?" Sacha asks.

"Yes," Wallace says softly.

"How do you stop it?" I question.

"You can't," Ernest says smugly.

"You ladies should step out while we handle the rest," Cristobal politely dismisses us. I want to let him handle the dirty work. Turning a blind eye would be so easy right now. But if I did that, how would I be any different from them? I bow my head.

"*I can't.*"

"*Dove …*"

"*We can't become them.*"

"And what should we do instead? Human law has no jurisdiction in this matter."

"Why not? They did kill a man. There will be prints and plenty of evidence."

"Which will all disappear thanks to their miracle worker. The Djinn will see to them as he already has. Loose lips don't sink ships, loose ends like these two do. I won't risk us, so you can feel better. They've flayed who knows how many people alive. Some people are past the point of redemption, and we could never trust them. Are you willing to risk your family on the flimsy hope that they won't retaliate later?"

"No." Lying would be pointless, and immature. I've lost this battle. Everything he's said was true. I can feel the approval of the court rushing up to side with him. They remain perplexed by my ability to hang on to my *silly* human notions.

"Come on, Sacha, let's see if we've heard anything from the others while we've been here." I ignore her questioning gaze. There are things that need to stay in the court.

Chapter Sixteen

A tri-ringed circle is drawn along the wide patch of grass. Swirling circles, interwoven knots, and elegantly looped Gaelic phrases have been carefully sketched in white chalk. Members of each main family stand in the circles while the court stands around us. We're a motley crew. Exhausted, battle-worn, and sleep deprived, we came to the same conclusion after twenty-four hours of nonstop debate: we needed help from a higher power.

Father, a Baal Shem, and a Synagogue full of faithful, holy Jewish men have yet to banish Agares back to his own plane of existence. His current followers might be temporarily disposed of, but the setback is temporary. He will escape eventually, gather his forces again, and complete the cycle. The men can't continue to hold him forever.

Five steps remain between the Djinn completing the puzzle box and ruling. The reality is sobering and too close for comfort. The only thing to do is disassemble the box, scatter it, and permanently trap Agares. It'd serve as a warning and make them think long and hard about attempting the same route he'd taken. There's one catch. The box can't be handled by human hands. The slimy bastards pay attention to details like they're lawyers. As dawn crests into the horizon, we're prepared to explore the loophole. Faeries don't have human hands.

So we're here to perform the ancient summoning ritual for the Fae. The complicated procedure requires an immense amount of power and very well may go unheeded. We're not calling out to a lesser Fae. We're begging a queen for the audience. My gut tells me Sebile will show. If only to be updated on the current state of things. The question I dread most is how high the price for her help will be.

The sweet smell of burning sage and cedarwood float through the air. Mémé begins an old Gaelic song. Her voice is crisp and clear. The lilting lyrics are hauntingly beautiful. I may not understand them, but the emotion poured into them speak volumes. The symbols glow as we begin to cast our circles. Power moves through the layers separating us, like ripples traveling across a lake.

Connected by intention and cleverly drawn designs, we're united as one unit. Magic hums in the air, electrifying my space. My hair curls as the heavyweight settle over me. Fresh beignets, wild honey, and a pitcher of creamy milk mixed with honey and nutmeg rest beside a golden goblet.

"Sebile, Queen of the Winter Court, Houses Esçhete, Morel, Duplex, and Blanchard have come to bring you a gift. If this gift is accepted, please show yourself."

The stars twinkle above us and swell. Light rushes forward in a shower of a particle like pieces. Sebile materializes as the show fades. One pencil thin eyebrow is arched. Her berry red lips form a thin line. The winter white gown contrasts with her dark corkscrew curls. Tiny flakes of snow drift down off around her. They're odd in the muggy, rainy weather we've kept out with a clever spell.

We've prevented a massive hurricane, but the storm depression has brought plenty of rain and light flooding. We continue to monitor the weather reports closely.

"Using the old ways? Clever." She sounds almost approving. "I trust you have not called me here on a whim."

"No. We've neutralized the Djinn."

"Score one for the Esçhete warrior."

"It was a group effort." I glance at the powerful people behind me.

"And modest. Not sure how I feel about that quality. A queen needs to remain center stage at all times." I disagree, but I'm smart enough to keep that to myself. "Did you call me here to brag about your victory then?"

"No, we've called you here to make a deal."

"Hmmm." She slinks her way over to the plate of beignets, brings the plate to her with her powers, and begins to devour the dish with dainty bites. She shakes one at me. "This is one of the few things humans have gotten right."

I smirk. We're on her timetable, and she knows it. She drizzles the fresh honey over the plate and drinks a tall glass of milk to wash it down. When the food is all gone, she cleanses her fingers with a look and turns her attention back to me.

"Why do you think I want to deal with you at all? You've taken care of the threat."

"Temporarily, yes. They came too close to achieving their goal. Neither one of us wants to see the Djinn rise and take over. With your help, we can put them out of commission on a more permanent basis."

"The enemy of my enemy is my friend. What's in it for me? When the human world finally burns itself to the ground, which it will eventually, I have my own kingdom to rule over."

She's playing hardball, and I put the ball back in her court. "What do you want?"

Her full lips part into a full out smile. "I thought you'd never ask. I want out. I'm bored, and humans are such good entertainment."

"You know I can't allow you to declare hunting season on the human race."

"Just the stupid ones. We'll call it natural selection."

"No."

She sighs. "We only want a little sport."

"What does that mean exactly? You want to trick them, or eat them?" I ask bluntly. I ignore the gasps of the others behind me.

Sebile wrinkles her nose. "That's like comparing the actions of your caveman ancestors to you. We want entertainment. Tricks are what we do. Not having an appreciative audience has been less than favorable. I won't grant safe passage to those who foolishly seek us."

I consider my response carefully. "If we rework the conditions of our deal and grant you more freedom to visit our realm, I'll require a blood agreement that you will monitor the activities of your people, and punish them accordingly by our standards of right and wrong." I sense the displeasure of others pressing in on me. I stand my ground. I'm the one in the hot seat. Perhaps they'll think twice before they doubt me or offer me up like animal sacrifice.

"In exchange for what?" Sebile asks.

"Imprisoning Agares in the Forgotten Place."

She grins. "My dear, I'd do that for fun."

"And disassembling the puzzle box and scattering its pieces where few are likely to every uncover them."

"That's all?" She narrows her gaze.

"Yes."

"I agree to your terms." She snaps her fingers. An obsidian blade appears along with an ornate silver goblet. She slices her palm. Her blood is as black as the night court she belongs to.

"I, Sebile, Queen of the Winter Court, do swear to banish Agares to the Forgotten Place and properly disassemble and scatter the puzzle box." She hands me the knife.

I slice my palm, and we allow our blood to drip into the goblet, sealing our deal. "I, Louella Esçhete, so swear to amend our deal to the Fae. May they enjoy this word with the understanding that force will be met with force."

Golden light surrounds us. Pop. An old-fashioned scroll and a white quill hover in mid-air.

"Let us seal the deal by blood and word after you've read it over of course." It's a physical copy of the words spoken out loud seconds ago. She holds out her hand and our palms press together, blood mingling as we sign the parchment together.

The paper glows and duplicates. One is rolled into a scroll-like fashion on the ground and the other disappears. *Efficient.*

"Come on, I'll fulfill my part, and my people will be on Bourbon Street before the night is over." She heals me with a wave of her hand.

My stomach lurches as we travel along what feels like a tube. Seconds later we arrive in the basement of the Synagogue where Baal Shem is taking another turn with the stubborn Djinn.

Father Axson and a small sea of Jewish holy men and priests form a pool of righteousness. I can feel the goodness in the air. These men have held a vigil here, lending their support and power to their elders as they try to send a demon back to hell. The men turn toward us, shocked.

"Wh-what is the meaning of th-this?" one of them sputters.

"I've brought reinforcements."

Sebile parts the men like the Red Sea as she gracefully glides across the floor to the circle. A priest makes the sign of the cross. "Not a demon," Sebile chirps.

She pauses in front of the circle. "You and I are going to take a little trip." She blows the salt forming the circle away and grasps the Djinn so fast it's a blur. He writhes in her grasp. The overhead lights flicker. The Djinn begins to turn to smoke and flee. She traps him, half smoke, half corporeal body. His bottom half is a twisting, spinning gray tornado, and his upper half is a decaying, grayish-green torso.

"Stay out of this, Faerie," he hisses.

Her eyes turn into purple fire. "You dare to address me with such disrespect?" Her voice is deceptively even. Calm before a vicious storm.

"I will come for you next once the storm destroys everything in its path. And then we will take—"

He coughs, clawing at the slender hand wrapped around his throat.

"I'm going to enjoy this, demon."

The building rocks on its foundation. The Djinn opens its mouth, and black tar spills out into the air like an oil burst. His aura is nausea-inducing. Snow falls down, obscuring them from view with a thick blizzard. I wrap my arms around my waist and wait. The unholy shrieks pierce my eardrums like swords. The snow stops abruptly. Fangs bared, Sebile stands tall, grinning. Black blood smeared around her mouth turns the beauty savage. She provides a handkerchief and wipes her mouth. "Problem solved."

"Meyn Gat."

The Jewish men bow as they pray and the priests make the sign of the cross.

"The box?"

"Was attached to him. I've freed it, and even now my people are working to deliver it to creative hiding places. My end of the bargain is done. Make sure you uphold your own."

The threat is very real and impossible to ignore.

"I will."

We disappear in a swirl of darkness, sending the holy men into a fresh round of praying. It's the last thing I hear before I'm returned to the center of my circle alone.

"What happened?" Mémé asks.

"She did what she said she would. Has the council been sufficiently pleased by my performance?" I stare at Zephirin, daring him to say otherwise.

"You have gone above and beyond, exceeding our expectations, Lou," Vale says softly.

"Then let it be known, I will no longer suffer snide marks, or questioning my every move. Without the Cortez Court, we may not have found the answers we needed in time to thwart disaster. Like it or not, our people are aligned for the foreseeable future. I don't believe it has to be a bad thing. I know we're all exhausted, so I propose we go home, get some sleep, and call a proper meeting in two days' time with all of our people. I want them to feel safe, and see that we worked as a united front. We may have vanquished the genie, but we've all noticed the balance isn't what it should be. This is the second major occurrence of darkness. Once is a coincidence, twice is a pattern."

I take the murmured noises as agreeance, and we break the circles. It's all I can do to stay upright as I walk toward the court. Cristobal places a hand on the small of my back and they press in closer to me, lending me their approval and affection. With the threat gone, I'm forced to examine my actions and admit I'm no longer the woman I was before I recognized the bond. It's changing me. For better or for worse.

"Are we going to talk about it?"

I set down the contemporary romance I've been trying to lose myself in for the past hour and frown. "What are you talking about, Sach?"

Leaning against the wall, she takes a sip of her beer. "The reason you've been over the house for the past week."

"Well, I do own it. Am I annoying you?" I shift on the cushion. Maybe she's gotten used to me not being around, and I'm cramping her style.

"Stop it. You know I love spending time with you. You tend to mix the days here and at the mansion up though." She plops onto the couch beside me. "Is Cristobal out of town?"

"No," I say glumly. One of the things I love most about Sacha is her bluntness. She won't let you run away from yourself.

Her brow furrows. "Okay. So what gives?"

I pick up the cat pillow and place it in my lap, toying with the tag. "Do you think I've changed since I got back?" I whisper.

"Yes."

My heart sinks, and my shoulders slump.

"Wait. Is that a bad thing?" she asks.

"Maybe." I shrug.

She grunts. "Why don't you tell me what you're really worried about so we can have a real conversation?"

I cringe at the C would. Conversation always means tough love with her. "When we were interrogating Wallace and Ernest, I didn't recognize myself any longer."

"I wondered if you'd ever bring that up," she says softly.

"You noticed it, too?" I study the smiling cat's face, afraid to look up. If I saw dissapointment or fear in her eyes, it'd kill me right now.

"None of us are perfect, Lou. We all get caught up in the heat of the moment from time to time. You're under a lot of pressure right now, and that case was tough. Literally, the fate of the universe was on the line. Why can't you cut yourself some slack?" She nudged me with her elbow.

I sigh and explore the ceiling. "It was more than losing myself at the moment, Sach. I liked it. I felt superior and completely removed from humanity. I saw them as creatures, not people. It was like I was ..."

"A vampire?"

"Yes." I exhale. My secret is out.

"In a way you are, though, aren't you?"

"What?" I look at her.

She holds up her hand. "Let me finish. What you have going on is more than simply being influenced by them because you're around them all the time. This connection is on a deeper level, right?"

"It is."

"Tell me how it works."

"That's kind of hard. Every couple is affected differently, and there's no manual. It's such a personal experience, no one's thought to document it, so we're discovering it together. It's more than telepathic communication. I experience the same emotions and thoughts."

"Sounds overwhelming."

"It can be. Especially at first. After a while though, you learn how to turn the volume up and down, and even block the other person out."

"Is it just you and Cristobal?"

"No. Well, it was at first, but now it's expanded to the others since I've agreed to become lady of the court."

"And it's the same with them? Thoughts, emotions, et all?"

"Yes. Why—" I point. "I see what you're doing here."

She laughs. "You're making connections to a lot of different vampires. That's a number of different wavelengths to adapt to. Is it surprising that your signals got crossed?"

She's made it sound so simple. "Looking at it from that perspective, you could be right," I admit begrudgingly.

She grabs my hand a squeezes it gently. "You can't go back to who you were before this, Lou. And that's okay. You aren't any less of a witch."

"I think you're the only one who believes that."

She clucks her tongue. "Since when do we care what others think?"

"I don't know."

"I think you're emotionally drained and overwhelmed. Avoiding Cristobal is precisely what you don't need to be doing right now. How you managed to keep him away this long is beyond me."

Shame sends the blood to my face.

"How did you manage that, Lou?"

"I might've been a stark raving bitch and threw down a ridiculous ultimatum."

She rubs her hands together with glee. "Dish. Any man who can inspire this much passion in you is impressive. You always think with your head. It's incredibly annoying at times."

I groan. "I told him if he didn't give me space and wait on me for once there wasn't going to be a coronation."

"And he believed you?"

I look up at the ceiling.

"Louella. What did you do?"

"I might've spelled him."

"To do what?"

"I made a raincloud appear over him everytime he tried to follow me," I mumble.

"You what?" She bursts into laughter. Her face grows red, and she clutches her stomach. "Oh. Oh, this is too much."

"After a day straight, he backed off, and the others were too wary of me including them in the spell to try to approach me in person."

"Well, that's one way to make sure he remembers he's dating a witch."

"Sacha."

The laughter starts up again. "Oh, my side."

She falls over on the couch. My lips twitch. Letting go, I laugh alongside her. "You should've seen his face when the cloud formed, just like in the cartoons, and all he could say was 'how undignified'." The salty drops pouring from my eyes help me purge the sadness with laughter.

"Oh, God. I could just see it from him." Struggling to catch her breath, she wipes away the tears. "You know you have to make it up to him, right?"

"I do." I exhale.

"Feel better?"

"Much. I think I did need the space. My head was so full; I couldn't think straight."

"I can understand that. I'm sure he'll be able to as well. You still need to come up with an amazing way to say I'm sorry, though."

"Ugh. I know."

"Why the grimace?"

"Because I'm embarassed about how I acted."

She giggles. "Welcome back, Lou."

"Stop enjoying this and help me plan an 'I'm sorry I was an asshole' apology. Would it be odd to take a man out to dinner?"

"You're the one groveling."

"You're a cruel woman. You know that?"

"I'll stop." She fixes her face into a more stern expression. "This is about him and what he likes. I don't think there's a right or wrong way to do it."

"I'll recreate our first date. We're getting so lost in responsibilities, the *why* we're together has all but slipped from view. I forgot the most important thing."

"What's that, Lou?"

"I love the impossibly old-fashioned vampire. Head over heels, stupid, crazy, love him. Enough to risk everything."

Smiling, she nods. "My job is done."

I tackle hug her on the couch, and she laughs. "Thank you for giving me the kick in the ass I needed."

"Anytime, my friend. I know you'd do the same for me."

"I'm looking forward to it actually."

"You and me both. My love life is currently D.O.A. With no prospects on the horizon." She rolls her eyes.

"That's not what the psychic said," I remind her.

"Ha. She didn't give any time frame on that. Enough about me, let's make plans. What was your first date like?"

"Well, by the time he wore me down enough to say yes, a simple date wouldn't do. He took me to New Orleans for an entire day affair."

"Oh my God, you are so screwed."

"Why?"

"Because your man is extra. Which means this whole groveling thing is going to be that much harder."

"He's worth it." The words are everything I needed to remember. I smile. For the first time in six days, my mind is a lot clearer.

Chapter Seventeen

Step 1: Send mixtape

Playlist:

Swallow My Pride—Ramones

Purple Rain—Prince & The Revolution

Dig—Incubus

Let's Stay Together—Al Green

Please Don't Leave me—P!nk

Try—P!nk

I Only Have Eyes for You—The Flamingos

Little Lion Man—Mumford & Son

Don't Let Me Down—The Beatles

I purchased a two-piece wooden puzzle with our names on it that snaps together. It's cheesy, but I know Cristobal will appreciate it. As stern as he is, the man craves love and affection. I wonder if it's linked to being virtually ignored as a child. The youngest son, he wasn't viewed as essential. They had an heir and a spare, so he was just more of the same. Often looked out for by the staff, he felt closer to the cook than his own mother.

I smooth out the blank piece of paper, grab a pen, and begin to write.

Cristobal,

I've spent the past week thinking. I needed time to do that. To process everything, take stock of my emotions and equalize. But I never meant to do it at your expense. I reached my breaking point, and I took it out on you. It was never my intention, and I sincerely apologize. I wasn't able to craft my words and express myself adequately at the time.

I wasn't prepared for the changes the bond has brought. They caught me off guard, and I exploded rather than decompressing and coming back later. Communication is something we need to work on. We're such different people, it can be hard to see eye to eye, but I'll keep working for balance because you are the love of my life.

I don't say it enough. I can't imagine life without you. I feel safe when I'm with you. I trust you above all others, and I admire your old-fashioned values and manners. Even when you make me want to pull my hair out. I want to make you feel as loved, special, and cherished as you make me feel on the daily. Please extend me the courtesy of romancing you.

Yours,

Dove.

I place the cassette tape in the box and add his favorite candy, la Violeta. The lavender scented candy is native to Spain. I sprinkle the water lilies inside, then seal the box. Cristobal has a particular and expensive taste. I'm a nervous wreck by the time I see the courier off and trying not to open the link too far. I need a distraction. After the intensity of the previous case, we decided to take a week off. My mind and my body rejoiced. I text Fel.

Are you up for lunch at Tia's? ~L

Oh, I haven't been there in foreverr. I'm down. What time? ~F

Now? I'm starving. ~L

Lol, all right, I'll meet you there. ~F

Tia's has been a fixture in Cypress since the 1920s. The menu is old-school but cooked to perfection. They're the epitome of comfort food done right. A trip here is a treat I occasionally indulge in. Too much of Tia's family recipes, and I'd no longer fit my clothing. The sugar, lard, and salad make the good food taste like heaven, but the calories remain pure evil.

I feel the gloom lifting as I park in front of the quaint building. Tia's Lunchroom is written across the building in simple black print. The boxy white building has weathered storms, change, and constant generations of patrons. As I park the car, I'm reminded of visits before with family and friends. Tia's is the place you turned to when you wanted a home-cooked meal without the responsibility of clean up.

I cross the lot and slip inside.

The white and black checkerboard floor and glass dessert case full of freshly baked pies await me like an old friend. Fel waves at me from a wooden both by the window. I make my way over and sit across from her.

"Hey, cousin."

She smiles. "You look and sound so much better than you did a week ago."

"Ditto."

"Trust me. I've been making the most of my break … sleeping in, reading, watching television. I'm living the life."

I laugh. "I've been doing about the same. It's sad that this is the first time I've seen you socially in ages."

"I know. One more *meeting* would've damaged my psyche beyond repair. There's only so much PC arguing a woman can take," Fel says dryly.

I laugh. "It feels like things are finally starting to settle. Even the weather. This is the first day without rain."

"Thank God, the flooding was starting to get out of control. I'd started giving it a little helping hand and making it drain faster," Fel admits.

"Wow, Fel."

"I've been practicing. I don't think you're the only one experiencing an upgrade in powers."

"How long have you suspected that theory?"

"Since we cast the sunrise circle and Vit came into his own. The power had to come from somewhere. I think if he'd been that inclined all this time at the least he would've done some sort of accidental magic.

"You think we've all leveled up?"

"Maybe. I know things shift to fit each matriarch. Your power is new and multi-layered now that you're bonded with the court. Maybe it's a trickle-down effect?"

"It's a logical conclusion," I say, wondering how we'd test it.

"Let's get our food ordered."

We walk up to the counter, and I waffle between the fried chicken and meatloaf for my dish. In the end, the meatloaf wins out. I go down the hot lunch line, have the woman behind the counter add mashed potatoes, fried okra, and mac and cheese to the tray. My stomach rumbles. I top my selection off with sweet tea, and a slice of lemon meringue pie.

A comfortable silence settles as we appreciate the food we're eating.

"Are you still on the outs with the vampire boo?" Fel asks between bites.

"Yes. I'm curious to know who you're on the ins with in the mansion, though."

"Percival mentioned it. We text back and forth almost daily."

"Oh my God, you're practically hanging out."

"No, we're not," she protests swiftly. "Unless you count library trips."

I chuckle, thinking about his courtship with Mémé. "I have it on good authority he does."

"Stop it. You're going to make me paranoid."

"Because it would be a bad thing or a good thing?" I observe her carefully as emotions run the gamut on her face.

"I'm not sure," she whispers honestly.

Holy crap, Percy, what is it with you and women in my family? "Do you want it to be more, Felicite?"

She shrugs her shoulders and stirs her iced tea with a straw.

"Because it's okay if you do."

"Is it though?" She shakes her head. "I'm not convinced that's true."

"What happened?"

"I don't know. We've been spending a lot of time together just researching and him teaching me. It made it impossible not to see all his qualities. He's smart, patient, funny, and handsome. Percy never loses his temper with me. He gently guides me to the proper understanding of things. I've never met anyone like him."

"It sounds like a good thing, Fel."

"It's a stupid schoolgirl crush I don't want to embarrass myself over."

"If you really thought that, you wouldn't be talking about this with me," I say gently. "Are you hesitant because he's a vampire or is there another reason?"

"Well, that and the fact that I think he's still in love with our grandmother. I'm no one's stand-in. It's no secret I favor her. I find it hard to believe it's a coincidence I'm the one he's showing interested in. If that's the vibe I'm getting from him. He's hard to read."

I hum as I think on what she says. "I think he'll always have love for her, but he's said himself their time was long ago, and ill-advised. That the world wasn't ready for their relationship."

Her face wrinkles. "He talked to you about it."

"Briefly in passing when he wanted to give me a pep talk about taking risks." I wave her off. "Don't worry, your vampire boo isn't spilling his secrets to me."

She scowls. "He's not."

"Yet. But you want him to be."

"I think I might." Her face falls. "Is that awful of me?"

"Felicite, no. You like who you like."

"God, is this how you felt with Cristobal at first?"

I nod. "Yes, but I was too starry-eyed to care much about the consequences. Young amour."

She shakes her head. "I'm ahead of myself. I'm not sure if he reciprocates what I have going on."

"I know him well enough to say if you don't give him a hint that you're open to it, he'll never approach you. He'd be too worried about offending or frightening you. He really is such a standup guy. You deserve someone who will treat your properly and cherish you. Percy will do that and more."

"Is that why you aren't discouraging me?" she asks curiously.

"Yeah, and I see how much you want to try this out with him. I understand your fear. It's a big step, and a lot of people won't understand or approve. There's nothing wrong with taking your time and figuring out what it is you actually want."

She nods and toys with the condensation on her plastic cup. "Do you think Cristobal was worth it?"

"Yeah. Enough for me to be groveling right now."

"What?" She sits up straight. "Now you have to share."

I laugh. "I made him a mixed tape for Christ's sake."

"That's adorable … and necessary. You were over the top."

I sigh. "I know I was. I feel like shit about it now."

"What did he say?"

"He hasn't yet. I sent it off by courier before I drove here."

"Now we wait?"

"Nothing else to do but that."

"You wouldn't change anything knowing what you know? Even with the hardships you've already faced?"

"I've been asking myself this very question. The only thing I would change is how I felt. I'd have been more upfront with everyone. That time of discovery was vital to who I am now. As for not being with Cristobal … If I'm honest, I can't even imagine what that would be like long term. I wasn't happy when I was gone. Content, busy, and successful for the most part, yes. We both know those things aren't the same thing as having joy. Being with him is complicated, but I do feel it's where I'm meant to be. Whether I feel that on my own or the universe hardwired me to feel that way I'm not sure."

"And it doesn't bother you?"

"I think it always will to a small degree. But the benefits far outweigh that."

She nibbles the inside of her jaw thoughtfully. *I tried to help you out, Percy. You deserve happiness, too.*

A tentative caress through our bond has me closing my eyes. I've missed this.

"I accept your apology, dove. I look forward to seeing what else you have planned."

"Clear your schedule, mi rey."

"Done, reina."

"I'll be by at nine o'clock sharp to pick you up. Dress semi-casually."

I open my eyes and grin.

"He got it?" she guesses.

I laugh. "He did. He accepted my apology. Tomorrow I'll initiate step two." I wiggle my eyebrows. "I'm having fun keeping him on his toes. Usually, he's the one wining and dining."

"What are you doing tomorrow?"

"Recreating our first date, which was basically a day and evening out in New Orleans."

"That will be fun!"

I nod my head. "What are you going to do about Perc?"

"You like him, don't you?"

"Yeah, the guy deserves some happiness."

"I'm going to spend more time with him and see what goes from there."

"Sounds like a solid plan."

"I never thought my life would be like this," she laughs.

"So awesome?"

"So crazy." She gestures wildly with her hands.

"Girl, you're an Esçhete. You know we don't do normal."

"Yeah, I've come to realize how very true that statement is over the past year."

I knock on the front door holding a single red rose. Gil answers.

"Aaaah, my lovely. You do not do things by halves."

I laugh. "Where's my date, Gil?"

"Being held up by the rest of the court who are utterly amused by this turn of events. Step in. You are truly a vision." Gil takes my hand. "Spin." I slowly rotate, and he clucks his approval of the lightweight boat neck, strapless, blush-colored dress with a pastel floral pattern across the top to the waist and along the top of my thigh down to the end of the dress that stops at my calf. I've ditched heels for a simple pair of pale pink canvas shoes perfect for walking the city.

I've pinned my hair off my face in a chignon.

"Do I pass inspection, my good sir?"

"Oui."

I laugh. "I've missed you."

"I see I've missed all the action while in France, but I have secured the things we will need for your coronation. Soon we will try on your dresses?"

"Yes, the date is speedily approaching."

"And yet you no longer seem nervous."

"There's something about fighting for your life that places things into perspective."

He hugs me. "Come, cherie." He pulls me in and shuts the door.

"Look at that, Mom and Pop are going to paint the town." Renee lets out a low wolf whistle.

"Stop it." My face heats, and he laughs roguishly. I think he was a pirate in another life. With his blinding white smile, mischievous nature, and the rock-like diamond in his left ear, it's not hard to imagine.

"You look good." He comes over and kisses my cheek.

"Thank you."

Ada and Ruby rush over.

"Is everyone here?" I ask.

"Oh, we weren't about to miss this for the world, poppet," Ruby drawls.

Ada laughs. "It's a big deal when we see the boss man thrown for a loop."

I grin, pleased to hear my plan is working so far.

"Where is my vampire boo?" I ask, knowing he can hear me.

"Your wh-what?" he sputters.

I giggle as laughter fills the space, shaking out the stale air of discord left behind after our fight.

"Welcome to dating in the twenty-first century," Luz says. Her full-bodied laugh is infectious.

I watch amused as Luz, Miles, Percival, and Larkin flank Cristobal down the hall.

"We expect you to treat him well you know," Marcellus says, joining us from the opposite end of the hall.

"I will."

He smiles. "I believe you." It's as close to approval from him as I'll ever get.

"Don't stay out too late or get into trouble while you're in the big city," Ruby drawls.

"I'll try not to," I respond to their heckling, but I only have eyes for Cristobal. The black slacks, white button-up, and gray vest fit him to a T.

I hold out the rose. "For you."

His lips twitch. "Like I gave you on our first date."

I nod.

"Thank you." He leans and brushes my lips with his. "I'll put it in water."

"We'll do that. You two go have fun." Luz takes the bloom and we're ushered toward the door after a few photos have been snapped.

I'm almost dazed on the doorstep. "What in the world?"

"I may not have been the best company of late." He clears his throat.

I reach down and squeeze his hand. "I'm sorry."

"We both have much to learn when it comes to how far we can push boundaries," he admits. "I love the fire inside of you. I don't want to extinguish it."

I lead him to the car and open the door. He bristles but allows it. I grin. "Thank you for being such a good sport."

"For today only," he warns.

It's more than I hoped for. I scramble around to the driver's side, and we pull onto the road.

"Fill me in on what I've missed."

"More preparations for the coronation, meetings, and Gils' phone calls every other day from France."

"Be honest, you sent him there with the black card to get him out of your hair."

He chuckles. "Perhaps."

"That's a yes from you."

We spend the road trip filling each other in on our week. He laughs when I lead him to Café Du Monde.

"I didn't realize you were such a sentimentalist, Ms. Eschete. Recreating our first date."

"I wanted to go back to the start. The craziness of the upcoming events and the Djinn really threw us for a loop. It became all about getting things done, surviving, and we lost sight of the best part ... us."

"Do you mean that?" he whispers quietly. Seeing him uncertain is a shock.

"Of course I do."

"There are times I worry I have pushed all of this on you, reina. Seeing you happy and initiating things has been good for my soul." He pulls me closer to his side, and I enjoy his slight warmth as we weave our way through the crowd to the building with the green and white striped awning, and a line out toward the street.

"I insist you let me pay."

I smirk. "Okay."

We make our way to a table outside, and I do a bit of quick magic.

"What was that?"

"A powdered sugar repellent," I answer honestly.

His full-bodied laugh is like sunshine, warming me from the inside out.

"Brilliant." Little is said as we finish our snack.

"I thought we could wander Jackson Square for a bit," I say, thinking of my odd new friend, Sabrina. She'd get a kick out of Cristobal, and I think vice versa.

"I haven't been by in ages. It'd be interesting to see who's still around these days." We leave our plates, and he offers his hand. I loop mine through it, and we walk across the street to the square full of people on lunch breaks, tourists, palm readers, painters, and more. We peruse the tables slowly. I catch a glint of dark hair and spot Sabrina at the very end of the line. I tug Cristobal's arm.

He smiles down at me. "What?"

"I want you to meet someone."

He arches an eyebrow as I break away from the candle table and lead him to Sabrina.

She looks up and grins with a slight bow.

"My friend has come back to visit me and brought more royalty I see. It's an honor, my Lord."

"This is Sabrina, Cristobal. Sacha and I met her recently."

"The pleasure is mine, Sabrina."

"I see you took my advice?" Sabrina says cheekily.

I laugh. "I did."

"I wondered if you would read for Cristobal."

He clears his throat. "Not many can."

Sabrina sits up straight. "I can, my Lord."

He arches a thick brow. "If you're sure."

"Please, sit."

He perches on the edge of the lawn chair, and I plunk down in the one beside him with glee. She removes the black velvet bag, and I feel the pull of the cards. There's more to them. They have a magical weight that intrigues me. She slides the cards over to him.

"I want you to shuffle them until they feel right for you. I will do a simple three card spread."

I admire his strong hands and long, artistic fingers as he shuffles the cards with ease and confidence. I can feel bits of his own magic sparking to the surface. I want to cozy up to him and rub against him like a cat. I settle for watching him like a stalker. There's been a shift for me over the past week. It's a combination of missing him, and our magic and souls beginning to settle in together.

He stops shuffling.

"Okay, now I want you to cut the deck four times, please."

Why four?

Sabrina smirks. "Because his soul is no longer just his own. No, I don't read minds. Your face was very expressive just then." She winks.

When he finishes, she spreads the cards in a fan. "Pick three, whenever you're ready."

He pulls three. She flips over the first. The passionate couple embracing brings heat to my face and neck.

"The Lovers. You've met your match. The two of you complement one another perfectly. Your love is flourishing, never take it for granted, because love-starved can turn." She flips the next card with five wands. "Hmm, the five of wands. You will face competition and scorn. Together you're very powerful, and others will seek to diminish or possibly possess that for themselves." Cristobal tenses as she flips over the final card. A beautiful woman with brown skin, big amber eyes, and full lips greets us. A crown of flowers is woven into her dark hair. "The Empress. She stands for fertility and feminine energy. You will overcome your rivalries and grow. Her energy will be good for you and your people. As you join his court, you are stepping into a motherly role. The cards are giving you a blessing of sorts."

"I need all of that I can get."

Sabrina laughs. "I can see the two of you are a good match. Don't worry so much." She pats my hands.

"Thank you, Sabrina."

He reaches into his pocket for a wallet.

"No, allow me to give this to you as a coronation present."

He laughs. "Clever. I will accept it as such. Thank you."

"Enjoy the city," Sabrina says as we stand.

We leave her with a wave.

"It's been ages since I had my fortune read."

"Did you like it?"

"It was incredibly enlightening."

"You know the next place you took me is what won me over."

His brow wrinkles. "Really?"

I nod. "Because it showed me who you were behind all the pomp and circumstance."

We catch a trolley to Storyland Park, holding hands as we work our way through the fairytale-themed park.

"What made you take me here?" "Other than the obvious irony of a witch and a vampire in a fairytale-themed place? I always saw you as magical, beyond your abilities. You were so pure to me."

I laugh. "I was until you took care of that."

He presses his lips together. "I'm sorry. But it's more than that. You still maintain this radiating aura of goodness."

"Even now?" I whisper.

He pulls me to his side and kisses my forehead. "Always."

"Do you remember what happened here?" I whisper, pausing at the pirate ship.

"You told me that Peter Pan was one of your favorite stories."

I nod my head. "And then you asked me if you could kiss me."

"Yes, and you offered up your cheek." I laugh.

"Damn right. It was the first date." I elbow him playfully.

"I knew then you'd always keep me guessing and amused in the best possible way. I'd grown so bored with things before I met you. It had begun to blur together."

I remain quiet, letting him process and speak in his own time. "I'd considered going to ground for a bit. That's why I had you make the protection spell, so I'd be safe there if I decided to go through with it."

"Cristobal," I whisper, stunned.

"No one knew. Eventually, we all do it. The press of years and responsibility become too much. You put those you trust in charge, and you let yourself reset. It's a painful process when the hunger sets in, but afterward, the bliss of nothingness."

My stomach lurches. "If I hadn't been the one to do the spell for you—"

"We might've missed one another completely. Never doubt that you are my light in the darkness, Louella. There's nothing I wouldn't do for you, and that will come across in fucked up ways at times. Just know I always have your best interest at heart." He cups my face and runs his thumb over the apple of my cheek. "I love you."

"I love you, too," I whisper.

"One day you and I are going to share the same name."

I groan. "Can we get through the insanity of this year first?" I rest my head on his chest as he laughs.

"Of course, reina."

We continue to walk, and I bask in the deeper level of understanding we've managed. Sometimes things have to break down, to be built up stronger.

Chapter Eighteen

I hug my knees to my chest and shiver as the heated water slowly fills the porcelain tub drug out into my garden. Today is all about preparation to receive the mantle of the matriarch. Tomorrow will be more than a title exchange. I'll be channeling a large quantity of power, mingling it with my own, and being judged by my ancestors. If they were to find me severely lacking, they could stop the ceremony. It's extremely rare, but not unheard of. I'm worried about what they'll see when they peer into my soul.

"You better start thinking happier thoughts, or you're going to freeze out here while we try to cleanse you of negativity," Fel says.

I wrinkle my nose. "Why do so many ritual preparations have to be performed nude?"

"Because modern day people are prudes," Mémé replies.

Ruby chokes out a laugh. "Oh, I like her."

"Everyone laugh it up." Luz pours in heated water, and I smile my thanks. Everything has to be done by hand for this. We have a large fire pit built, and multiple cauldrons are going. Sage, chamomile, rosemary, lavender, lemon balm, and plenty of sea salt float around. Modern items won't play a part in preparations until the celebration.

"I feel like we're trying to make a Louella tea," I mumble.

"It'd be very floral," Sacha speaks dryly.

I snicker. "Are you trying to say I shouldn't be a floral and sweet flavored tea?"

"You have your bitter moments," Mom adds.

I bat my lashes. "Why thank you, Mother. I knew I was a delight to raise."

Mémé laughs. "It's good you have so many women here to support you. It means you're loyal and loved. I couldn't think of a better way to go into this. You'll need them to keep you on the right path. This is your circle of trust. None could have entered the garden today if they had any ill intent toward you."

Just when I think I know everything, Mémé drops some more gangster-style shit that blows my mind.

As the water warms up, my muscles relax, and I forget about everything else. My body tingles and my aura drinks up the healing magic, herbs, and vibrations from the quartz at the bottle of the tub. It's been a long year full of ups and down, enemies and growth. People think growing pains stop when you leave puberty. I know better. There are scars on my heart from misunderstandings, words spoken in anger, and the awareness that the person I was is undergoing another conversion and I have no clue who will emerge. Letting go of preconceived notions of how things should be, saved me plenty of anxiety, and cleared the blockage I had when trying to bond with the court.

Much like a wedding, the people you trust most are the ones to attend you before the ceremony. It's supposed to be for witches only, but I have a workaround; Ruby, Ada, and Luz have a magic all their own. Therefore, technically they could not be banned from the process. I've learned a lot about rules, laws, and how to bend them from the court, much to the council's chagrin.

"This is to cleanse her aura you said?" Luz asks Mémé.

"Yes, we want to prepare her for tomorrow. When you become matriarch, it's a physically and mentally draining process. She'll receive power, memories, and if she's really lucky blessing. It's a lot for one person to handle."

"Yeah, I could see how that would be true," Luz says.

I smile reassuringly. She has a tough exterior, but when it comes to those she cares about her heart is tender.

Bundles of sage burn on the fire, giving off their distinct scent. Concentrating on letting the worries and negative thoughts go, I close my eyes as my skin tingles. The sun rays kiss my skin, and the herbs do their job, calming and cleansing. My energy is restored, the clutter is removed from my headspace like unwelcome cobwebs, and I begin to feel an intense connection with the world beyond our own.

"It's already beginning." I feel like I've been connected to a battery. Everything is amped. My heart knocks against my chest as my powers surge. Mémé leads a chant. I slip deeper into the water.

I submerge myself, using the salt and handmade lavender soap to symbolically scrub away the impurities and prepare myself for what I will soon receive. Flashes of memories explode in my brain like memories set on fast-forward. I twitch, sloshing the water.

"It's happening fast," Mémé whispers.

"Is she okay?" Ruby asks.

"Yes, she's starting to receive the things she needs to know in order to do the job. We do the ritual the day before to keep all the unpleasant side-effects that might occur in private."

It's like being plunged into icy water. I lose touch with my physical body and find myself standing at the entrance of a forest with Alida waiting.

A long, white gown brushes the tips of my toes. The sleeves caress my fingertips. "Hi."

"Hi." She hugs me.

"You feel solid," I marvel. "And I can hear you."

She nods her head. "I hoped I would be the one to greet you."

"Why is this possible?"

"Because we're not on your plane or mine. We're somewhere in between where many rules no longer apply. I want to show you something. For when the time comes." She holds out her hand.

Taking it, I allow her to guide me through the woods where we now regularly cast circles. "I know this place."

"Yes, but not where I'm going to take you."

We move past the space for casting, through the thicker, dense forested area. I feel the pine needles under my bare feet. A bird caws.

"That's a raven," I whisper, recognizing the sound.

"Have you figured out why that bird is special to you?" Alida asks.

"It's one of Cristobal's forms."

"And your spirit guide. Whenever you need help, it will come to you. Often it's one of your ancestors in disguise."

"The Fae land," I say, remembering the strange disturbance when I tried to choose a door.

"Yes, one of us was there. You're never truly alone because we walk through all the trials and challenges with you." Her words are comforting. "Can you hear what the raven wishes to tell you?"

I tilt my head back and find the large bird perched on a low hanging branch a few feet above my head. It cocks its head to the left and the right as we size one another up. It caws and flaps its wing.

"Yes?"

It straightens. I feel a sense of pleasure before it takes off to the next tree and comes back. On the third fly back, it clicks.

"You want me to follow you?"

Caw. It leads us deeper into the woods, pausing to caw every few feet.

"Where are we going?" I ask Alida.

She shrugs. "We'll have to wait and see."

He leads us to a tree that's glowing white. "Ghost tree," I whisper. The light-colored bark is known to reflect the moonlight, giving it an unearthly appearance that earned its nickname. The raven flies to the ground. His dark beak pecks at the soil.

"What are you doing, buddy?" I ask softly. He caws at me and returns to his pecking.

Can a bird have an attitude? He's making a hole.

"Are you digging?" I kneel down beside him and grab a flat rock. Together we continue to dig. I lose track of time until I hit something substantial. I brush away the dirt on the surface to reveal what looks like a wooden box.

"Remember," Alida whispers.

"What?"

A hand on my shoulder makes me jump in the water.

"You back with us?" my mother asks.

I open my eyes and see her worried expression.

"There she is," Mémé says.

"What just happened?" I mumble.

"You drifted off for a while."

"I was somewhere else with Alida."

"She may be one of your spirit guides," Mémé chirps. "Come on, pruney, it's time to get you out."

Mom and Fel help me out and wrap me in a homespun cotton towel. Once I'm dry, they drape a white cotton nightgown over my shoulder. It falls to the ground, and I experience a moment of déjà vu. *Remember.* Raven, digging … A ghost tree. I pull the memory from the haze and tuck it away for later.

"You'll continue to drift in and out for the rest of the evening. There will always be one of us with you to keep you grounded," Mémé says.

They help me over to a white tent pitched up with wooden poles. Cristobal followed the rules without skimping on comfort. I chuckle as I'm helped into the bed raised on a wooden platform. This is glamping at its best. A fire crackles outside, and a small mountain of comforters are pulled back, so I can climb in.

"Sleep. You'll need all your strength tomorrow." My mother

kisses me on the forehead, and I struggle to keep my eyes open as the others bid me farewell. Weariness wins, and I close my eyes, returning to the in-between space where half dreams wait.

Faces, voices, and time-periods blur together as the ancestors speak to me throughout the night. I wake feeling like I've been trapped in a fever dream. I push the comforters off my body. We've been wrong. The ancestors admire tradition, but they're hungry for change and also worried about our lineage. These are messages to ponder after the next two days have commenced. Every matriarch faces their challenges. I think mine will be revitalization.

The curtain is swept back.

"You're already awake?" my mother says.

"I dreamt all night long. It was strange." I brush my hair away from my face.

"Bad?"

"No, nothing like that, just odd. I spoke with a lot of our ancestors."

"That's good. Means the bonding has begun and it's strong." Mémé follows in behind Mom.

"Do you still see them, Mémé?"

"Occasionally. It's never been so vivid as it was the night before my coronation."

"That's good. I don't think I'd ever really get a good night's rest again if this was my new normal."

"It was so vivid?" Mémé asks.

"As clear as we are right now."

Her eyes widen.

"Is that bad thing?"

"No, I think you will be exactly what this family needs." Her eyes water. "We should go, time moves swiftly, and we have to prepare you for the sunrise. Traditionally coronations were performed at the start of the new day to symbolize a fresh beginning. Modernized, they tend to take place in the evening, but not mine. I'm going old school.

That means adhering to the original customs. Making bigoted bastards get out of their bed at an unusual hour is merely a bonus."

The dense area is crowded. Witches stand among the trees, in the trees, and along the walkway that's been cleared leading up to the massive oak tree where the exchange of power will be made. Dressed in various stages of finery, they're all barefoot in accordance with tradition. It's supposed to keep us all grounded by earth and in tune with one another.

The people stretch out before me for miles. A lot of people wanted to see a coronation. They don't come around often, and I'm a wild card. Everyone wants to be there in case I fail epically. It's a sad but true thought.

"Are you ready, reina?"

I throw a smile over my shoulder and nod. The court is there for protection if necessary and medical support. In essence, I'm bonding myself to a position. We're uncertain how that will react to the bone already in place.

My dress is blue, the color of water. The strapless dress is an ombre-style that mimics the ocean going from a deep blue to teal. A white pattern mimics sea foam and waves. My hair is adorned with a crown of blue orchids.

Mémé is waiting at the end of the aisle in front of an altar. She gives the nod, and I slowly make my way toward her. I send a gentle mist creeping along the forest floor. Flowers bloom and the sound of the ocean is heard as I pay homage to water and spring. The coronation walk is about proving your worth. I add a hint of salt-water scent and the feel of sea spray. It comes easily. The conversion process is alive and altering me with each step.

I flow from water to air and summer. A warm wind rushes through the area, blowing away the scent of the sea and the mist. Warmth encompasses the crowd. The smell of wildflowers rolls over us. Sunflowers spring up five to six feet tall and my blue dress turns a deep yellow. Lace appliqué flowers cover my arms and the sheer front of the dress, leaving my back bare. The mermaid-style skirt flows out around me. I focus on Mémé and her encouraging smile. I can feel her pride and excitement through the temporary connection linking us for the transfer.

I use it as my fuel and push myself harder. Autumn erupts in a shower of red, gold, and orange leaves that form on the trees and rains down on the crowd. Their whispers and murmurs make me smile. Vines push up from the earth and pumpkins grow, big, fat, and round. The scent of pumpkin fills the air, and I pay homage to earth with an emerald green dress with a trumpet skirt, bell sleeves of sheer material, and a corset top that accentuates my curves. Leaves and vines wind their way across the boat neck and sides by my hips. A crown of autumn leaves circles my hair.

A crack of thunder shakes the space. Tiny snowflakes begin to rain down, growing in intensity and size until the entire pathway and forest have been turned into a winter wonderland. My dress erupts in a violent display of flames. The red burn away the green. The one-shoulder gown has a trumpet cut at the bottom and hugs my curves. It stands out against the snowy backdrop. I reach inside for an offering worthy of my ancestors who I sense are here and the change to head my family. Glowing green tendrils of power flow from me, coating the ground and the surrounding area. I reach the end of the aisle and kneel before Mémé.

"We ask the ancestors to guide, keep, and bless this new matriarch as she takes the position of many proud women in her lineage who have come before her." A cold gust of air makes me shiver. I open my eyes and gasp. I'm surrounded by the filmy images of women of all shades, sizes, and time-periods.

"The spirits show their approval," Mémé whispers, dazed. "Rise, granddaughter, and receive what is rightfully yours."

I stand, and we join hands. She stares into my eyes, and I feel the last of the power begin to transfer. She squeezes my hand, and I set my feet, supporting her. Soft white light washes over us, and it's done.

"You have all witnessed it. So mote it be," Mémé whispers.

"So mote it be," the crowd choruses. Mémé and I move over to our family gathered around the altar. I take the head of the space.

"To our ancestors who came before us," I lift the bottle of expensive wine and pour it onto the earth, "we thank you." I feel a new kinship with the women who showed up for me today. Seeing them turned them into more than a vague concept.

"And now we go make nice with everyone talking shit about us right now."

Vit laughs so hard he has to bend over and clutch his belly. "What?" Mom screeches.

"Oh, was I the only one thinking it?" I ask.

Mémé laughs. "Straight shooter. I like it."

"If you can't be real in front of your family, who can you be real with?" I ask.

"You're not too old to have your mouth washed out with soap," my mother mumbles.

"Sorry, Mom. Had to blow off some of this excess energy."

"They'll be waiting to rub elbows with you," Mémé says.

I nod. We've set up tents similar to the ones for Equinox with heating, a catered brunch, and champagne. Taking it outside made it more organic and less opulent, which I appreciated it. I'll get enough of that in a few weeks.

I offer Mémé my arm. Back straight, she's the picture of decorum in her white suit with matching jacket, but I can see her waning. It took a lot out of her exchanging power.

"You want to make a run for it? I'll let them blame it on me," I say quietly.

She laughs. "Non, I want to eat my fill of this fancy breakfast we're paying out the nose for."

I laugh. "Fair enough. Let's go do our best to eat our weight in crepes and whatever other tasty things they whip up." Relief courses through me. Months have led up to this display. A few more hours of mingling, making nice, and performing more magic, and this coronation will be officially done. Next comes the hardest part ... living with it.

I fight the urge to pinch myself as I stand in the church foyer between Luz and Marcellus. As his next in command, they have the task of making sure I'm delivered to Cristobal like a blushing bride. The deep purple, off the shoulder, gothic gown shimmers beneath the light. The silk has a boat neck and bellows out into a massive ball gown. A black, Spanish-style veil with scalloped edges frames my face. Black was too vulgar, and red was in poor taste, so purple, the color of royalty, was the best choice for the coronation dress.

We've gone over the ceremony so many times I could perform it in my sleep. Still, the thought of doing it here in front of a crowd full of upper-crust vampires has me nervous.

"Relax, you're stunning, and you know what to do," Luz says.

I squeeze her hand. "Thank you."

"Don't let them smell fear, kiddo," Marcellus adds.

Straightening my spine, I take a deep breath. I have one coronation under my belt. I can do this. The door swings open and Percival and Gil grin down at me. "We're ready."

The two hold the doors open. *Here we go.* Ruby and Ada lift the back of the train, and we begin to move. I focus on the man waiting at the end of the aisle in a black tuxedo with a gray vest tailored to perfection. I smile politely at the vampires all turned to face us. Every bench in the cathedral is packed. They all want to get a glimpse at the witch binding herself to a lord. I can't blame them. We're an oddity.

Keep it pretty, relaxed, and graceful. My steps are sure and small. I ignore the looks of disdain or contempt. I refuse to let anyone ruin this day after I worked so damn hard to pull it off flawlessly. The corner of Cristobal's lip twitches up. My fake smile melts away and becomes a real one. His eyes twinkle.

"You are magnificent, dove."

"So are you."

When we reach the end of the aisle, Cristobal offers his hand and helps me up the final three stairs. Two crushed velvet pillows rest on the floor in front of us. The vampire officiating is dressed impeccably in a black three-piece designer suit. He is short but muscular with long, dark, curly hair, a hooked nose, and dark eyes fringed with long lashes. The translucent blue flames dancing around him mark his age as scarily old. I narrow my gaze in an attempt to bring them into focus.

"What do you see?" His accent throws me for a loop.

"I'm sorry?"

"When you look at me. What do you see?"

I look to Cristobal who nods.

"Your aura. It's incredibly powerful."

He gives a dark laugh that shows off his fangs. The cathedral echoes him as the vampires join in on his mirth. The jokes on me right now.

"Wonderful. Perhaps she is as talented as you claimed, Cristobal. I am pleased to be the one to perform this ceremony." He nods his head. There's more at work here. I trust Cristobal, but I loathe being in the dark. He brushes my hand with a fingertip.

"Finding your mate is a luxury most of us never know. Do not squander the gift you've been given. Protect one another at all costs, or you may live to regret it. Eternity can be a lonely sentence, yes?"

Cristobal nods in understanding. The words go over my head once more. The officiant clears his throat. *Who is he?*

"We are gathered here today to witness a rare thing, bond mates joining together as lady and lord of a court. Let us begin the ceremony."

Cristobal helps me kneel, and I arrange my dress prettily before I sit up. He takes my hand and kisses it. Right now, I know they can all hear my heart racing a mile a minute.

"It's nice to know I can still make your heart skip a beat," Cristobal says, breaking the tension. I giggle. He's breaching his own protocol to make me feel better. I slow down my vitals and lift my chin.

"Good girl," Cristobal praises me.

The officiate opens the weathered leather-bound book in his hands. The man speaks the words in an old language I don't understand, and then he translates.

"Do you swear by blood to work together for the betterment of your court? To teach, protect, and nurture them?"

"We do."

"Will you remain loyal to your death to them? Forsaking all others?"

"We do."

"Hold hands." I place my hand in Cristobal's. The officiant looks behind us. "Bring forth the cords prepared with their blood." *Everything is all about the life-giving nectar with them.*

He takes the cord from Percival and ties our hands together.

"Up until this moment, you have been separate in thought, word, and action. As this cord binds your hands together, so shall your lives be bonded as one." The rope begins to burn. I gasp in shock. It's a cold burn, unsettling, but not quite painful. Swirls of green energy wind around our hands.

"Frumoasa," the officiate whispers.

"What is this? Some trick?" Etta's voice is like nails on a chalkboard.

"Our powers are saying hello," I say softly, knowing all of them can hear us. My energy rises to answer his. The blue and green tendrils dart after each other like playful pups. They move through our bodies, wrestling with one another until they find a happy compromise. The discomfort stops, and the colors mingle to make a greenish blue before they settle back into our bodies.

I exhale.

"Wow," I whisper shakily.

I hear the members of my court chuckle.

"Bring forth the chalice."

Renee and Miles walk up. Everyone played a part in our day. I wink at Renee who grins even harder. Renee kneels beside me, and Miles mirrors him next to Cristobal.

"Today your blood will mingle and become one."

Larkin steps forward with a sharp blade. "Let this blood oath taken in front of all be an outward sign of your promises here today."

Larkin makes a cut on Cristobal's palm. Miles catches the droplets in the silver chalice. Larkin repeats the process, and Renee grabs mine.

"When you accept this blood into your body, you bind yourself to the contract agreed upon." When Cristobal's wound seals shut, he leans forward to lick mine. The anticoagulant goes to work and my skin mends. Renee and Miles hand over the chalices. We link arms and drink. His blood is a fire ringing its way through my body. Like a shot of espresso, it reinvigorates me. His eyes go heavy-lidded. I look away, pleased. Let them smell how we make each other feel. Etta has a front row seat. I wish I could turn around and see her face without being a basic bitch.

I unbind our wrists with magic. Cristobal places the cord in his pocket and rises, offering up his hand to help me stand. We turn, and he addresses the crowd.

"Meet the Lord and Lady of Cortez Court, Cristobal Cortez and Louella Esçhete." The vampires clap politely.

"We thank you for being here to celebrate this momentous occasion with us. I think we all dream of one day finding our bond mate. We have entertainment, food, and wine prepared for you at our home. We hope you'll join us, so we can thank each one of you in person," Cristobal says with a small smile.

"Come with me to the office, and we'll sign the paperwork?" The officiate leads us in the opposite direction away from the crowd to the side of the building where the office rests. *"Do vampires file paperwork?"*

Cristobal nods. The members of our court follow us, forming a wall of protection. I notice the officiant has his own people as well. Once the door closes, Cristobal turns to me. *Who is this man?*

"Can you perform a silencing spell, dove?"

Closing my eyes, I weave a quick muting ward. "Done."

"I'm sure by now you are wondering who I am. I will see if you can guess."

The last thing I want to do is offend him by guessing horribly wrong.

"Who did I tell you would survive long after a nuclear war broke out?"

No.

My eyes widen. I glance from Cristobal to the man.

"I … V-Vlad?" I choke.

He bows. "At your services."

My jaw drops, and he laughs heartily.

"How? Why?" I shake my head, confused.

"I've made many deals during my recent travels."

"I agreed to do this for a fee. I have waited a long time for some-one like you to come along and help me with a task. One day soon I will come and ask a favor."

I nod slowly.

"By officiating, he was giving his approval of our union."

Holy shit I was kind of married by Dracula. Now I can't stop staring at him, despite the rudeness factor. He glances up as Cristobal fills out his part of the paperwork and catches me staring.

"I'm sorry." I study my hands.

"Sign here, dove." We prick our fingers and add a few droplets beside our names.

Vlad signs the bottom. "I will send this to the archives."

"Thank you again, Vlad," Cristobal says.

He nods. "You'll forgive me for not attending the celebration. I do not enjoy large crowds of strangers vying for attention and talking politics. I will give you time to settle in before I call upon you."

"We're at your disposal." Cristobal bows.

Vlad studies me once more. "You will be my savior or my ruin, Ms. Esçhete."

He's gone before I can respond.

"What?"

"Yeah, he has that effect on people." Cristobal laughs.

"What did you agree to do?"

"It's more about what you can do. Don't worry, it's not a big deal."

"You know our opinions vary greatly on that statement often."

"Not this time."

He pulls me from the room, and I'm bombarded by hugs. I let the issue go. I have an evening of schmoozing and avoiding traps to get through. Swept away on the infectious excitement, I exit the cathedral in high spirits. A few months back I wasn't sure if we'd live to see this moment, and now it's already in our rearview mirror. I can't say what the future holds for me, but I know it won't be dull, and I won't be alone. Can anyone really ask for more than that?